NEVER A WINNER

NEVER
A
WINNER

Paul Henke

WINSTON BOOKS

Winston Books
98 Tunis Road
London W12 7EY

© Paul Henke 1987
Published 1987 by Winston Books

British Library Cataloguing in Publication Data
Henke, Paul
Never a Winner
I. Title
823′.914 [F]   PR6058.E51/

ISBN 0–9512288–0–3

Photoset, printed and bound by
Redwood Burn Limited, Trowbridge, Wiltshire

*To my beloved wife Dorothy
and my son Oliver*

Chapter 1

He paused at the entrance, glanced around the room, noted there were less than half a dozen customers and walked towards his brother standing at the bar, his back turned to him. 'Mine's a lager,' he said, clapping him on the back.

'Steve!' His brother spun round to shake his hand. 'Good to see you again, damned good. What time did you land?'

'I got to Heathrow just after six. Strong head winds delayed us half an hour. At least, that's what the pilot claimed. I got the new tube and here I am. Sorry I was so late.'

'Don't be daft, man – thank you.' He broke off to pay for the beer. 'What's a couple of hours in two years?'

They stood there grinning idiotically at each other. Since the death of their parents nearly ten years previously in a senseless road accident – the other driver having been too drunk to stand, never mind drive a car – the two brothers had grown very close, each acknowledging the other as his best friend, a rare event in any family. To look at them they were as different as chalk from cheese. Steve Barber stood six feet in his socks, blond and good looking, without an ounce of fat on his lean body; that was only to be expected after seven years as an officer in the Royal Marines, specialising in the Special Boats Service. Philip was two years younger, dark haired like his mother had been, and a few inches shorter than Steve. He was a very junior partner in a small solicitors' firm – in fact had been there less than two months – and had the beginnings of a small paunch, the price he had to pay for his wife's Cordon Bleu style of cooking.

1

'How're things?' Steve asked, having sipped his lager. 'Is the company a good one?'

'Excellent. We've more work than we can handle at the moment, and it's getting better all the time. It means we can start refusing some smaller cases and concentrate on the more remunerative ones.'

'Glad to hear it. And Sue?'

'Couldn't be better, considering. In about another six weeks, God willing, you'll be a proud uncle.'

Steve smiled fleetingly, though the humour did not reach his eyes. He looked levelly at his brother. 'No questions?'

Phil Barber shrugged. 'I think it would be a good idea to talk about it though I guess I know all the details from your letters.'

'Yes, you probably do. However, if it wouldn't bore you too much I'd like to tell you how it was, just for the record.'

Philip nodded understandingly, realising that his brother wouldn't have said anything to anyone else. They only ever confided in each other, one of many small facts that had made and kept them close friends.

Steve gazed reflectively into his glass for a moment, then looked up.

'It began about six months ago,' he said, 'just after I arrived in Singapore. As you know, we were visiting the old ANZUK base there preparing for an exercise with the Aussies, Malaysians and Singapore Defence people. It promised to be the usual fiasco of politically inspired non-events; in fact we began to look on it as a break and rest from our usual tough programme. The second night we were there, our new Colonel arrived in the mess with his wife in tow.'

As he talked on, the words already beginning to relieve some of the pain, he was back to the night it had all started, when the various officers, resplendent in their mess-dress, with their wives or girl friends alongside, met their new leader. As usual, the British officers had been complaining because arrangements had been made for the families of the

2

other officers to be flown to Singapore for the duration of their stay. The British, however, continued to be treated like poor relations; not even a special RAF flight or low rate commercial flight was laid on for them. The Ministry of Defence defended its inaction by claiming that defence cuts left nothing available for the sort of frills the officers were demanding, so the Marines, like the rest of the forces, would have to manage as best they could.

For all that, the gaiety and laughter in the mess that evening were spontaneous and real. Barber had a pint in his hand when he was summoned for by the Adjutant to meet their new Colonel and his wife.

'Sir, allow me to introduce Lieutenant Steven Barber,' he said. 'Steve, this is Colonel Bradshaw and his wife Louise.'

He held her hand a few seconds too long as he gazed into her blue eyes, his throat suddenly dry with desire for her. She was beautiful, with glossy black hair worn in a becoming page boy bob, and a slim but curvaceous body, shown off to perfection by her clinging dark green dress. An electric spark of understanding flashed between them, and somehow he knew she would be his one day soon. It took all his will power to prevent himself devouring her with his eyes while he indulged in the necessary small talk.

Presently, in a voice that was soft and slightly husky, she said, 'We must meet soon, Lieutenant Barber, and you can tell me all about your exploits in the SBS.'

'I'm afraid, ma'am, they amount to very little. I suspect your husband's stories would be far more entertaining than mine.'

'Only if we're talking about military matters,' she replied. 'Come along, Mike,' she took her husband's arm, 'let us do some circulating for a change.'

The Adjutant cocked an eyebrow at Steve, murmuring, 'She's a rum one and no mistake. Still, what can you expect if you marry someone fifteen years younger? Watch out, my lad. She'd eat junior officers for breakfast, along with the cornflakes.'

On that word of warning he departed, leaving Barber to wonder about the woman and ignore the advice.

After the dinner there was dancing to a Royal Marine four piece band, the younger element tapping their feet impatiently through the obligatory waltzes and foxtrots, and surging enthusiastically onto the floor when the beat changed to rock and roll. Steve knew he'd had more port than was wise, and that the whisky he was now consuming was making him drunker by the minute. He couldn't remember whether Louise asked him to dance, or vice versa. All he knew was that the lights had dimmed, a smoochy number was being played and she was in his arms, warm and scented and soft. She willingly allowed herself to be manoeuvred into a corner behind a large potted plant, and gave him her mouth for a kiss that left them both shaken and trembling.

'This is madness,' he muttered. 'Sheer unadulterated madness. When can I see you?'

'I don't know: tell you later. I'd better go now before I'm missed.'

He stayed where he was as she slipped back across the crowded floor. The alcohol had been dissipated by the brief encounter, his senses restored. For the rest of the evening he stuck to tomato juice, waiting impatiently for the message telling him where and when they could be alone.

As the evening drew on, and she didn't even seem aware of his existence, rebuffing him when he asked her for another dance, he was first bewildered and then angry. Who the hell did she think she was, turning him on as she had and now dismissing him like an importunate schoolboy? It was lucky for him that the evening was ending, for he resolved to get drunk and started on the whisky again. He was on his second double when the band played the last waltz, followed by 'God Save the Queen'. The lights came on, the bar closed and everyone was bidding each other goodnight.

Steve found himself alongside the Adjutant, saying goodnight to the Colonel and his wife. As she placed her small hand in his, leaving it there for a moment, he closed his fingers over the scrap of folded paper and, poker faced, waited for them to leave. His heart was soaring, his mind cursing. It would be madness to become involved with her. Good God – he'd only just met the woman, and here he was acting like an adolescent in the throes of calf love!

In the heads, he unfolded the note. 'Ring 328 tomorrow afternoon,' it read.

They became lovers on their first meeting. Steve was completely captivated by Louise, and was sure he was in love – but when he told her so she became angry and threatened to put an immediate end to their relationship unless he promised not to mention the word 'love' again. He agreed, terrified lest she carry out her threat, and the affair lasted four months almost to the day.

They couldn't get enough of each others' bodies, and when they were together caressed and touched each other continuously. They were very discreet to begin with, but as time went on they grew careless. It wasn't so much their preparations for meeting that gave them away – they still proceeded with the greatest caution – but their attitude towards each other in public. Their gestures, looks and smiles all added up to one thing for a certain man; the Adjutant. Steve had even received what amounted to a week's warning before the final débâcle.

'Come in, Steve.' The Adjutant greeted Barber at the door to his office. 'Grab a seat.

They sat opposite one another at the narrow, service issue desk in the sparsely furnished office, and the Adjutant's expression warned Steve that something unpleasant was about to come.

'In most circles, Steve, what I'm about to say would earn me a torrent of abuse, an instruction to mind my own business and mean the end of a beautiful friendship. Unfortunately, when the Regiment is involved to the extent it will be if a certain situation continues, I'm afraid I have to say something, and you won't be able to tell me to mind my own business. You know what I'm talking about?'

5

'No sir,' lied Steve, his mouth tightening.

'Don't play games with me, old boy, I don't like it. I'm talking about your affair with Louise Bradshaw, as you know damned well – and if I'm aware of it, I've no doubt others are too, or if they're not they soon will be.'

Not a muscle twitched in Steve's face to betray the agitation that was going on inside him. He'd already dismissed the idea of denying the Adjutant's charge, for he knew him well enough to be aware that he'd never make such an accusation unless he was positive of the facts. And anyway, they were the facts, so what was the point?

It's got to end, now, for the sake of us all and before it's too late,' the Adjutant was saying. 'Good God, man – imagine the scandal if it got out! It would have repercussions that are too serious even to contemplate.' He paused, then went on in a tone half authoritative, half persuasive: 'It must be this way, Steve – it has to be. Nothing is worth ruining your career for, to say nothing of the Old Man's, probably, and if not that, then at least his self respect. He's the best colonel this Regiment's had in a long time, and you know it. He loves his wife deeply. Think what it would do to him if he discovered she was being unfaithful to him. Think what it would mean to the rest of us.'

Steve sat there grim faced, saying nothing. He listened to the voice going on and on and on, knowing the Adjutant was right but at the same time rejecting what he was saying. Finally the Adjutant concluded: 'Go away and think about it – but don't take too long. If you finish it, nothing more will be said, I promise you that. . . . If you don't then I'll take steps myself to ensure the end of it. Another posting. . . .' He stopped, anger bubbling to the surface at the sight of the impassive face in front of him. 'Now listen, Steve, and listen well. Nobody, but nobody is going to upset this Regiment. We've got a hard enough time with the low morale of the men as it is, what with lousy pay, bad conditions and little prospect of either ever improving. If this got out, after the laughter would come the knowledge that it wasn't only the

6

men who were enjoying the joke of the Old Man's sexy wife being balled by one of the other officers, but everyone who could read a newspaper – if it got that far. And that I have no intention of allowing. After the laughter comes the shame; the snide jokes about the Colonel not being man enough to keep his wife happy, the ribbing from other Regiments, and the fights that would ensue.'

The Adjutant paused, then went on in a milder, more reasoning tone: 'Believe me, Steve, I know what I'm talking about. I've seen it happen more than once; men proud of their Regiment in trouble because of that pride. I know it and you know it – so stop being so damned selfish and try and think of others for a change.'

The continuing lack of response from the officer opposite him fanned his anger back to life. 'Very well, if you won't meet me in this, then I'll come all the way. You'll keep your flies zipped and stay away from that randy little bitch. If I see you anywhere in her vicinity, let alone in the same room as her, I'll have you on extra duties so fast your feet won't touch, and for so long you'll forget what shore leave is. Do I make myself clear?'

'Yes, sir,' came the wooden reply.

He tried once more. 'Please, Steve. Just give me your word you'll break it off and we'll forget this conversation ever took place.'

'I'm sorry, sir, but that's impossible.'

'Then get out!' gritted the Adjutant through clenched teeth, restraining himself with difficulty from hitting the other man. 'No – wait. This is off the record, Barber. I think you're a louse; a selfish bloody louse. If the Old Man learns of what's going on I'll have your guts for garters, and that's not a threat, it's a promise.'

Steve's mind was in a turmoil as he walked out into the humid heat and made his way across to the wardroom. Alone in his cabin, he lay on his bunk and tried to sort out his jumbled thoughts. So it was known. So what? So he know what. All that the Adjutant had said was true. He, Steve, had always known that this situation would arise one day, but had convinced himself that when it did he'd be able to cope – would know what to do. Well, here it was – and he didn't have a clue. He could always ask Louise to come away with him, of course. He'd resign, naturally – but then what? He had no idea how to support himself away from the security of the Marines; in fact had never given it serious consideration. He looked at his hands. One of the best pair in the S.B.S. at the killing game . . . at least in the practice of their art. He usually came first or second in the unarmed combat competitions that were frequently held, and was the best by a fair margin in the sharp shooting, whether with a rifle or a pistol. His paper work was adequate – with the help of his section's sargeant – but his leadership was excellent; his men were ready to follow him anywhere. He knew where his strengths and weaknesses lay, and recognised the fact that Louise was amongst his weaknesses. He'd see her, talk to her, reach a satisfactory agreement; which latter, in his mind, could only mean going away together, eventually.

They met on the other side of the island. When she heard what had happened Louise was concerned, but not unduly upset. When Steve tried to talk about a future together she brushed him off, and sensing her mood, he wisely dropped the subject until they'd returned to her house, safe in the knowledge that the Colonel had flown to the north of Malaya for an important defence meeting. They both drank too much at dinner, merely pushing the food around their plates, and afterwards Steve began again:

'Louise, you know I love you. You say you love me too, yet you won't even consider leaving to come away with me.'

She made no reply, but sat gazing moodily into her half empty glass.

'For Christ's sake, Louise, can't you answer?'

She raised her eyes then, and the total indifference of her look staggered him. He couldn't believe it. Later, replaying the scene in his memory over and over again, he came to re- alise that it was at that precise moment he had realised she

8

didn't love him; never had and never would. At the time however he wouldn't acknowledge it and fought against the truth, convincing himself there was some other reason for her lack of response to his idea of their going away together.

They made love, and Steve convinced himself that it was going to be all right; they'd work it out somehow. Afterwards she lay beside him, smoking, not speaking, he content just to watch her, his troubled feelings dormant for the moment.

Was it a sudden draught that made him sit up, or some sixth sense? Whatever it was, he found himself looking into the face of his Colonel.

He was unprepared for the transformation both of character and physique that took place before his very eyes. The tough, dapper man seemed to age and shrink; he leaned against the doorjamb as if to support himself, and said in a low, broken voice:

'Why, Louise? Why again? I thought . . . I thought after last time there'd be no more . . .'

'Sir, it's not what you think,' Barber began. 'We love each . . .' He broke off, quelled by his superior officer's icy stare.

'Shut up, Barber. Get dressed and get out. Now.'

Disconcerted, Barber turned to look at Louise. She looked back at him, an expression of indifference, boredom even, on her lovely face. Suddenly he knew that the scene being played was not a new one. He was a realist, and though the truth in this case was very hard to accept, he did so immediately. He knew she'd only been playing with him, and with the knowledge came a bitterness for what she'd done not to him, curiously enough, but to her husband. The words 'Why again?' echoed in his mind.

Part of a silent tableau, Barber slipped from the bed and began to dress. What was there to say? What could any of them say? As he buttoned his bush shirt and turned to leave, the Colonel edge away from the doorway.

'I'm sorry, sir,' Steve said. 'Dreadfully sorry . . .'

9

'Shut up and get out,' the Colonel interposed softly.

Barber glanced over his shoulder to see if there was any response from Louise. As he did so, her mask of indifference slipped, and her face was contorted by a look of hate and fury, directed at her husband.

'Yes, just get out, Lieutenant, and leave me to my oh so bloody righteous husband!' She sneered. 'My homosexual, man-loving husband who hasn't touched me for over six months.'

Barber shocked by the venom in her voice, turned to the Colonel, expecting an outraged denial. The Colonel, however, merely stood there making stricken, soundless mouthings, while Louise continued:

'You thought I didn't know, didn't you? Well, I found out nearly a year ago, and ever since then the very sight of you has made me sick with loathing. The last time you . . . violated me, if you remember, I was ill for days afterwards. That was you.' She drew a deep, shuddering breath. 'You're vile – vile! I wanted to die when I thought of what you'd been doing at that club of yours. You're nothing but filth, and I hate you. You, with your sanctimonious whining about my very normal sexual behaviour! You bloody queer . . .'

Barber didn't stay to hear any more. He left the house sickened, appalled, utterly depressed. He couldn't think, couldn't feel, couldn't get his brain out of the quagmire into which it seemed to have become trapped. All that long night he lay sleepless on his bunk, not knowing, not even able to imagine what would happen once the day started, as it inevitably would. God – how he wished the night would go on for ever!

The sound of the steward knocking on the door of the cabin next to his brought him back to reality with a shock. Realising he was still dressed, he scrambled to his feet, quickly stripped off, wrapped a towel around his waist and was brushing his teeth at the wash basin when the steward entered with his morning tea. He nodded his thanks, wryly applauding his own correct behaviour. The Marines certainly trained their officers well.

10

He rubbed his eyes wearily, trying unsuccessfully to rub away the gritty sensation beneath his lids. Somehow the incident had removed the fog from his mind and he could think clearly; for that, at least, he was grateful. Perching on the edge of his bed he sipped the lukewarm, sugarless tea and took stock of his position.

He would have to leave the Corps; of that he was certain. Whatever turned the Old Man on was his own affair – Steve couldn't care less. What he did care about was the Marines, and one thing he was sure of was that the Colonel was a far more useful officer than he himself was or was ever likely to be. With regret he remembered the Adjutant's warning. He'd been so right. . . .

Christ – what a fool he'd been! Steve resolutely pushed back the feeling of self pity within him. It was his own fault, and by God, he'd sort it out. The first thing he must do was talk to the Colonel, and arrange a transfer to another unit. Assure him that he'd never breathe a word about what had happened. He'd probably be away within the week.

This decision taken, albeit regretfully, Steve felt a certain sense of relief. Little did he know he'd be away within six hours, carrying with him an enormous burden of guilt that was to stay with him for the rest of his life.

★　★　★

Shaved and showered, Steve set out for the Mess, automatically noting the overcast and humid day; ideal for the first phase of the exercise that was to take place that day. He was quite looking forward to the challenge, after the period of intensive training. He was to lead his attack team across fifty miles of Malaysia, carry out a sneak swim-attack against eight anchored ships. Eight men, loaded down with eighty pounds of hardware each, living off the land and risking an encounter with the enemy every step of the way. To succeed . . .

He shook his head. Everything was changed now. He'd brought the consequences of his actions on himself, and though he'd never considered himself an honourable man in the strictest sense of the word, he knew he had to make the offer. He hoped against hope that he'd be allowed to continue with the exercise – but somehow he doubted it. His sergeant would have to manage; at least he could be confident he'd do a good job.

As Steve entered the mess, a military ambulance came round the corner and sped along the road leading to the senior officers' temporary quarters. He glanced after it, only mildly interested, then picked up a *Singapore Times* out of the newspaper rack and strolled in to breakfast. He nodded a greeting to a number of the other officers he knew and sat down with the paper in front of him. After reading the same paragraph for a third time without having understood a word, he gave up, and sat chewing on a piece of sausage and gazing gloomily into space. What a stupid bastard he'd been! Angrily he again pushed the thoughts from his mind. The stupid cliche, 'A man's got to do . . .'

The tap on his shoulder startled him.

'What? Oh, it's you, Bill. What's wrong?' he added quickly, alarmed by the look on the Adjutant's face.

'Come with me,' was the terse response. Without waiting for a reply the Adjutant strode out of the room, Barber hurrying to follow him. He caught up with him outside his office door, but wisely waited for his superior officer to speak first.

With the door closed and the desk between them, the Adjutant paced back and forth the small office, a movement which would have seemed comical in such a confined space had it not been for the agitation on his face. Barber waited.

'I could kill you!' the Adjutant said, abruptly, stopping and facing Barber.

The latter, feeling the blood drain from his face, stammered, 'Wh . . . what did you say?'

'You heard me. Look . . . look at these.' He held out his hands in front of him; they were shaking. 'I want to smash something, break something – because I'm afraid if I don't I shall attack you. Do you know what you've done? What

you've caused? Of course you don't, you self centred...'
He stopped, his mouth working. 'They're dead. Both of
them.'

'Who are?' Barber said weakly, already knowing the
answer.

'Who the hell do you think?' snarled the Adjutant. 'And
you killed them. She deserved what happened, but not him.
Christ – what am I saying? It shouldn't have happened to
either of them, especially this way.' He sank into a chair and
put his head in his hands. 'Oh, God, Steve,' he groaned.
'You should've listened when I told you. I told you to drop it.
Now look what you've done. Christ, what a bloody mess!'

'What happened, Bill?' Barber asked quietly. The shock
of the news seemed to have frozen his heart, but his brain
was icy clear.

The other man shook his head slowly, then raised it to look
Barber in the face. 'I'm only guessing, but it looked as
though the Old Man killed her and then committed suicide.
The police seem to have arrived at the same conclusion but
they're checking, just in case.' He shook his head again,
warily. 'I feel so tired...' Suddenly he banged the desk violently with the palm of his hand, startling them both with a
crack like a pistol shot. 'But I meant what I said a few
moments ago, Steve. For the first time in my life I was
capable of murder. I could have killed you, and been glad to
do it. That feeling has passed now, but by God, I loathe your
guts. If it's the last thing I do, I'll make sure you leave this
service, and the sooner the better. I virtually begged you to
leave her alone; if you'd listened, this would never have happened. The best officer the Marine Corps has ever had would
still be alive, and...' He broke off. 'Oh – what's the use!
You know what's going to happen as well as I do. You will
remain in these barracks until after the official enquiry, and
then return to the U.K. You will also tender your resignation, which I shall personally hand to the General in
London the day after tomorrow. I think I can promise you a
speedy exit into civilian life.'

13

'Just a minute ... sir,' Barber interrupted through clenched teeth. 'Just who the hell do you think you are? You've hung, drawn and quartered me before I've even been charged, let alone tried. The Colonel and his "lady" may both've been murdered, for all you know, and the whole thing rigged to look the way it does. So don't start accusing me of being responsible.' He didn't believe a word of what he was saying, but he carried on anyway. It was in his nature never to give up without a fight. 'I would suggest also that you keep your ideas to yourself, otherwise you'll find a lawsuit slapped on you so fast you'll wonder what hit you; then see what'd happen to the Regiment. Furthermore our precious Colonel...'

He stopped abruptly. What was the point? Even if the Adjutant believed the story that his hero was a queer, it could only cause him extra misery – and to what purpose? Barber knew he was through with the Marines, no matter what he said. At least he could leave them with a little more dignity than they'd have anyway once the story got out.

'Furthermore what?' the Adjutant demanded, his eyes narrowing.

'Nothing. Forget it.'

'Barber, if you try to sling muck at the Colonel I will kill you.'

'For God's sake, Bill – don't be so bloody melodramatic. You aren't going to kill anybody, least of all me. I deeply regret what has happened, and assure you you'll have my resignation as soon as I can write it. Meanwhile ... sir ... I suggest you pull yourself together and start the right balls moving in the right directions, before the situation gets out of hand. When you've calmed down, and if you wish to talk to me further about this, perhaps you'll either send for me or come yourself. And now, as you obviously have a lot to do, I'll leave you to get on with it.'

Without giving the other man time to reply he left the room, closing the door behind him with a firm click. Reaction set in, and he felt his body beginning to tremble. He

14

walked quickly across to the cabin, went in and thankfully locked the door behind him.

Somewhere he lost four hours. Throughout that time he lay on his bunk, not thinking, not feeling. The series of shocks his nervous system had sustained during the last twelve hours or so were beginning to take their toll.

At last, for the second time within a short period, he felt his mind beginning to function properly again after, it seemed, wandering through a thick fog.

One thing was certain; he'd never get the chance to take part in the exercise now. Even as the thought went through his head he felt disgusted with himself for his selfish attitude. He forced himself to think of the Colonel, and how he'd felt the evening before. He'd realised some time ago that Louise had had other lovers, but he'd had no way of knowing her husband was aware of it too. Perhaps it was unfair to judge her too harshly; after all, it must be hell for a woman to discover that her husband was homosexual. She could have divorced him, though; they could've gone away together . . . But no – she didn't love him. She'd never loved him. It had all been a joke; the declarations of love . . . their passionate interludes in bed . . . the sheer fun of being together.

He tried to hate her for it, but knew that it would be a long time before he would be able to come to terms with himself and what she'd really meant to him. He'd loved her. For all her faults, he'd loved her.

Chapter 2

Steve stopped speaking and shrugged. 'You know the rest. The enquiry came to the same conclusion as we had; the Colonel killed Louise and then took his own life. As far as the civilian authorities were concerned the case was closed – but as far as the Marines were concerned, I had a lot to answer for; unofficially, of course. The Old Man had been a protégé of the General's. Naturally nothing was put down in writing; they just promised me the lousiest jobs available, and no chance of promotion. My resignation was accepted with delight and sighs of relief...' He broke off, and shrugged again. 'So – to cut an even longer story short, what with all that happened, here I am.'

Philip Barber nodded. 'You know,' he began hesitatingly, 'with my connections and your cooperation we could fight this all the way. Expose the truth, get your commission back – or insist on adequate compensation. After all, your only crime was that you had an affair with a married woman, which is a common enough occurrence these days, and certainly doesn't warrant the kind of treatment you've been subjected to. If we proved your Colonel was queer...'

'No, Phil,' Steve broke in, 'I've no intention of doing anything of the sort. Sure we could kick up a rumpus – and then what? I couldn't rejoin. At best, life would be hell; at worst ...' He shuddered. 'Ugh – it doesn't bear thinking about! the publicity's been bad enough already. This would be ten times worse – and what would I achieve? A certain amount of notoriety, maybe a bit of cash; it's just not worth it.' He looked his brother in the eye. 'And most important, I don't want to.' He held up his hand as his brother started to interrupt. 'Hang on – I'm not quite such a fool as you think I am. You see, Louise was the Colonel's second wife. He has a fifteen year old son in school somewhere in England, and I reckon life's been difficult enough for him without learning something like this about a father he rarely saw, and whom he probably idolised. Consider the possible consequences, Phil. I'm sure you'll agree that any small gain I might make is simply not worth it.'

Phil thought for a moment, chewing his lip; then he nodded slowly. 'Yes – I suppose you're right.'

I'm glad you think so. Now – let's turn to pleasanter subjects. What are you planning to do over the weekend? I thought all three of us might go up to the cottage in Scotland; if we caught the late train we could be there by breakfast on Saturday. What do you say?'

They made plans for the immediate future, skirting around the question of Steve's lack of qualifications, lack of money and lack of prospects. There weren't many jobs going for a young, tough ex-marine officer, expert in demolitions, under-water sabotage and most methods of killing a man without really trying. Still, as Steve said, something would turn up.

They'd refilled their glasses for the last time and were thinking about leaving when Phil, looking over his brother's shoulder towards the door, gave a groan.

'Oh no! I thought those creeps never came in here.'

Steve glanced over his shoulder and saw three youths with short dyed hair, wearing 'punk' gear and clearly looking for trouble. The smallest of the three approached a table where an old man was quietly sipping his brown ale, leaned forward, snatched the glass out of the old man's hand and drained it. Then, wiping his mouth with the back of his hand, he belched loudly and turned to grin at his two friends. They grinned back and nodded in the direction of a young couple.

'The two with the little punk are brothers,' Phil said in a low voice. 'The other's their cousin. This has been a favourite trick of theirs for quite some time. If anyone hits back, the other two use it as an excuse to beat that someone up. It's been known to get very unpleasant. People usually ignore them, and after a while they get bored and leave.'

The three had walked across to the table where the couple were sitting. The younger punk picked up the girl's drink, scowled at it and poured it onto the floor. Then he picked up the boy's pint and began to drink. The boy half rose, his fist drawn back, but the girl pulled him back into his seat.

'Scared, sonny boy?' sneered the smaller punk. He turned to the barman. 'Hey, this beer's like piss. Good for only one thing, ain't it, sonny boy?'

So saying, he poured the last few dregs of beer over the young man's head. The young man looked up, his eyes smouldering, but when the girl said something in a low voice he sat back, not looking at his tormentors.

The three laughed and looked about them. Steve caught the eye of one of them and turned back to his brother.

'Phil, if they start on us leave everything to me . . . okay?' He saw his brother hesitate. 'Listen,' he continued softly, 'when I want legal advice I'll come to you. In this situation, leave it to me.' He smiled gently. 'I'm going to enjoy this.'

The younger of the three punks stopped at their table. Steve didn't move as his brother's pint was raised and drunk. The punk then picked up Steve's tall lager glass and raised it to his lips. As he started drinking, Steve hit the base of the glass with all the force he could muster. The glass shattered and sliced through the youth's cheeks almost to his ears. Beer and blood flowed down his studded leather jacket as with a scream he fell back into the arms of his mates. They staggered, and he slipped to the floor, and lay there howling and squirming in a widening pool of blood. The other two, quick to recover, squared up to Steve, but he was ready for them.

'I shouldn't try anything if I were you, else you'll both end up in hospital.' His even tone, his complete confidence made them hesitate.

'Do as my brother says,' put in Philip. 'Just pick up your cousin and get out of here.'

They looked at him, took a hesitant step forward then simultaneously turned around and helped their injured cousin to his feet. His cries had subsided to loud moans, but blood was still pouring from the jagged lacerations to his face, which he was trying to hold together with shaking fingers. Throughout the incident no one else in the bar had moved or spoken.

At the door the three paused, and one of them turned to the Barber brothers.

'I'll get you for this, you fucking bastards!' he cried. 'Jus' you wait . . .'

Steve grinned. 'Any time, punk, any time. In fact, how about now?' He took a couple of paces towards the door and laughed aloud as the three scurried out. 'Come on, Phil, let's get the hell out of here before the fuzz arrives to see what all the noise was about.'

As they left, by a different exit, the hushed silence in the bar erupted into pandemonium.

They walked a few hundred yards in silence. Finally Phil remarked. 'You moved fast.'

'Uh-uh – I should have taken all three of them. I've got a feeling we haven't heard the last of them. 'Damnation!' Steve thumped his fist into the palm of his other hand. 'I can't stand turds like that. I'd like to put them through a bacon slicing machine, starting with their feet.'

His brother gave a grunt of laughter. 'I hadn't realised you were so bloodthirsty.'

'I'm not really.' Steve put an arm around his shoulders. 'In fact I feel quite sorry for poor sods who end up doing that sort of thing for kicks. There must be something wrong with them. In fact if they were slightly more mentally deficient they'd make good SAS men.' He laughed sourly at his own joke. 'Oh, come on – let's forget about them. Look, that off-licence is still open. Let's pick up a bottle of plonk and take it home with us. I'm sure Sue could use a glass with dinner.'

It was a fortnight later that Steve Barber received the 'phone call from Sue. They'd had an enjoyable weekend in Scotland, and though Phil had pressed him to stay with them he'd declined, and instead had found himself a cheap bedsit in Hounslow, on the outskirts of London. He'd signed on the dole, and by eating frugally could afford the rent and a good supply of whisky to keep him company during the interminable days. He'd been offered two jobs so far, both in a managerial capacity, but had turned them down. He was dissatisfied, lost without the direction of the Marines, and slowly sinking into a state of apathy.

He heard the telephone ring, and looked at his watch. He really ought to rouse himself and get ready for an interview that afternoon – but the effort seemed too much. Instead he poured himself another large drink, added a dash of water and took a mouthful. The whisky had no effect as it hit his stomach. Strange, he thought, such a large amount. His descent down the slippery slope was becoming daily more rapid – and there was nothing he wanted to do about it.

The shrill voice of his inquisitive, shrewdish landlady penetrated his morose reverie.

'Mister Barber, do I have to come all the way up there to get you? Can't you hear me? Telephone for you.'

'All right,' he yelled back. 'I'm coming.' Old cow, he thought as he struggled off the bed. He looked around him in disgust at the threadbare carpet and tatty wallpaper as he made his way down two flights of stairs to the front hall. Self pity was welling up within him as he picked up the receiver. He paused, and looked at the landlady hovering in the background.

'Thank you, Mrs Benn.' He waited until, with a loud sniff, she marched into her living room and carefully half closed the door. He knew she'd be listening on the other side, but he didn't really care. One minor victory was enough for one day.

'Barber speaking,' he said into the mouthpiece.

Sue's voice came over the line, gasping with sobs. 'Steve! Oh Steve! It's Phil . . . he's in hospital. He's . . . oh God!'

Steve had turned cold. 'Take it easy,' he said. 'Calm down, take three deep breaths and tell me what's wrong.' His brain was racing, the adrenalin in his blood over-riding the effect of alcohol. He waited for his sister-in-law to control her weeping and continue in a faltering voice:

'Phil has been badly beaten up. He's in hospital under-going an emergency operation. He . . . he's in a pr . . . pretty bad way. The d . . . doctor has given him a fif . . . fifty-fifty chance of pulling through, and even then God alone knows what s . . . sort of s . . . state he'll be in.' She burst into sobs again. 'Oh Steve – who could have done such a thing, and why?'

'Now hold on, love. I'll be right over. Are you in the hospital just now, or at home?'

'In the hospital. Saint Bartholomew's . . . in . . . in . . .'

'I know it. I'll be there in an hour. Now don't worry – he's going to be all right. Don't forget he's got the strength of the Barbers in him.' The words sounded inane even to him.

'Th . . . thanks, Steve. I'll feel better when you're here.'

He hung up, ran up the stairs, grabbed his coat and glanced at himself in the mirror, before leaving. God – what a sight! He'd be more of a hindrance than a help if he turned up looking like that. Hastily stripping off, he shaved, had an all over wash, and put on a decent shirt, suit and tie. As he did so he thought about his brother, and rage welled up in him, rage so strong it caused a tight knot in his jaw, and made his fingers tremble as he tied the tie. He knew who was re-sponsible, all right. Well, this time they were for the chop. He'd get the bastards if it was the last thing he did. Whatever injuries Phil had sustained at their hands would be paid back, with interest. He took a deep breath to steady his nerves and remove the tension from his body. I won't kill them, he thought. They'll just wish they were dead.

21

He got on the underground at Hounslow West, and as the train rattled towards the city he began planning what he intended to do. It wasn't callousness on his part that he didn't think about his brother, it was an attempt to keep down the anguish he was feeling. Concentrating on his hatred for the punks kept down his worry, stopped it clouding his brain, and more importantly, stopped him from remembering it was his fault. All for the price of a couple of pints his brother was . . . was . . . He pushed the thought aside. Why, oh why hadn't he just let the bastards take the beer and leave? But no – he'd had to be the big man, the hero in his brother's eyes. He shook his head in exasperation. No dammit, that wasn't the reason at all. He'd never tried to be any sort of hero in front of anyone, let alone Phil. He'd reacted as he had because he'd felt it right to do so. Those punks had had a lesson coming to them, and he'd been in a position to give it. Their next lesson would be their final one.

He was so deep in thought he almost forgot to get off the train at the next station. He took a taxi to the hospital, and a short while later was with his sister-in-law, whom he found sitting outside the emergency theatre, a half-empty cup of cold tea in her hands.

'Hullo Sue . . . any news?' he asked softly.

She looked up, startled, then sprang to her feet. 'Oh Steve – thank God!' She bit her lips to stop them trembling, trying to be brave. 'No – there's no news. They've been in there for hours, at least it seems like hours. I'm so worried . . .'

She looked so pathetic, standing there in her maternity smock, her body swollen in the eighth month of pregnancy, her face strained with grief and worry. Steve put an arm around her shoulders, saying softly, 'Don't fight it, love. Have a good cry if it will help.' His words broke the fragile shell of self control, and she leaned against him, sobbing bitterly. He patted her gently without speaking, and when the storm of tears eased, led her back to her seat and sat down beside her, holding her hand.

'He'll be all right,' he began. 'I'm quite convinced . . .'

22

She laid her fingers against his mouth, saying softly, 'Hush, Steve – you don't have to say any more. Thanks for trying, but I realise the possible consequences of this sort of ... of injury. He's been viciously kicked in the head and abdomen ... so ... possible brain damage, and possible organ damage. I don't know exactly what that means, of course. Do you?'

Steve shook his head mutely.

'I've been sitting here,' Sue went on, 'imagining life with a new born baby and a cabbage of a husband. The thought scares me to death. I pray he'll be all right, but prayer doesn't much help because the injuries are already there. In a couple of hours I shall know, one way or the other and I'm so scared of knowing that I just want to run away and hide. Does that make any sort of sense to you?'

Barber found her forced calm, her detached way of talking more alarming than any outburst of emotion.

'I understand what you mean, Sue, if it's any consolation,' he said, 'but all I can say is that you've got to hang in there, never stop hoping. Phil will be all right.' He paused, and for the hundredth time since her 'phone call debated whether or not he should tell her about the incident in the pub. 'How would you feel if the people who'd done this were caught and punished?' he went on presently. 'I don't mean by the police, but in a similar way to the way they've hurt Phil?'

She looked at him for a moment, puzzled. 'But how can they be caught? No one has any idea of who did it, least of all the police. The only person who can identify them is Phil, if and when he recovers sufficiently. Even then he may either not remember or not have seen their faces. So your question is somewhat academic, don't you think?'

He shook his head slowly.

'What do you mean by that? Do you know who did it?' When he didn't reply she continued, 'But that's absurd. How can you possibly know?'

'I don't know for certain,' Steve told her, 'but I can make a damned good guess. Haven't you wondered why Phil was attacked? After all, he had no enemies to my knowledge, and certainly none who'd want to inflict this kind of damage on him . . . True?'

She nodded. 'So where does that lead?'

'I don't suppose he told you about the fracas we had in the pub a couple of weeks ago?'

When she shook her head, he took a deep breath, let it out slowly, then began to relate what had happened.

'I wasn't sure whether to tell you or not,' he concluded. 'Cowardice, perhaps; I didn't want you blaming me to such an extent that if things did turn out badly you'd end up hating me.' He paused, then added with a grimace, 'I couldn't blame you if you did, of course. With hindsight, maybe I shouldn't have done what I did – but I think if you'd seen the looks on the faces of the other people in that pub when they were being terrorised, you'd understand why I did react like that. I wish I hadn't, now. I'm bloody sorry, I don't know what to say.'

Sue covered his hand with her own cold trembling one.

'Phil didn't tell me anything about it,' she said. 'He probably didn't want to worry me . . . that's typical of how thoughtful he is . . .' She broke off, her lips quivering. Presently she went on, 'I don't think Phil will blame you, so why should I? But I do wish you hadn't done it,' she added quickly looking away.

'You're an incredibly generous person,' Steve told her softly. 'I know it's one of the qualities Phil has always admired in you. Anyway, I think it will be best if you forget what I've told you, just in case the police have cause to question you further. I'll just say that the bastards who did this won't get away with it . . . Okay?'

She smiled wanly. 'Okay, if that's . . .'

Just then the doctor pushed his way through the swing doors of the theatre. Neither of them moved as he approached them, a tired, sad look on his face; Sue's hand found Steve's once more, colder and more tremulous than ever.

24

'You must be the patient's brother,' the doctor began. Steve nodded. 'Good. Well, it's a bit early to say yet precisely how he'll do, but I can tell you that it's not quite as bad as I at first feared. He has suffered extensive injuries, but most of them should heal quite straightforwardly. There are, however, three areas for concern.' He looked down into Sue's strained, attentive face. 'I'm telling you all this, Mrs. Barber, because I think it's only right that you should know, so that if . . . Well anyway, as I was saying: there are three areas for concern; damage to the kidneys, the testicles and the brain. Your husband has severe renal bruising, mainly on the right side. At first we thought he'd lose the kidney, but further examination has shown us that this is not necessarily so. With proper treatment and care there's more than a 60/40 chance that it will mend all right. His right testicle is also badly bruised, but again with correct treatment he should be all right. The area that causes us most concern is his head. He has a fractured skull.'

'Oh God . . .' Sue whispered.

'It's quite a serious fracture, but, I hasten to add, not as bad as a number I've seen where the patient has made a complete recovery. Part of the bone on the right side of the skull splintered and has damaged some of the nerves. Although we can prevent further damage, unfortunately we can't repair what has already been done. The damage is by no means extensive, but it's in an area where it's difficult to predict what the outcome will be.'

'What's the worst that can happen, doctor? I think I'd like to know, if you please.'

He glanced at her narrowly, disturbed by her icy calm.

'I can only guess, and say that at the worst, partial or complete paralysis of the left side. But, and I must stress this, that is taking an extremely gloomy view. It's more likely that he'll merely suffer a weakening of, say, his left hand or arm. Only time will tell, though.'

'Thank you, doctor. When may I see him, please?'

'Not before tomorrow; he probably won't regain consciousness before then. If you arrive at about two o'clock, you should be able to speak to him, if only for a few moments.' He bent closer. 'Mrs. Barber! Are you feeling all right?'

Sue's face had become even paler than it had been when Barber first arrived at the hospital. She closed her eyes, gripping her brother-in-law's arm as she began to sway.

'Easy, Mrs. Barber,' the doctor said, motioning to Steve to support her. 'I'll get a nurse.'

Sue moaned and leaned forward, clasping her hands across her swollen belly. 'My baby . . . please . . . my baby. Don't . . . don't let anything happen to my baby. Not now . . . please not now.'

'Hold on, Mrs. Barber. Help's coming.' The doctor strode across to an internal telephone mounted on the wall, and spoke urgently into it for a few moments. Then he hung up and turned round, smiling encouragingly. 'Now, don't worry about a thing, you're in good hands here. We'll have you admitted and examined in no time. I'm sure there's nothing to worry about. This reaction is only to be expected after all you've been through, in your condition. I've arranged for a colleague to look at you. We'll just whip you up to the maternity ward where they know about these things – it's not my field you see – and make sure everything's all right. Ah – here's the wheelchair. Just sit in here . . . that's it. You'll be more comfortable than trying to walk.'

She looked imploringly at Steve, who gave her hand a reassuring pat. 'It's okay, love, I'll wait here for you,' he told her. 'Don't worry.'

She nodded, and bit her lip as pain stabbed again.

'I'll come with you,' the doctor said to the porter, and they hurried off towards the lift.

Steve sat down, feeling very much alone, and tried to control the trembling of his hands by putting them between his knees and pressing until they throbbed. His rage against the people responsible for his brother's condition had passed the homicidal point and now glowed in a white hot fever, leaving him determined to take revenge, but in a way which couldn't be connected with him. He dwelt with grim pleasure on the form the punishment would take. Should he inflict physical or mental damage? The latter could be more permanent, but took longer to achieve, risking the chance of his being discovered. No; he needed an action that could be completed in a few hours while inflicting the maximum possible damage, both mental and physical.

An idea slowly took shape, but before more than the barest outline could emerge the doctor returned, looking more tired and haggard than ever.

'How is she?' Steve asked anxiously, getting to his feet.

The other man grimaced, waggling a hand, palm down. 'Touch and go, I'm afraid. I understand she's in her eighth month, so it's not as bad as it might have been. The baby has a strong, steady heartbeat, so even if it is born prematurely it won't matter—too much.'

'Thanks, Doc.' Steve shook his head. 'God – What a mess! One thing, were you on the level earlier on – about my brother I mean. You weren't keeping anything back because my sister-in-law was there?'

'No,' the doctor assured him, 'nothing kept back. Of course there may be other factors we haven't discovered yet, but I've told you all I know so far.' He held out his hand. 'I have to go now, Mr. Barber; I have a ward round to do. Oh – and if you go up the stairs over there on the right, your sister-in-law is on the next floor up. They'll let you see her for a couple of minutes.'

Chapter 3

Steve was allowed to see his brother for only a few minutes the following day. Phil, though conscious, could not speak; nevertheless he did manage a sickly grin of recognition. Steve sat beside his bed, made some encouraging small talk and reassured him about Sue, who was to be allowed to visit him in a little while.

When the nurse put her head around the door and told him it was time to go he nodded and stood up. As he did so he leaned forward and whispered fiercely to his brother, 'Listen Phil – if the police ask you any questions, tell them you have no idea who did this? Okay? I'll take care of it myself – and this time there'll be no comeback from the bastards. Okay?'

'No, Steve,' his brother croaked. 'Don't do it, p . . . please.'

'I must. Now don't worry – I can take care of myself. It means I won't be in to see you for a week or so but . . . don't worry,' he repeated lamely.

'Not . . . worth it, Steve . . . not . . . worth it.' The effort of talking was making Phil sweat. 'Don't . . . ruin your life.'

'Come along please, Mr. Barber,' the nurse urged softly. With a final wink and a wave Steve left the room.

He paid a brief visit to Sue, and found that the crisis had been averted, and that her pregnancy was following its normal course. Having reminded her too about not talking to the police, and promising to telephone in a couple of days, he left the hospital with some relief, hating its smell of antiseptics and anaesthetics, and its atmosphere of sickness and pain.

★ ★ ★

For the next five days Steve Barber, dressed in the scruffiest clothes he could find, unshaven and with hair unkempt, slouched around the pubs in the area where he'd met his brother. No one took any notice of him as, unobtrusively, he narrowed the area of where the punks, as he now thought of them, hung out. By the fifth day he was sure he would meet up with them eventually in one of two places.

On the Friday evening he was sitting in a corner of a popular bar, packed with loudly boisterous working men, most of whom appeared to be dockers, when he caught a glimpse of a face he was sure he recognised. He was gratified to realise that, apart from a slight increase in awareness, he was totally unmoved by the thought of what the next few hours might bring.

Shouldering his way to the bar, he managed to order another pint as last orders were called, and with the lower half of his face buried in his tankard, scanned the crowded room. He spotted his quarry sitting in a corner, involved with his brother in a heated conversation with a third man. Not looking their way again, Barber placed his tankard on the bar, pushed his way through the crowd and out into the street. The pub had two doors, both opening on to the dark, dank street in which he now found himself. The earlier heavy rain had stopped, leaving the roads wet and glistening, with street lamps reflecting in the puddles. The sky was overcast – there was no moon. The pub stood at the end of a row of terraced houses on the corner of a T junction. Steve had already scouted the area, and knew that the roads to his left and right were cul de sacs, each containing a dozen or so houses. Paths led out of the cul de sacs, running alongside a railway embankment for fifty or sixty yards before joining up at the end of another T junctioned road, where there were more houses.

He stood in the shadows, watching the doors as the people

29

began to leave, most of them more or less the worse for drink. He wriggled his toes, trying to keep warm, his hands thrust deep into his raincoat pockets. The chill, damp air was beginning to make him shiver, but he forgot his discomfort when he saw the two brothers step through the door, followed by the man with whom they had been arguing.

Keeping perfectly still, well hidden in the shadow of a doorway, he waited to see which way they'd turn. Their voices were still raised in dispute as they turned past him, walking up the cul de sac. They were, it seemed, talking about football.

Have a good argument, boys, Barber said to himself, because I doubt if you'll enjoy many more. Keeping well behind, he followed them to the top of the road, where he heard one of them say goodnight before letting himself into the end house. The others replied with a goodnight, and some remark was made that indicated they'd all be meeting again at the pub the following night. By the light of the last street lamp before the beginning of the path, Steve recognised the two brothers. He watched them disappear around a bend before returning the way he'd come, smiling grimly to himself.

★　★　★

'Gentlemen, I apologise for calling this meeting today; I know how precious Saturdays are to all of us. Unfortunately, it couldn't be helped. The Prime Minister was panicking on the 'phone to me last night, and demanded that we present her with the facts and the solution – if, that is, a solution is called for. She wants to see us all at Number 10 first thing Monday morning.'

The other three men seated around the table nodded gloomily.

'Typical,' said one. 'She's put us off for a week, and now she ruins our weekend. The bloody woman has no consideration at all. At least the Opposition, when they're in power, give us some thought; or they used to. Don't know what this one's going to be like.'

30

Pearce, a permanent undersecretary at the Ministry and responsible for liaison between the internal security organisations and the government of the day, glared at his companions as if daring them to contradict him. No one did.

Chief Superintendent Jim Carmichael felt it wasn't his place to say anything. Although after nearly ten years of dealing with these people he knew he was treated like an equal, he still kept his opinions to himself, reticence he'd learnt from an eternity spent in Special Branch; at least his wife claimed it seemed like an eternity.

The third man, Walters, began fiddling with his pipe. He was a nervous man who was always playing with something; his pipe, his watch chain, his pen knife. When agitated he developed a small tic in the corner of his right eye, and junior members of his department ran small sweepstakes on how early in any day the tic would start. So far, there'd only been one recorded before lunch time. Walters was the assistant to the man chairing the meeting, and tipped to take his place one day.

Chapman, at the head of the table, was a small dapper man, a career civil servant and now, with only three years to go before retirement, head of the political espionage and counter-espionage department. Although his brief was world wide, affairs at home took up more and more of his department's time; so much so, in fact, that there was talk of setting up an entirely new department to deal solely with political counter-espionage in the UK. Left wing infiltration of trade unions and the Labour party was already causing the Prime Minister grave concern, especially as the more moderate Labour voters were beginning to take heed of what was happening, and looking to the Alliance for a way out. At the same time her own conservatives were becoming restless with her inability to bring down unemployment. It was rumoured that they too would probably ride with the Alliance next time. If balance of power fell to the Alliance then proportional representation would follow. It would mean an end to the two party system (something neither she

31

nor the Leader of the Opposition wanted) and result in the type of hung parliament that had plagued European countries since the last war. No. It suited the system to keep it as it was. More to the point, it suited the people running the system. Which was why the attacks on the Liberal and SDP were as vitriolic from both sides of the house. The status quo had to be maintained at all costs. Walters would help to keep the system intact, Chapman was sure of that, which was why he would be appointed to head the department; a fact not yet known to the rest of his colleagues.

'You're all fairly conversant with the facts, or at least with our beliefs,' began the Chairman. 'Because we have only the one file, and that kept by the Chief here, I suggest that, at the risk of boring you all, we listen to the story as we know it, and the solution we intend proposing on Monday, Jim.'

He nodded towards the Chief Superintendent, who began without preamble:

'Gentlemen, as you all know, the subject was born of wealthy parents in Hampshire. After a public school education he went to Oxford, where he read political science and history. After a closeted and pampered life, he appears to have become dissatisfied with the capitalist society in general and his own life style in particular, and like may young men of that era, became a member of the Communist Party. He visited Russia on a number of occasions during the early fifties, and was a very active member of the party. In '54 his parents died in a car accident, under somewhat mysterious circumstances, and our man left for Russia, vowing never to return. As you are all aware, he did return three years later, renounced the Communists and joined the Labour party.'

Carmichael paused and held up a thin document. 'In here are the sworn statements of once active trade unionists telling us exactly how the balloting was rigged and why the subject was elected to the post that started him on his highly successful career in politics. In a word, orders; orders that came from Moscow. With heavy union backing he was quickly nominated for a seat in the House of Commons, and

32

having been offered the safe Labour seat in Hull, was certain to end up as a member of Parliament pretty soon. In hindsight, a number of interesting points appear. It was easy for him to drop his old friends. He had renounced his background and was living in a comparatively remote part of the country. He never returned to the south of England and appears to have deliberately avoided the area. One or two old friends did try to get in contact after his return but were fobbed off. He has had no contact with his past up to the present time. His time in Russia has been played down and if it is ever mentioned he claims that having seen the system from inside, as it were, he knows better than most how bad it is. Recently, he has been heard to say that for a nation such as Russia, with its diversity of peoples, languages and cultures it is the only system that could work. And what a wonderful job is being done to improve the lot of the people etc. etc.'

Carmichael paused, and looked around the table. 'One point, gentlemen,' he went on. 'I can't find out why he was offered that seat when he was. As a relative newcomer, you'd expect him to have to fight hard for such a constituency; plum seats like that are usually reserved for the more senior members of the party. Although we have no proof, it's been suggested that it could have been achieved by a certain amount of coercion and bribery in the right quarters; however, that's sheer conjecture, too far in the past and must be left to the imagination. The fact remains that he got the seat, and has proved to be an able politician and a good man for his constituency. Indeed he did so well that he came second in the party leadership nominations three years ago.

Again Carmichael paused, surveying the three men before him. Walters was playing with his watch, Pearce sat with his head thrown back, his eyes fixed on a spot on the ceiling, and Chapman seemed lost in a world of his own; a pose that had disconcerted Carmichael at first, until he learned that not only was he being listened to most attentively, but also that the information he was conveying was being carefully and accurately assimilated.

He cleared his throat and resumed: 'We would never have suspected anything; after all, there was no reason to. Apart from the periods he spent in Russia there's been nothing especially remarkable about the man's career, unless the whole picture is analysed. Then it becomes disconcerting to say the least. A great many of our politicians and trade unionists have been, and in the case of the latter, still are, paid up members of the Communist party. Some are even on record as saying that they'd like to see an end to the Capitalist system of this country, with the nationalisation of all industry and land. However, I digress. As I said, unless carefully examined, the career of the subject is not particularly unusual. After all, we need to go back more than twenty years to find the slightest indication of any criminal activity – that of rigging the ballot box – and that is damned difficult to prove.

'As you are all aware, just over a month ago the Americans agreed to shelter and interrogate a Russian defector. Although the man had approached us originally, we felt it safer, with the political climate at present prevailing ("God," Carmichael thought, "I sound more like a bloody civil servant every day!"), to ... er ... let the Yanks look after him.

'Now, the reason the defector wished to come to us was because he'd been specialising in British Political affairs at the KGB; as second in command of his section, he had a lot to tell us. You know what an agonising decision it was, to let the Americans have him, but I'm sure you all agree there was no choice. They may be having a good laugh at our expense because of what they're being told, but that's nothing compared to the howls of rage that would have gone up, not only from them but also from the rest of NATO, if we'd been made to give him back.' Again he held up the small dossier. 'It took the Americans four days to produce this, and it proves conclusively that the present deputy leader of the Labour party is not the Honourable Edward Parker, but a Russian substitute. Everything, from the fake accidental death of Parker's parents, to the seducing of Parker himself to go and live in Russia, to the finding of the right man to take his place, to the fixing of his election to the House are all shown clearly in here. The concluding paragraphs, which no one apart from myself and Mr. Chapman have read, are highly illuminating.' He glanced at Chapman's assistant. 'Mr. Walters, sir, you asked at the beginning of this affair, why should the Russians bother? Why take the risk, when Europe appears to be headed towards communism anyway? It's simple. If you look at the powerful Euro–Communist parties of Italy, France and Spain, you will see that more and more they're having less and less to do with Mother Russia. Indeed, while paying a very half hearted lip service to Russia, the European Communist parties go very much their own way; which, of course, Russia doesn't like one little bit. Now, even if Britain became so left wing that her policies could hardly be distinguished from those of the Russians, we would still be our own rulers – and that is not, as you are all aware, acceptable to Russia; she wants Europe to be under the direct control of Moscow's ruling Politburo.

'The Russian leaders came to the conclusion that if a man achieved sufficient seniority to enable him to affect this country's policies, no matter what his political views, he would tend to end up doing his best for this country, even if that best was only from his own point of view; therefore a Communist Britain would still rule itself, and go the way of the other Euro–Communists – a totally unsatisfactory state of affairs as far as Moscow is concerned. However, what if the man in the influential position was not only a Russian at heart but also by birth? A man whose loyalty could not be doubted, could not be swayed?' Carmichael paused, allowing his point to sink in. Then he went on:

'The planning and effort that went into the project in the early days was enormous, and it was pulled off in a way they could only have dreamed about twenty years ago. A minor point, gentlemen.' Again he paused, and this time all eyes were on him. 'To ensure continued loyalty, the subject's parents are kept in Russia, and are visited once a year by their son, in Copenhagen. The visits only last a few days, and are apparently highly charged with emotion. Oh – and there's one more point. As far as we know, and as far as the Russians themselves know, neither the subject's wife, nor of course, their son, know he's a Russian.'

Carmichael stopped speaking, noting with a certain amount of satisfaction that this time there were no protestations, as there had been when Walters and Pearce had first been told of what was suspected. Familiarity with the facts made additional information easier to take.

'How far have you got with cross checking this information?' Walters asked, after a silence that had lasted almost a minute.

'We've made a start on the more obvious bits. By that I mean, for instance, Russian involvement and reactions in Africa during the period Parker was a junior minister with the Foreign Office. It's not conclusive, of course, but a correlation of the facts gave rise to some pretty interesting hypotheses. By themselves they would mean nothing, but taken all together, I believe them to be pretty damning.'

'I see. I assume we can take it for granted that the Russians are aware of what's going on? That being the case . . .' He paused significantly, and Chapman took up the point.

'Precisely,' Chapman said. 'I think we can all work it out for ourselves. I've authorised a watch to be kept on Parker until further notice. We can expect some sort of contact, but how or where . . .' He shrugged. 'We'll just have to see. We've examined what we think Parker's possible reactions might be, and between us, Jim and myself have arrived at the same conclusion.' He grinned. 'We haven't a clue.'

Carmichael said. 'There are a number of options available to him. He could brazen it out. After all, what we know and what we can prove in a court of law are two different things. His political life would be over of course and with it would go his social standing, perhaps even his family. The forces unleashed by this revelation to him personally are incalcu-

36

lable. Whether he could recover from it is doubtful. He could cut and run. He would be hailed as a hero of Russia, retire with a pension to a suitable dacha and write his memoirs whilst drinking himself to death.' The wry tone was not lost on his audience. 'Finally, a fake death, nobody and he quietly retires to Russia. No hero's welcome, no propaganda coup by the Soviets, in short nothing really gained after twenty years. In fact, a lot lost just as they are about to pull off the big one.'

In the ensuing silence Carmichael covertly studied the other three men. He wondered what they were thinking. This whole business had been a shock to them all, and he knew that it was going to cause further, even greater shocks in the very near future, especially when they heard the solution he and Chapman were proposing.

'Jim,' Pearce began, 'I know I asked this at the very beginning, but ... there's no doubt about this? I mean ... no doubt at all?'

'Fred, you know as well as I do there's always room for doubt. The evidence we have would be very difficult to prove conclusively in court – but we aren't attempting to do that. If we supposed the whole thing was a gigantic Russian fraud, an attempt to discredit us in the eyes of our allies, it could well succeed. Let's assume Parker is exactly what he appears to be. The Russians would have chosen his name because he fits the bill so exactly for their requirements. We examine the evidence presented by this so called Russian defector – and interpret the results exactly as predicted. So what do we do? I guess they'd expect us to show our usual misguided sense of fair play, put the man on trial and end up a laughing stock ... us and our allies; assuming, of course, our defector friend is a plant. That's really the decision we have to make – and the result of that decision is a foregone conclusion. I've spoken at great length with our American friends, and in their opinion ... he's real.'

'Two things you've said cause me a certain amount of ... er ... trepidation,' said Walters. 'The first is that we're not trying to prove anything in a court of law. Correct?' Carmichael nodded. 'The second is that our decision is a foregone conclusion.' Again the nod. 'Would you like to explain both points, please?'

'Before I do,' began Carmichael, 'on the evidence so far presented, we have to reach a decision. Is Parker the man the defector claims he is, or is he really Edward Parker? Unfortunately time is short; we must decide today – now. Once that decision has been taken, we move one of two ways. I'll outline whichever one we decide upon – and incidentally, Mr. Walters, answer the points you raised.'

The ensuing silence was broken by Chapman who, seeing the indecision on the faces of his colleagues, said, 'As far as I'm concerned, I believe it. That is to say, I believe Parker is a Russian.'

'We don't want to be too hasty in this,' Pearce spoke with a heavy frown marring his features. 'We have to be certain there is no doubt whatsoever.'

Carmichael nodded. 'It has only been three weeks since we started our own investigation but there is no doubt. Taken as a whole, viewed at from this new angle then a lot of Parker's background becomes clearer, more understanding.' He paused searching for the words. He knew it was true but he also knew he was not putting it across very well. How could he get these people to feel it like he did? How could he make them see the meaning behind the dry sentences? The bare facts? It was why an arrest and a court appearance would do nothing except embarrass the whole of NATO and her allies.

'We have done an analysis of what it could mean politically. It has been discussed with the Prime Minister and the opposition leader,' he paused. 'The brief given to me leaves no alternative though they never actually said so in so many words.' He saw the uneasy looks passing between the others. Surely, they seemed to say, the solution could not be that. It was unthinkable. Not in Britain.

'The analysis is somewhat stark but we believe to be accurate. If Parker is denounced then there will be a huge outcry in this country. Reds in the beds will be the least of it. How many more are there? In what positions? Who can we trust? Our paranoia will be fanned to a conflagration which will stop where? One thing is certain, it will mean an end to the two party system of this country. There is no doubt that the swing to the Alliance will be huge. If that happens and they are seen as an alternative government there is no doubt that vast numbers of Conservative voters will flock to them. These are presently the people who vote the way they do because they see no real alternative. They would never vote Labour but on the other hand are disgruntled with Maggie and Co. With the Davids in power then proportional representation will follow and,' he paused significantly, holding up a finger to emphasise the point, 'the probability is that neither the Labour nor Conservative parties will hold power in this country again this century and probably beyond. Neither party wishes to soldier on like the Liberals for nearly eighty years before they get another chance at power. At least with the way things are at the moment they can be sure of power every decade or so at least. So there, there is hope. The other way there is none at all. So Parker can blow apart the whole of the present day political system.' Again he paused and looked around the table seeing the deep consternation there. 'Curiously enough, when I first knew about this, I thought that the Prime Minister would want the Labour party smashed. It was only after a meeting with her that I realised the meaning of Real Politik. It was she who pointed out what would happen across the country if any of this got out. She saw the implications far clearer and with, shall we call it, a more penetrating vision? than I had. The sum of it was that this must be kept under wraps at all costs.'

'What about the Welsh boy wonder?' asked Walters. 'Does he know about it? And anyway,' he suddenly sat up straight and looked unblinkingly at Carmichael. 'If Kinnock wins the next election it will be he who is Prime Minister and not Parker. If they are in power surely the situation could be defused. Parker forced to resign. Or even blow open the case. Labour would have the best part of five years to live it down. It would not be insurmountable. The scene could change so quickly. As Wilson said, a week is a long time in politics.'

'He would not have a week. Our constitution allows for the deputy Prime Minister to take over on the death of the Prime Minister without the necessity for another election. Kinnock would be dead before he is even sworn in and Parker would take over immediately.'

Carmichael was satisfied with the shock waves he had created, sweeping across the faces of the other men, bouncing back and forth.

'All right then,' said Pearce. 'Why not simply demote him now. Send him back to the backbenches. Let him know he is out in the cold.'

'Because the Russians will then know that we know. He will cease to be of any use to them. They could change that with one last smash at our system. Expose Parker once he is safely in Russia. Create panic in our political system.'

'But to what end?' asked Pearce with some exasperation.

'Let me recount the political lesson I had from the Prime Minister,' said Chapman. 'The Conservatives are strong on defence including nuclear power. We make an effort, at great cost, to sabre rattle at the Russians. Many of the people like it. Good old Great Britain isn't such a spent force after all. We are independent and still a force to be reckoned with.'

'But that's sheer bloody nonsense?' Pearce said with a great deal of exasperation.

'Of course it is,' replied Chapman evenly, 'but it's how too many people see it in this country. On top of that we have a very patriotic working class. The opposition know that. Which is why if they came to power it would suddenly become too difficult to do away with nuclear weapons. Unfortunately, although many of the senior members of the party say so, conference does not. Once in power conference will be ignored. At least as far as that subject goes. Political analysts in the East and West know that. And I don't mean the so called political analysts writing their columns trying to sell newspapers. I mean the real thinkers who inform governments and important institutions as to what will really happen in any given situation. If you doubt me then just look at France. After the scare there, we are closer to the socialists than we were to their last lot. That is in spite of the fear of what Communist party ministers would do once they were in power. Mitterand moved quickly to prevent them from having any real power and now look at what's happening. This government would be proud of some of the changes that's been going on over there. So you see, in the foreseeable future our defence policy will remain at or near its present level. There is one possible exception. One unknown. Unknown because there are not enough hard facts, not enough data, not enough understanding of what will happen if the Alliance gets in. They could disband our nuclear armaments because they are committed to doing what their conference says. And they will do it. Liberal voted for unilateral disarmament last time. It would probably be carried out. Russia would love that to happen of course. Proportional respresentation will mean that within Europe we will go the same way as the Belgians, the Danes and some of the others. Hung parliaments trying to compromise all the time with nothing significant being achieved. That point is, in my opinion, somewhat debatable but nevertheless a factor to be taken into account. And of course let us not forget the Russian character. How well it would suit them to stir the pot and see what happens. After all there are so many imponderables that we don't really know what will happen. An educated guess is about all we can achieve. The Russian propensity for mischief making must not be ignored.' Chapman looked around at the others. He could see that his words had an effect. Their minds were already working overtime, seeing the perspective more clearly now. Seeing other ramifications. Not liking what they saw.

'It's a no win situation,' said Walters evenly. He looked from Carmichael to Chapman.

'There is one way out,' Chapman replied. 'It has been

41

sanctioned, tacitly I may add. However, it's a situation that neither the Prime Minister nor Kinnock can see another answer to and so,' he suddenly spoke more heavily, more ponderously, as though an unseen weight had suddenly landed on his shoulders. 'There are a number of rules we will follow. There will be no more records kept of this case, and when it's finished the files held by Jim will be destroyed. If anything should come out about the affair then it will be denied with the utmost vigour on both sides of the house.'

'I am beginning to perceive what your solution is,' Walters interrupted 'and to say I'm not going to like it is an understatement, to say the least. However, Chief Superintendent, spell it out if you please.'

'Right, Sir,' Carmichael took a deep breath. 'If Parker is arrested and committed for trial, or he escapes to Russia, which we suspect he may try, then the outcome will be the same. Both are unacceptable for the reasons given. Therefore the man must die.'

The bluntness of the last words caused his listeners to gasp in horror and dismay, even though they had known what the proposed solution was to be. Walters thumped the table savagely, exclaiming, 'No, by God – I won't have it! Are we to sit in judgement, convict a man and sentence him to death without any proper trial? We're supposed to be a civilised country, we've abolished the death penalty, we treat prisoners humanely, actively support human rights campaigns wherever we can – and now this. It's monstrous. Monstrous, I say! We're proposing to take away a man's life, and . . .' Walters began but was interrupted by Chapman. 'Don't be naive! "Take away a man's life." Men's lives are constantly being taken away as a result of political decisions. Our soldiers are being murdered in Northern Ireland for political reasons. Look at the Middle East, Afghanistan, Cambodia, Africa etc. Need I go on? So don't talk so emotively. It does not become our position nor the seriousness of the situation. The man is an enemy agent. He can cause great political and economical damage to this country, yet you won't sanction

42

his death. Think, man! Just think of the potential harm if he lives.'

'That isn't the point,' Walters said stubbornly. 'The point is, it's barbaric. You're giving the man no chance whatsoever of defending himself. I concede that certain political decisions in the past have led to the deaths of many people, but that's no excuse for the retrograde step you are now advocating. Let's suppose we arrest him. The worst that would happen would be a change in the political scene of this country, possibly for the better. Maybe it is time to rid ourselves of our nuclear weapons. Why not try an alternative to what we have? It surely could not be worse than the upheaval we suffer every time the main parties play musical chairs and swop round?' He looked belligerently around him.

Pearce, who until now had been quietly chain smoking, interrupted. 'Look Dennis – although I understand how you feel, I'm afraid I can't agree. At least we know and understand our present system, for better or for worse. The political fallout world wide could be devastating. It is such an imponderable that I don't believe we dare risk it. If political change came about as a result of the ballot box then that is one thing. If it came about as a result of the biggest scandal ever to rock the western world then that is another.'

'I see,' said Walters quietly. 'In that case you leave me no alternative. I shall withdraw from this meeting, and give the Prime Minister my reasons for doing so when we see her. Though I've no doubt she'll have already heard the details before then,' he added, with a significant glance at Chapman.

'No doubt,' Chapman agreed blandly. 'I think you're making the wrong decision, although I sympathise with your feelings. As this is a reasonably democratic meeting I'd suggest that you abide by the majority vote, as has always been the case.'

Walters gave a shudder. 'Democratic? It's more like the worst kind of dictatorship! However, I suppose you're right in that sense. I want it put on record...' He broke off, uttering a mirthless bark of laughter. 'I forgot – there is no record. Very well, I'll stay. I suppose I'd better listen to your half baked ideas, even if I don't agree with them.'

'Good. That's a step in the right direction at least,' said Chapman. 'Now, Jim – outline your plan as it currently stands, if you please, and bring us up to date with the situation.'

'There are two options open to us,' replied Carmichael. 'The first is to stage an accident. This, despite what's shown on television and written about it in novels, isn't as easy as it may seem. If an iota of suspicion is aroused, the most carefully arranged accident can usually be disproved. Naturally, we have experts within the department who could arrange it, but once we do that we increase the likelihood of his death becoming generally known. Remember, Parker is a highly respected member of the community and it may be extremely difficult to persuade the right operatives of his guilt. Someone may talk at the wrong moment, in the wrong place. I'm not suggesting it's at all likely, but I think we should face the fact that it's more than possible. I believe that to ensure silence, to ensure that nobody except we four and the Prime Minister knows the truth, we arrange to have him terminated.'

'Good God!' Walters interrupted. 'Is that the euphemism for murder in current use in the best government circles? Terminated?'

'Yes,' replied Carmichael, tersely. 'Now, as I was saying . . .'

'Just a moment.' This time it was Pearce who interrupted. 'How can you manage that? Surely, you don't propose mur . . . murder, I mean terminating him yourself?'

Carmichael shook his head. 'No, you're quite right Fred; I don't. Nor do I intend that any of you shall do it either. No, it's quite simple. I believe I know just the person.'

'You're talking in riddles, man,' protested Walters, becoming exasperated. 'You've just said no one else apart from us, the Prime Minister and the leader of the opposition will know, yet now you're introducing a seventh person. How can you be certain he won't talk? Hell – it just doesn't make sense.'

'If you'll just give me time to explain,' Carmichael retorted, mastering his impatience with difficulty. 'Once the deed has been done, only the five of us will be in a position to say anything. You see, I intend to kill the assassin as soon as he has done his job.' Correctly reading the expressions on the faces of Pearce and Walters, he hurried on, 'Now before you say anything, just hear me out. If anything goes wrong there can be no doubt that we may be in more serious trouble than we are already. If we allowed the assassin to escape, he may either be caught and, in an attempt to save his own skin, tell everything he knows, or alternatively he may try to blackmail us. Only his death can ensure that there will be no blackmail, and no fear of future leaks.'

'Where do you propose getting this expendable item from?' Walters enquired sarcastically. 'I presume you don't have a ready stock of them, for use in an emergency like disposable syringes, for instance?'

'I intend procuring a man from the armed forces,' Carmichael replied calmly. Clearly his plans were well thought out. 'You all know as well as I do that the trained killers of, say, the SAS have only escaped imprisonment on murder raps because they're in the army. Their brutal instincts are legitimately catered for in places like Northern Ireland, Mozambique, Afghanistan, the Middle East and so on. We all know of the unofficial use to which they're put in these places. However, that's not the point. In the limited time at my disposal I found three names that could fit the bill. The first, Lampluff, is serving a life sentence in Parkhurst prison for the murder of his platoon commander, whom he confessed he loathed. He's a brute of a man, lacking intelligence but with a certain low cunning. To say he's expendable ... well, he is. Controlling him may be difficult, if we decide to use him, but will not be impossible.

'The second one I have in mind, currently under surveillance, is a man named Barber. I'll come back to him in a moment. The third man, Syers, is a known alcoholic, an ex-sergeant in the paratroopers. He took to drink shortly before he left the service, when he realised he wasn't to be allowed to sign on for a further five years. His Commanding Officer reckoned he was too brutally sadistic for their liking. Every leave he was in trouble for beating his wife and kids, getting drunk, assaulting the police. He kept his nose clean in the service – that's why he eventually made sergeant. He's an expert in killing in all its forms, but the Army considered he was more trouble than he was worth, and got rid of him. He hasn't settled down at all well in civvy street, and I'm sure he would very quickly readapt for this special job and probably do exactly what we require.'

'They don't sound a very inspiring pair,' remarked Walters. 'If that's the best you can do, I don't think we have much chance of getting away with it. What about the second man you mentioned – the one you have under surveillance? What was his name? Barber?'

Carmichael nodded, 'I've been keeping the best 'til last. He's another who doesn't appear to have settled very well into civilian life.'

While he talked, a part of his mind wondered about Walters' sudden change of heart. It hadn't taken much persuading to get him to stay.

Chapter 4

'What the hell do you mean, you've lost him?' Carmichael barked down the 'phone at the Special Branch Sergeant. 'Where's he gone?'

'If I knew that he wouldn't be lost, would he?' retorted the young officer, wet enough and cold enough to forget he was addressing his superior.

Carmichael kept his temper with difficulty. With forced calmness he said, 'Careful, son, you're forgetting yourself. Now – tell me what happened.'

'Well – sir – we were being extra careful, like you said, using a full squad in the surveillance team, and everything was going well until an hour or so ago.'

Automatically Carmichael checked his watch. 20.30 hours when they lost Barber. 'Okay, so what went wrong?'

'We followed him from his digs and had no problems at first, despite the pouring rain. He was obviously dressed for the weather, in some sort of heavy combat type jacket and trousers. The kind of gear a lot of young people wear nowadays, know what I mean?'

'Yeah, I get the picture,' said Carmichael thoughtfully.

'Anyway, we followed him down into this pretty grotty area between Whitechapel and the end of the embankment . . . I'm not exactly sure which district I'm in. There's nothing readable in this box; in fact it's a bloody wonder the 'phone works at all. He walked down Awdrys Road, past a pub on the end, turned left and . . . and that's it,' he finished lamely.

'What do you mean, that's it?'

'Exactly what I say. We can't find him. We're positive he didn't enter any of the houses in the short street he turned into. The end of the street becomes a pathway leading alongside the railway, and about fifty yards beyond that it becomes another street. I sent one man around to the other side, another's been up and down the path a few times and two more have gone across the foot bridge over the railway. That's about half way along the path, and leads to a small locked park with no way of getting round or into it.'

Carmichael sighed. 'All right Harris. You've done your best, I'm sure. Knock off for the night, but arrange a continuous watch on his digs. He'll probably turn up in the morning. Let me have a full report some time tomorrow. I'll be here in the office all day.' The correct routines had to be followed, even if he did intend destroying all written connection with the case as he got it . . . just in case he forgot some later on. He became aware for the hundredth time what a precarious position he was in, his career well and truly on the line. It wouldn't be the first time, he thought ironically . . . though it had every chance of being the last.

'All right, sir. And sir . . . sorry.'

The line went dead before Carmichael could reply. Damn. He didn't like suddenly finding himself in the dark. He liked having things just so, following the paths he'd predicted and planned for. He hadn't counted on this latest development, especially as he'd intended calling on Barber the next evening, to put forward a little proposal.

★   ★   ★

The heavy rain meant Barber had to be closer to the path than he'd intended, in order to be able to recognise his quarry in the dark. From the ditch where he crouched in the grey twilight, he'd watched a man hurrying up and down, apparently searching for someone or something. Since then, no one had appeared. He blessed and cursed the rain simultaneously; he was getting soaked to the skin, but it would help to muffle any noise he made when the punks appeared.

He'd checked they were in the bar, and now waited patiently for them to show, realising as he did so that he may be waiting in vain. They could use another route, go on somewhere else, even take a taxi home – he had no way of knowing. All he did know was that it wouldn't matter. One day soon they'd come, and he intended being there when they did.

He thought about Philip, still critically ill but, according to the hospital, making steady progress. It was still too soon to be sure about possible paralysis; Wednesday was the test day. Steve prayed he'd be all right, and thanked God that Sue at least was okay. A train rattled past on the Southend line, and Steve grinned evilly, as he did whenever he thought about the next few hours. He touched the rope by his side, assuring himself it was still there, along with the two rags, then settled himself again to wait in patience. This was one wait he didn't mind; not like the endless times he'd had to do it in the Marines. He was aware that, thanks to this action, he'd pulled out of the decline into which he'd been sinking. Once it was over he intended to find a decent job, and stop wallowing in self pity. He'd contact a friend of his, another ex-marine lieutenant who was now working for a diving company somewhere abroad. Bob would be able to fix him up with something, he was sure. He'd heard there was a lot of money to be made in the diving industry, and if that was so, and if he could get among it, he'd be able to look after Phil and Sue, at least until they found their feet. Wryly he realised that could be many months, of course. He didn't mind helping, didn't give the money a thought; just hoped he'd get the type of job he needed. The medical bills could be expensive.

By now it was pitch dark. Hearing footsteps he tensed, peering into the night, then relaxed when he realised only one person was approaching. As the figure hurried past he knew he'd never be able to identify the two brothers when they did come, unless he got much closer. He was prepared to do just that. Checking his watch he was relieved to see it was past closing time. Soon now, very soon, he thought.

A couple of times he convinced himself someone was coming, but each time as he prepared to leap up and step onto the path it proved a false alarm. Another passing train had him on his feet before he'd identified the noise and, cursing his nerves, he settled back once again. Even as he was relaxing, the noise of the train receding, he became aware of two figures only a few steps away, hurrying heads bent through the rain.

Barber jumped up, one step behind them. The noise he made caused them to spin around, and he switched on his torch, illuminating the startled faces of the two brothers. His finger slipped off the flash button as he swung the heavy metal torch into the side of the head of the man on his right. The solid, satisfying clunk brought a fleeting smile as the man dropped soundlessly. The other's cry of alarm ended abruptly in a strangled gurgle as a hand like a steel band gripped him round the throat, and a pile driver fist buried itself in his soft belly. The grip around the punk's neck prevented the air in his lungs from escaping, and the consequent agony almost made him faint. Doubled over as he was, he hardly felt the chop on the back of his neck that sent him into blissful oblivion.

The punk Steve had felled with his torch gave a low moan. Steve bent over the still form, found a nerve in his neck and after a few seconds' pressure the punk passed out. Grabbing him by the arm and leg, Steve threw him into the ditch. Straightening, he looked up and down the path, then hearing nothing, picked up the other brother and slung him across his back in a fireman's lift. He stepped across the ditch, carried his burden about ten yards over long grass and a tangle of brambles, then threw the dead weight down, not caring how it landed. He paused for breath, then made his way back to the other inert form. He was bending over him, gripping his coat and about to haul him up across his shoulders, when he heard someone coming. Releasing the coat he dropped down on the body, the unconscious man emitting a soft grunt. Barber realised it was the approach of a torch that had alerted him and cursed silently, hoping that whoever it was wouldn't notice him lying there on top of the punk. The last thing he wanted at this moment was the ministrations of a good samaritan!

The light came closer, sweeping from side to side. Barber held his breath as the beam reached him. It swept from the other side, across the narrow path and on to him as he hid his head in his arms, his body tensed, ready to deal with the unwanted, innocent intruder.

The footsteps were alongside him and the torch beam a couple of yards ahead when Barber gently breathed out and relaxed his muscles, letting the flow of adrenalin subside before getting to his feet. Quickly slinging the body across his shoulders, he carried it to where he'd left the other one, threw it down and returned to collect the rope and rags, moving rapidly but with caution.

Once he'd gagged them both, tied their hands behind them and their legs together, he relaxed. Now all he had to do was wait.

When the first one moved he drew his knife, jammed the point in the punk's neck and applied pressure. The pain penetrated the layers of darkness around the punk's mind, and his eyes snapped open.

'Don't move, don't struggle,' said Barber softly. 'Otherwise you're a dead man.' The other stiffened and lay still. 'Good. Continue doing as you're told and you may live.' Similar treatment of the brother brought similar results. Steve propped the pair into more comfortable positions facing him and showed them the knife, holding it before the face of first one, then the other.

'In a while,' he told them, 'I'm going to use this to cut you up in a way that will take away your manhood and leave you scarred for life.' At his words both youths began to struggle frantically, then stopped as the slip knots around their necks and connected to their feet tightened, cutting off their breath. Barber waited a few seconds, then released the pressure. When their breathing was more or less back to normal he settled back on his haunches, facing them.

51

I want you to know,' he continued softly, in a conversational tone, 'why I'm going to do it, and then I'll tell you exactly what I'm going to do, in detail, so you can think about it before I actually start. You bastards put my brother in hospital a week ago. Shall I remind you about it, in case you've forgotten? I was the one who cut up your cousin's face in the pub . . . Ah – I thought you'd remember. You bided your time, didn't you, and then avenged yourselves on my brother. He's in a really bad way. In fact, he's still in hospital, on the critical list. However, fortunately you weren't very scientific in the way you went about things; just brutal. He's going to live, and he's going to be reasonably all right. Well – I say reasonably. He may end up a partial cripple. Now, let's assume the worse, and that is exactly what does happen. Naturally, I'm going to pay you back – with interest, of course. I'll let you ponder for a few minutes on how you think I'm going to do it, and then I'll tell you. Some time after that, I'll do it.'

Barber sat back, looking from one pair of frightened eyes to the other. After a moment the punk on his left closed his eyes. The other stared back at Steve, as a mesmerised rabbit stares at a stoat. Soon he began to tremble, each tremor causing the rope to tighten and interfere with his breathing. After a few seconds, when he was no longer able to draw breath, Barber leant forward and once again loosened the noose.

'I don't want you to choke to death, Sunshine,' he said chummily. 'That would spoil the pleasure I'm going to get when I start on you.' He lapsed into silence, continuing to stare at them.

After half an hour had gone by one of them murmured and squirmed. Barber leaned forward, about to warn him to keep still, then realised what was wrong. He chuckled humourlessly. 'Of course – I hadn't thought of that. You pair have been drinking all night. Want a jimmy riddle, do you? Is it agony yet, lads, or just discomfort? Well, I'm afraid you're going to have to manage – for about another hour, that's all. Why an hour? Well – it's quite simple. You see, at one

52

o'clock I shall cut off all your clothes; you can then pee yourselves to your hearts' content. You'll probably do the other
as well, not because you need to but from pain and terror, I
hope. At least, that's my intention.

He paused, smiling benignly from one to the other. 'Let
me tell you what's in store. When your clothes are out of the
way I shall begin by cutting your Achilles' tendons. They run
down behind your heels, you know; keep your feet walking
properly. That won't be too painful, but you'll probably be
spending the rest of your lives in wheelchairs. Just to make
sure, I shall also sever the tendons in the backs of your
legs plus the ones in the backs of both hands – they're the
ones that make your fingers work – and also cut off both your
ears. By this time you'll be experiencing a fair amount of
pain, but even so, it may not be enough to make you shit
yourselves.'

He paused, then went on, 'By the way, you may be wondering where I learnt this sort of thing; you know, stuff like
pain thresholds, what to do and so on. Well, I'll tell you. I
was an officer in the Royal Marines, and because I was in
what's called the SBS – Special Boats Service – I was considered to be a high risk number for capture and interrog-
ation. Although pain inflicting methods have come a long
way in the last ten years or so, they usually involve sophisticated equipment and drugs. Those methods are used by the
enemy to gain information, and we're instructed in them and
also in some of the more ancient forms of torture; helps us to
resist them, you see. To a limited extent they work, but
somehow I don't think they help much in alleviating the
pain. You will, naturally, discern a subtle difference in your
case. I'm not after information; I merely intend to inflict the
maximum amount of pain possible within a limited period of
one hour. That may not sound very long, but believe me,
when your body is screaming in anguish, it can seem like an
eternity. I'll just leave you to ponder on what I've said for a
bit, and then we'll begin.'

Barber fell silent, his gaze not giving away the fact that if

53

his very life depended upon it he could never carry out his declared intention. Presently he said:

'It's time, gentlemen; I fear I must begin. That's quite funny, don't you think? I fear. Of course, I don't fear as much as you do.' He began to cut through the clothing of the punk he considered the toughest. 'Ugh!' he exclaimed, lying. 'You've already shit yourself!' As he said this the punk's brother, beside himself with fear, did just that, loudly. Barber chuckled grimly. 'See what I mean about psychology? I lied.'

Tears were streaming down the young man's face as Barber began cutting off his clothes. His brother, already naked, was shivering uncontrollably, whether with fear, or cold, or both it was impossible to tell. Barber did not care. His own actions, along with the stench filled him with sick loathing, directed, he knew, at himself. Gritting his teeth, he finished what he was doing. The weaker of the two began to moan, the noise sounding loud in the night even through the gag. Barber placed the point of his knife against the narrow chest, muttering, 'Shut up! One more sound out of you and I'll begin right now.' When the noise continued Barber drew the knife along the chest, down across the abdomen and under the balls. 'Shut up, you bastard, or else I'll flick my wrist and cut 'em off,' he hissed. The sudden flow of warm water made him start and the knife sliced into the loose flesh. The moan became a muffled scream and the punk fainted. Nausea rose in Barber's throat at the sight of the blood spurting out. For a second he had an impulse to release both his victims – but the moment passed. He decided not to wait any longer.

The other brother had been watching, unblinking. Now, as Barber turned to him, the fear so far successfully contained erupted, and urine soaked his legs and stomach. Barber bared his teeth in an evil grin for the benefit of the terrified man, and squeezed his neck until he lost consciousness. Pulling the hood of his foul weather jacket over his soaking hair, Barber heaved the man on to his shoulders and struggled to his feet. With the rope in his other hand, he carted his burden back to the path and on to the footbridge across the railway line. Securing the spare rope around the punk's waist, he retied his hands to each leg and checked the gag. When he'd finished, he used the rope to lower the man onto the rails fifteen feet below, and then raised him four feet. Hauling the rope across until the man was just swinging to one side of the line, he secured the end of it. Panting, sweat mingling with the rain on his face, Barber cut off the end of the rope, left it there and went back for his other victim.

The latter had recovered from his faint. Seeing Barber, he began to tremble violently. Steve bent down and spoke to him softly.

'In a moment I shall make you unconscious. When you come round you'll find yourself hanging alongside the railway. Between now and daylight there will be at least half a dozen trains along that track. You may survive; on the other hand, bouncing along a moving train will probably kill you. I hope not, but we'll just have to see, won't we? I shall look forward to reading about it in the papers. Now – shall we begin?' He was to be haunted for the rest of his life by the horror and the fear in the young punk's eyes as he put his hands on his neck.

Hurrying as fast as he could with his burden, Barber suspended the man alongside his brother, but on the other side of the track. Finally, after ensuring he'd left nothing behind that could identify him – though not wasting time trying to conceal evidence of where he'd been, knowing the police would have a complete picture shortly after they arrived on the scene – he left.

He felt sick at heart. He knew what he'd done wasn't worth it; nothing was. He could go back; it wasn't too late. He could spare their lives. Whatever happened, they'd probably never be the same again. Why take it so far? Then he remembered Philip; remembered the fear and pain he'd suffered, the anguish both his brother and sister-in-law were suffering now, wondering if Phil would be a whole man again, able to walk, father more children . . .

Try as he would, Steve could not convince himself that what he had done was right. He knew it wasn't; knew, moreover, that he'd allowed himself to be dragged down to the level of the two animals he'd left hanging by the tracks. Was that it, in the final analysis? Was he really no better than they? Had his intelligence, his education, masked the same sick kind of mind as the other two? Yes! cried his conscience. No – no! his mind replied. Hell – he hadn't started it. He was finishing it. Violence begets violence. They were only getting what they deserved . . . an eye for an eye . . . retribution shall be mine, sayeth the Lord. Damn the Lord, Barber said savagely to himself.

He'd already turned and was heading reluctantly back when he heard the train. Praying and cursing simultaneously, he broke into a run. He knew if the train was on the track they straddled he couldn't be in time – from the pub to the bridge was too far. He was panting with exertion, sweat pouring down his face when he stepped on to the bridge. The train was passing underneath, and he saw the nearest body bouncing along under the carriage windows, each flash of light making the scene look like an old silent movie. It wasn't silent, though. The rattle of the train took away the eeriness of the tableau, endowing it somehow with a degree of inhuman normality. It became too much for him. With a muffled groan he turned and dashed back the way he had come, along the path and into the road, all precautions forgotten in his headlong flight. Luckily, the rain was heavier than ever, the wind whipping up a storm. No one saw the soaked, bedraggled, blood-stained figure running through the night – and even if they had, they'd be more likely to think he was the attacked rather than the attacker.

At last he slowed down, forced himself to take a grip on himself. He had things to do, and there was little time left in which to do them. Taking out his sodden street map of London, he found where he was and started back, walking now, quite calm and rational. All right, he'd inflicted injuries; probably killed two men. Killing was something he'd trained for all those years, and now he'd done it. It was the first time. For him it may not be the last. He hoped it would be.

Back at the path, he found the sealed plastic pack of clean clothes he'd hidden there earlier. Teeth chattering with cold, he stripped off completely, including shoes, socks and the gloves he'd worn throughout. Then he quickly dressed in the clean gear, each item sodden by the time he put it on, and finally, having donned a new pair of gloves, he stuffed the other clothes into the bag. For the first time he noticed the blood, and realised it must have come from the second body he'd carried – the one he'd more or less castrated.

Stuffing the bag inside his raincoat, he hurried away from the area. It was beginning to get light as, following his A to Z, he made his way down to the Embankment, not far from London Bridge, visible in the growing daylight less than a mile up river. Pausing at the building site, he opened the bag, filled it with stones and bricks and resealed it. Having checked that there was no one about, he hurled the heavy bag as far as he could into the river. It floated for a few moments, the current swirling it round, and for one gut aching second he thought it wouldn't sink. Then the water closed over it and it was gone.

For an hour Barber wandered along the Embankment, his mind in a daze. He'd done what he'd set out to do – and now what? He felt the old despondency take hold, the lethargy he thought he'd beaten, and the more he tried to shake them off, the tighter their grip became. What's wrong with me, he thought? Why can't I direct my energies away from the physical, away from the need for violent action? He caught himself. Violent? Since when had he needed violence? No – not violence; physical exertion, strenuous exercise with a purpose, like in the Marines. Overcoming hardships, achieving an objective, being stretched to the limit of endurance; these were the things he wanted, craved. But he had nothing now; nowhere to go, nothing to achieve. No goal, no aim. He couldn't erase these thoughts from his mind, couldn't struggle out of this morass of self pity, all pervading, all encompassing self pity.

The rain stopped and the sun was breaking through by mid-morning, when Barber arrived back at his digs. The thought uppermost in his mind now was his need for a drink – a long, strong drink. Back on the slippery slope . . .

Indifferent to his surroundings, he failed to notice the car parked at the corner of the street. Even if he had done, he probably wouldn't have attached any importance to it. The vehicle was as nondescript as the two Special Branch surveillance men inside.

Chapter 5

'With Jemel, Hassan and Wafik in jail, all is lost!' The young man's anguish showed in his tear-brimmed eyes. 'We've always needed them, always will. Without them, what can we achieve?'

'What about the message? What did they say?' the blonde girl, the only European in the room, asked anxiously.

The Palestinian speaker, standing with his back to the wall, held the attention of his companions as he felt in his pocket for the letter smuggled by the defence lawyer out of the prison where their three leaders awaited trial.

'It says: "To our brothers and sisters. No matter what the outcome of the trial, you must continue the fight. If you don't our lives will have been wasted, the years of struggle of our people rendered useless and the hopes for our own land dashed. If we don't force world action on our behalf, nothing will be done. We shall continue to be outcasts with no identity, nowhere to call home. We hand the torch of our people's freedom to you. Follow our last plan, finish perfecting it and put it into operation – carefully. If you are successful, not only will our cause have taken a giant step forward, but we may be with you in the end. I send my undying love to Enis. Tell her I think of her constantly. Long live the cause. Jemel."'

He finished reading and looked up. The blonde girl was gazing at him, tears streaming down her cheeks.

'Enis, we can't do it,' he said helplessly. 'Without them it's just not possible. Jemel is the ideas man; he could always see what to do. Don't you see that?'

'No, I damn' well don't!' she replied fiercely, wiping her cheeks with the backs of her hands. 'Somebody lend me a handkerchief. Thanks.' She blew her nose and dried her eyes, then got to her feet, her body taut with anger. 'You all heard. From prison they call out to us, plead with us to carry on the fight – and what do you all do? Cower! Hide! Give up! One setback and you all collapse. Well, you shan't – I won't let you. We must carry on.' Her contemptuous gaze swept over the dozen young men and women sitting around the room, but none would meet her eyes. 'Look at you!' she went on scornfully. 'I came into this fight for love of Jemel and I shall stay because of that love. You are all here because you profess to love Palestine. Well, all I can say is, you don't know the meaning of the word. If love is not worth struggling for, fighting for, if it isn't worth the heartbreaks, the setbacks, then it isn't love at all. It's nothing. Nothing!'

As she shouted the last word her listeners raised their heads uneasily, beginning to protest.

'Oh – please,' Enis went on, with a dismissive wave of the hand. 'Spare me your excuses. The facts speak for themselves. I knew before I came here this evening what the outcome of this meeting would be. Jemel kept you together, gave you direction; without him there's nothing left. I'd prayed it would be different, tried to persuade myself that Jemel's thoughts, ideas, spirit would continue to inspire you – but I see I was wrong.'

The contempt gave way to pleading.

'Listen – we can do it. It's in the letter – the answer. Let's take the plan, use it. We can do it, I know. Just think – we could have them back with us, free, our cause once more on everybody's lips. This time it will be bigger and better than anything we have ever tried. We learned our lessons with the liner. We must now use those lessons to our advantage.'

She stopped, sensing that she was getting through to them, but probably not in a way that could be sustained. She'd spoken harshly to try and bully them out of their defeated mood. It was understandable, how they felt. With Jemel

Hassan and Wafik arrested for conspiracy to cause actual bodily harm, possession of firearms and explosives, it was no wonder their followers felt lost, helpless. Their confidence was shaken. How had the police got on to them, penetrated their secret hideaway without anyone having an inkling that something was wrong? Was there a traitor in their midst? That was unthinkable. No – the explanation must be that, after the liner débâcle, they were being watched far more closely. Too closely possibly ever to get away with blowing up Israeli offices in Europe. The damned Israelis. The Nazis had had the right idea about them. They had learned their lesson well from the liner débâcle. They had analysed and probed. They had discussed and planned. It had been a good plan botched up. World attention had once more been brought to bear on their plight. But still nothing happened. Didn't the world realise that ignoring them would not make them go away? Didn't the world realise that justice was screaming to be done? Didn't the world know of its collective guilt? They were all guilty; guilty of apathy, guilty because they were indifferent to the plight of a whole nation, a people who wanted only to have a place they could call home. Her love of Jemel had caused her to accept without question all he thought, all he said.

'How ... how are we going to go about it?' someone asked hesitantly.

'I don't know yet,' Enis replied. 'We have the concept, the idea – all we need are the details. Jemel has always maintained that, with the right plan, ten people would be sufficient. Ten of us here could do it, I'm sure. We know where to get hold of weapons, explosives. What I want is for us to leave this meeting committed to the idea, that's the most important initial step. Once we've achieved that we can go ahead, make arrangements, finalise our plans ... and strike. Let's try. Please, for God's sake let us try!'

For the first time since the meeting started, her listeners began to exchange speculative glances. Their shame of the knowledge that they'd all intended to give up was super-

61

seded by a sense of purpose, a hope of achievement. Was it possible? they asked themselves, each looking round at his or her neighbour. They weren't assessing what they saw; a group of troubled, young and inexperienced faces. The faces of people who had lived without hope, moving between camps, prisons by any other name. They were seeing the idea, the triumphant end; victory. They were seeing themselves as the heroes and heroines of their people: they did not see the possible bloodshed, the horror, the maiming, the killing; the chaos, the panic as 1500 people faced death for a reason they could not or would not understand. They were blind to the condemnation they would receive from their elders; blind to the hatred they would generate in the civilised world. They were blind to the biggest tragedy of all, the playing into the hands of the Israeli government, yet another propaganda coup. Further proof that the Palestinians were not a people fighting a despairing lost cause but a bunch of murderous thugs, untrustworthy, not fit to govern themselves. They were too young, too naive to see the real results of their intended action. They only knew that after years of negotiating, of listening to Arafat and his promises, that now was the time. Now before they became too old to say 'this is my home! this is where I shall live for the remainder of my days! this is where my children shall be born!'

'I've been giving it a great deal of thought,' Enis said, conscious that all eyes were upon her now, shining with eager anticipation . . .

★   ★   ★

Barber picked up the bottle and weighed it in his hand, looking in disgust at the cheap brand name of the whisky on the label. He felt terrible. When he arrived at his room he'd drunk a half tumbler of the amber liquid straight off, flung himself on his bed and instantly fallen asleep. It was dark when he woke, and looking out through the grimy window, he'd seen it was a beautiful night, the sky clear and rain-washed, the wind a mere breeze. Unaccountably a feeling of well-being had swept over him, strong enough to take him to where he was now, about to pour the remainder of the whisky down the sink. He knew if he continued where he'd left off there'd be little hope of recovery. He'd got out of the first fit of depression, been given another chance – why throw it away? Resolutely he unscrewed the cap. His mind was made up; he wasn't going to ruin his life. He still had Phil to care for – that was the least he could do. As for the two punks – well – as far as he was concerned it was good riddance. Society wouldn't miss them.

A knock on the door stilled his hands as he was about to begin pouring.

'Who is it?'

'Mr. Barber, could I have a word with you please?' The unknown male voice made him start guiltily, and his heart began to pound. That calm, authoritative voice sounded to him like officialdom. His mouth was so dry he couldn't reply. Instead, with shaking fingers he recapped the bottle, and still with it in his hand, opened the door. At the sight of the burly figure of Chief Inspector Carmichael, panic almost took over. This man had 'copper' written all over him. Nevertheless he was alone. If they'd been after him there'd be a squad, not one man.

'Mr. Barber, may I come in?' Carmichael was saying. 'I have something very important to say to you, and I'd prefer it if we were a little more ... er ... private.'

Following his meaningful glance, Barber could see the top of his landlady's head, where she stood partly concealed in the dark of the stairway.

'Come ...' he croaked, cleared his throat and began again. 'Come in.'

Once inside the room, Carmichael didn't bother to conceal his disgust at the surroundings in which he found himself.

'Not exactly the place I'd expect to find an ex-Marine officer,' he commented, wrinkling his nose.

Barber, in full control now, hid his surprise at the other's

63

knowledge of him and grinned. 'True,' he replied. 'Nor will you, this time tomorrow.'

'Oh? You're moving? I didn't realise you'd found a job.'

'I haven't yet. And what's all this about anyway? You seem to know a hell of a lot about me. Just who are you?'

Without answering, Carmichael opened the palm of his hand to display his warrant card. It came as a shock to Barber, despite his intuitive knowledge – and the fact that the man was Special Branch came as a greater shock. Not a muscle of his face moved to betray this however.

'That piece of card means as little to me as it would to most of the people in this country,' he said drily. 'For all I know you could have got it out of a corn flakes packet.'

'True. But it's hardly likely, is it?' Carmichael responded good humouredly. 'However, I take your point. I do assure you it is real.' He stopped.

'Look – do you mind if I sit down? I have a proposition to put to you which you may find highly interesting.' Without waiting for a reply, he crossed the room and sat on the edge of the bed. Barber remained standing and said nothing.

'Curiously enough,' the Chief Superintendent went on, 'even though I've rehearsed in my mind many times how to approach you, how to convince you, I now find it difficult to know how to begin.'

'Try the beginning,' Barber suggested, without a flicker.

'Yes, well – that's easier said than done. I suppose I'd better start by reminding you of the contents of the little buff coloured form you signed before leaving the Marines ... The Official Secrets Act applies.' Carmichael was pleased by the other's total lack of reaction. He was a cool one, and no mistake. 'What I'm about to tell you,' he went on, 'will sound incredible ... fantastic even – but I give you my word it's perfectly true. My word is all you have to go on, of course.'

Barber waited, impassive.

'A short while ago a senior Russian KGB man defected to the West. For reasons that don't concern you, we had him for a short while before he went on to the Americans. The information we've been given has been, to put it mildly, a bit of a shock. By "we" I mean the British; not the Yanks, not even NATO; just us. It's startled us so much that we have to act quickly and decisively. We have double checked the information of course, and we are satisfied.'

'What it means,' Carmichael concluded deliberately, 'is that a very senior member of the opposition is more than a Russian agent.'

Barber looked puzzled. 'More? How can any traitor be more than a Russian...' He broke off, as the answer dawned on him. 'My ... God!'

Carmichael smiled, pleased. 'Exactly. You are, as I suspected, an intelligent man. You don't need to have everything spelled out, which is...'

'Wait a moment,' Barber interrupted. 'Let's just make certain we're talking about the same thing. A senior member of the opposition is a Russian. Correct?'

'Correct. To be precise, it's the deputy leader of the Labour Party.'

'But still only the deputy leader,' said Barber.

'Not for long. If or when they win the next election, Parker would take over as Prime Minister immediately.'

'Don't talk rub...,' Barber trailed off as realisation dawned.

'Yes of course,' a half smile played about his lips. 'An accident of some sort no doubt. Interesting, I can imagine the results. Nuclear disarmament, a rift with and finally a total breaking away from NATO and the EEC. More union power, a huge bureaucracy of civil servants and an infiltration of State control, which would eventually become total. We'd end up another Hungary or Czechoslovakia, and after us, France, Italy ... Who knows where it would end? I'd guess there'd be a Russian dominated Europe by the middle of the next century; say in about 70 years from now.'

Carmichael nodded solemnly. 'In the latest of many such exercises carried out last year, the country's top political analysts arrived at the same conclusion. Naturally, not wanting to admit or even to be seen to conceive the possibility that it could happen in Britain, they took the substitution of the French Premier as their subject, and arrived at the following conclusions. If France fell, so would Britain, or vice versa. Italy would be forced economically to elect a Communist government, Spain would have a bloody revolution, backed by the other by now Communist countries, and it too would fall. Belgium would take longer, but could conceivably become a Soviet satellite within ten years of the others. The Netherlands and Germany would be the most difficult. Not impossible, mind you; just difficult. With the pressure that would be available though, they could be forced to do Russia's bidding, and ten years after that, Russia could probably invade and overrun the rest of Europe, including Scandinavia, by conventional means.'

'I follow your argument,' said Barber, 'but disagree with one major point. The Germans would never allow themselves to be overrun. They'd use nuclear weapons first, and even Russia wouldn't dare risk that . . .'

'Assuming they have the weapons.'

'What do you mean? Of course they'll have the weapons. America will see to that.'

Carmichael shook his head slowly. 'No, that's where you're wrong. Just think of the time scale. We're looking at – what – 20 years after we've gone Communist. The pretence about who our masters really are will be over. Russia will be firmly in control of half of Western Europe, and the Americans, regardless of what they would like to think, will be forced to the inevitable conclusion that Russia will subjugate the remainder, eventually. There'll be no hurry; no need for it. When you know you're going to win, why take chances? The isolationist forces already at work in the USA will meantime gather enough momentum to force Congress to pull out of what's left of Europe, and ensure that no nuclear ability is left here.'

'Can they do that? I mean, take away for instance Germany's ability to produce the bomb?'

66

'Why yes – by the use of economic sanctions. That way, the rest of free Europe can be forced to do as America says.'

'Some freedom!' remarked Barber, with a mirthless grin.

'Unfortunately that's the way it is; or rather, the way it could be.' Carmichael paused, then continued. 'This is what I think – for what it's worth. Eventually, the whole of Europe will end up Communist but – and this is important – it will be a different brand of Communism from that of the Russians. Euro-Communism will mean nationalised industry and land. It will come about democratically, via the ballot box. I see Italy falling, then France, and ourselves not far behind. In their case, I believe it will be called Communism; in ours . . . who knows? . . . Social Democracy, maybe – but whatever it's called, the result will be the same. Nevertheless, I do believe we shall be our own masters. Russia and all it stands for – lack of human rights, secret police, psychiatric wards – will be told to get stuffed. The status quo as it now stands will, to a certain extent, remain, but not the other way. The other way, the abrupt change of policies, the rapid disintegration of the EEC and NATO, will be too much. That's the key to their strategy; speed of change. The rapid transition will bring about USSR domination; the slower should enable us to keep our independence.'

'It's an interesting hypothesis,' Barber said quietly.

'It's more than that. As you're well aware, these sort of political games are going on all the time, being played by virtually every European country. Every country arrives at the same conclusion – forecasts the same result. There's even a term for these conclusions; projected facts. Certain circumstances must result in certain conclusions. Does it make any sort of sense to you?'

'Uh-huh.' Barber nodded. 'Too much so. I've heard similar arguments in political debates within the forces, particularly at Staff College, where most of our studies were political. Even then, many of us found the concept staggering . . . frightening.'

'I hadn't realised you did that sort of studying in the

67

Marines. At least, then, I don't have to try and convince you of the outcome of what I've told you.'

'The outcome of what you suggest is reasonably clear,' said Barber, 'but there are one or two other points that need clearing up. The first is that I don't believe your story. It's inconceivable to me that the substitution of a man like Parker could have taken place. He has already held several high posts in previous governments and didn't appear all bad from what I can remember.'

'You may find it more credible when I've told you the facts.' Carmichael took out the dossier and went through the evidence against Parker. Having heard the details, Barber nodded dubiously.

'It may be true then. I concede that. But it still doesn't tell me why you're here. Why tell me any of this? Why not just arrest the man, bring him to trial and expose him for what he is?'

'There are very complex reasons, mainly political, which we need to go into. Get me a coffee and I'll explain.'

An hour later Barber was shrugging his shoulders and saying, 'So what? That still doesn't tell me why you're here.'

'Work it out,' was all Carmichael said.

As the realisation hit him, Barber blinked rapidly. 'My God. No arrest. If there's no arrest, and there's no return to Russia then there is only one option. Elimination and you want me to do it. Of course.' Carmichael was looking at him like a fond uncle whose favourite nephew had just done something particularly clever. Barber seemed to be in a reverie for a moment and then he snapped out of it. 'You must be out of your tiny, poxy minds. You and whoever else dreamed up this charming little scheme. You're asking me to commit murder to save the political system of the country? To . . . to . . .' he was almost spluttering with rage, 'after all that's happened to me? I couldn't give a toss for this country. Why should I?'

Carmichael and Barber discussed and argued for a further hour. Finally Barber said, 'I understand the arguments, I see why you have to take the steps you suggest. But you can count me out. I just won't do it.'

Carmichael nodded and almost absently said, 'Tell me, when did you last hear from your brother?'

Watching Barber closely, he was gratified to see at last a change of expression.

'My brother? Leave him out of this. He's in hospital in a pretty bad way.'

'I know. I spoke to the doctor in charge this evening, and the news wasn't good.'

'What do you mean?' Barber demanded. 'Phil told me yesterday he was going to be all right; he'd be left with a certain weakness in his left hand and arm, that's all.'

'Yes – that's what the doctors wanted him to believe, to encourage him. Later, when he's stronger, they'll tell him the truth. Your brother will be completely paralysed down his left side.'

'Jesus H. Christ!' Barber's face drained white. 'You can't mean . . . yes, I can see you do. Is it certain? Is there no hope at all?'

Carmichael had wielded the stick; now it was time for the carrot.

'There is hope,' he said, and went on, as Barber's tense body relaxed, 'but it's expensive.' The other's jaw tightened again. 'There's a doctor in Switzerland who does marvellous work on cases like your brother's. There's no guarantee of success, of course, but it's the best chance he's got, and the treatment has to be applied immediately, before there's any scarring of the damaged nerves.'

'I see.' Barber nodded, his face impassive again. 'So how much will it cost? I've no doubt you just happen to have the figure.'

'As it happens, I do.' Carmichael paused. 'There wouldn't be much change out of £10,000, or, if you prefer it, 30,000 Swiss francs.'

'Which also just happens to be the amount you intend offering me for the job.'

'That's right. It'll be paid into a Swiss account in Berne, as soon as you agree.'

Barber shook his head. 'I want twenty thousand, in cash. And there's no argument.'

Carmichael sucked his teeth. He appeared to ponder and then nodded. 'I agree,' he said curtly. He did not tell Barber that he had already decided to pay as much as thirty thousand pounds if necessary. With an operation as important as the one contemplated there was plenty of funds available. It was a very tempting offer but still Barber hesitated. Carmichael had given in too easily. Was there any significance in that? If there was then he couldn't see it.

'And if I don't?'

'If you don't you'll probably be confining your brother to a wheelchair for the rest of his life. It's your choice, naturally.'

'You have all the answers, don't you?' Barber didn't try to disguise the bitterness in his voice. 'For all that, I have a few more questions. First – why me? Why not one of your own men? You'd have far better control over him and over events, and it would also save you a considerable sum of money. I'm not stupid. I realise the difficulty you'd have to get that sort of payment authorised.'

Carmichael smiled. 'No authorisation is required. We have the funds. We've been salting away small amounts from official sources into a special fund since 1950; totally unaccountable, and for use by only a handful of men, mostly my opposite numbers in other departments. From time to time calls are made on the fund. No reason is given, none asked for.'

'You're a very trusting bunch.'

'Somewhere along yet another line, we reach the point where such trust is necessary. To our knowledge it hasn't been abused – but that's by the by. As to your other query, the answer is even simpler. This whole thing is unofficial. There will be no records kept, no acknowledgement of our involvement in any way. It would be extremely difficult to get hold of one of our men at such short notice; one, that is, of the right calibre. An excuse would have to be found, heads of departments would have to be informed – and not only heads, but their deputies, and even section leaders. Our bureaucracy demands it. Checks and counterchecks; a system no one man could abuse.'

'You're abusing it,' Barber said quietly.

'Not so. I'm by-passing it. There's a world of difference. Sometimes such a move becomes necessary. Secrecy becomes the key word in an operation, and this is one of those times. The requirement is known by the other services, hence the setting up of the fund, along with certain other facilities which you'll hear about later.'

'But I haven't agreed . . .'

'My mistake. I'd assumed it was a foregone conclusion, especially in view of the money.'

'You've assumed too much. It so happens I'm in the process of negotiating for a job with a diving company abroad. It may take me a little longer to acquire the amount you mentioned, but I reckon I could do it in about six months.'

Carmichael was worried. He'd misjudged this man; he'd been so sure he could get him. His outward calm remained unruffled, however. 'Six months is probably too long for your brother to wait,' he said. 'I suggest you think about that.'

'I'll consider it, but I very much doubt I'll change my mind.'

'I see.' Carmichael paused, looked at the backs of his hands then looked up. 'That puts me in rather an awkward position, doesn't it? Here you are with all this information. Very tricky . . .'

'Not tricky at all,' Barber retorted with a shrug. 'The Official Secrets Act will keep me quiet. I'm not convinced this caper falls within the Act – but as far as I'm concerned it does, and I assure you I'll say nothing to anyone.'

They both knew that fear of the Act was groundless. With the right coverage, no court in the land could ever convict. Officialdom was stepping outside the law, and that was far more frightening than any Act, or even any ordinary criminal activity. The knowledge suddenly frightened Barber. It came to him in a flash. Secrecy . . . but he knew. He was outside their control, a source of danger, a threat. Which posed the greater danger; to do it, or to know about it? Carmichael's story had only been part truth. He could understand their inability to find a suitable operative – but there was more to it than that. They didn't want to lose their man; hence their decision to find an outsider. An expendable. Him.

Carmichael got to his feet. 'If that's your last word, I'll say goodnight. Only think about it, and contact me not later than tomorrow at six. Here's my number.' He handed him his card. 'Thanks for listening to me, at least.'

'I shall follow developments with interest. I'm sure you'll find an answer to your problems sooner or later.'

'I'm sure I will. Don't bother seeing me out, I can find my own way.'

The abruptness of his departure left Barber with a feeling of unreality for a second; then the full realisation of what it all meant hit him and he sank down on the edge of the bed, his mind in a turmoil. Heroes in books were portrayed as strong, silent types taking murder, mayhem and political intrigue in their stride. It wasn't like that. It was sickening to get involved, to know your life was being laid on the line, remorselessly, in cold blood. Nothing in the Marines had prepared him for this. Fighting an enemy you could see, knowing if you returned to your own country you'd be free to come and go as you pleased; that was one thing. This would leave him not only beyond the law, but their target for immediate execution. Carmichael was a ruthless bastard – no doubt about that – and he, Barber, knew too much. There was no control over him except one . . .

He suddenly wondered what would happen after 6.00 p.m. tomorrow? An accident? A bullet maybe? Who would do it? An operative or Carmichael himself? After all the death of Barber was a non event compared to the death of Parker. Except, that is, to Barber himself. Jesus H. Christ . . .

He sat there, shaking – and suddenly the fear left him, to be replaced by ice-cold fury at the way he was being used. He knew what he had to do, and he knew it must be done before morning.

Less than a dozen sheets remained on his writing pad, so he was forced to write in an uncharacteristically cramped style. His watch showed four o'clock in the morning by the time he had finished, sitting back to rub his tired eyes and stretch his aching muscles. Every word he could remember was written there. Now all he had to do was let Carmichael know the information existed, to be released if he died unexpectedly, no matter what the cause. He grinned wryly. He hoped he wasn't accidentally run over. The irony would keep him amused for eternity.

Chapter 6

Joan Carmichael hated having to wake her husband, knowing how late he'd worked the previous night. She shook his shoulder gently, murmuring in his ear, 'Come on, love – time to get up. It's half past seven.'

Carmichael grunted and fought his way groggily through the layers of sleep until he could push himself up. It was after three by the time he'd got to bed, having spent hours reassessing the other men he had on his files, wondering which to approach. The trouble was, now that he'd met Barber no one else would do. He had fallen asleep still racking his brains for a way of inducing the ex-Marine to work for him before six o'clock. After that there would be no choice.

'Breakfast in fifteen minutes. I've put out your blue suit ready for you.'

'Eh? What for? It's not . . .'

'Today,' Joan said gently, 'you have the meeting with the Prime Minister. Remember?'

'Oh yes, of course. Thanks.'

He gave her a wan smile, and she bent down and lightly kissed him.

'All in a day's work. I've even run a tepid bath for you; it should help to wake you up. The newspaper's in there ready for you.'

He was still so tired he only skimmed through the main story; something about two men being strung up across a railway line. One was dead, the other critically ill in hospital. The police expected an early arrest. He snorted. Probably meant they didn't have a clue.

As he shaved and dressed his mind was still wrestling with the problem of Barber. If only there was some way to force him . . .

He was half way through his breakfast when the 'phone rang. Knowing it would be for him he got up irritably to answer it.

'Yes?' he barked.

''Morning, Jim,' Chapman greeted him. 'Sorry if I'm disturbing you.'

'It doesn't matter,' grunted Carmichael, making it clear by his tone of voice that it did.

'It's just to let you know that the meeting this morning is cancelled.'

'Cancelled or postponed?'

'Cancelled. I spoke to her last night and explained the situation. She agreed with me. It would be better not to have the meeting, especially with Walters likely to get on his high horse.'

'Okay, whatever you say. I'll stop by and see you later this afternoon with my news.'

'Fine. Give my love to Joan and tell her I look forward to seeing her again one of these days.'

'Sure.'

Chapman had met Carmichael's wife only once, about a year previously, at a cocktail party; since then, he concluded every telephone conversation with the same message; the upper class civil servant being polite to the middle class. Carmichael had passed the message on the first time; now he didn't bother. He and Chapman were on different sides of the social fence, and as long as they worked well together, that was all that mattered. The idea that industrial democracy might one day invade the Civil Service made Carmichael smile.

★   ★   ★

Throughout the day something nagged at Carmichael's mind; some fact, something important lodged firmly in his

75

subconscious. He tried worrying at it, trying to find what it was, then dismissing it, hoping it would appear unexpectedly. It didn't. It just stayed out of reach, making him irritable and short tempered, quite unlike his usual, equable self.

He was convinced that somewhere was the key to get Barber for the job, and he needed to find it – fast.

★ ★ ★

Steve Barber slept until midday. When he woke, the memories flooded back. Unhurriedly he got up, dressed and got ready to go out. He had a great deal of respect for Carmichael, and didn't make the mistake of underestimating him. If he were in Carmichael's shoes he'd have a tail on him, at the earliest opportunity. As he left the house his mind was busy with the problem of how to lose one's shadower.

Initially, the difficulty wasn't in losing him, it was in identifying him. Steve took the tube to Oxford Street and wandered around window shopping. It took him an hour to decide that either there was no one following him, or he couldn't spot whoever it was – which left only one thing to do.

Pausing in front of one large store, he bent to do up his shoe lace and, as a crowd pushed past him into the shop, quickly mingled and went with it. Half ducking, not looking back, he pushed his way through the throng of shoppers to the other side of the building, hurried out into the street and across to Tottenham Court Road tube station. He took the Northern line to Leicester Square, waited until the doors began to close and then slipped out, careful not to push open the doors again as he did so. The train pulled out, no one else having left it, and Steve took the Piccadilly line to South Kensington, pulled the same trick and caught the circle for King's Cross.

On the main line station he found a photocopier, took three duplicates of his notes, sealed them in envelopes and walked for nearly a mile, posting them in different boxes. The first was addressed to his brother's firm, the second to his bank and the original to a friend still serving in the Marines. He intended to keep the third copy himself, to show to Carmichael if necessary. One problem now remained; to let the Superintendent know what he'd done before anything happened to him. But first he intended calling on Phil, to see how he was progressing.

★ ★ ★

'What do you mean, you lost him?' Carmichael demanded angrily. 'How the hell did you manage that?' An apologetic voice quaked on the other end of the line. 'I see. And you don't think he knew he was being followed, just taking general precautions? Bollocks! You cocked it up. He must have known you were there, otherwise he wouldn't have acted like he did. To lose the front tail in Leicester Square is understandable, to do the same thing again in South Kensington is sheer bloody ineptitude. All right – call it off. Cancel all further surveillance and write a termination of OP report.'

He hung up, pensive as well as annoyed. Barber was a clever devil and no mistake. Twice in less than 48 hours he'd given his men the slip, and they were experts in the job. First down Whitechapel way and now . . .

Christ – that was it! The fact, the nebulous thought that had been annoying him all day. He pulled his newspaper from his raincoat pocket and read the cover story carefully, his smile broadening with each successive paragraph.

★ ★ ★

'Hullo, Phil,' Steve Barber's smile couldn't disguise the worry in his eyes. 'How are you feeling?'

'A lot better. It only hurts when I laugh.'

'In that case I'd better not tell you any funny stories. Have you seen Sue?'

Phil nodded. 'She comes in every day. We're certainly get-

77

ting our money's worth from the N.H.S. It's quite convenient really. Her mother's staying with her to look after the house and have a meal ready for when she goes home . . .'

His voice trailed off. Presently Steve said: 'What did the doctor say? How long will you be here?'

'Quite some time yet. You know what these medical men are like; the Hippocratic oath includes one of silence as well.'

Steve forced a smile. The answer hadn't surprised him; his brother looked terrible. He was still connected to an intravenous drip in his arm, and a nasal tube, issuing from his right nostril, was taped to his cheek. His face was as white as the bandage that swathed his head. He had been moving his right hand slightly as he spoke, but his left remained still and heavy on the counterpane.

'I couldn't get anything out of them either,' he said. 'If you ask me . . .'

'Steve,' Phil interrupted, 'what happened? did you . . .?'

Just then, to Steve's relief, a nurse came into the room. 'I'm sorry, Mr. Barber,' she said, 'but I'll have to ask you to leave now. The doctor has left strict instructions that your brother must not be allowed to become overtired.'

'I understand,' Steve got to his feet. 'I'll come again soon, Phil. And you're not to worry. Everything's under control.'

He pressed his brother's left hand, lying cold and lifeless on the coverlet, and left quickly before the tears in his eyes betrayed him.

Steve wandered aimlessly around London, not noticing where he was or where he was going. It was with something of a shock that he realised it was after 1800 hours, and time to ring Carmichael. The third phone booth he tried wasn't vandalised.

'May I speak to Chief Superintendent Carmichael . . .' he began.

'Speaking.'

'Ah. This is Steve Barber. I rang to tell you I won't be taking up your offer. I . . .'

'No no, Barber. That's just where you're wrong. You will be taking it up; in fact you'll be carrying out my instructions to the letter.'

His bland certainty infuriated Steve.

'Are you deaf?' he demanded. 'I've just told you I'm not going to do it, and that's final. I don't need your blood money. I'll make my own, working as a diver.' His next suggestion to Carmichael, a physical impossibility for any man, was greeted with a chuckle. The sound warned him, but even so he was totally unprepared for the next words.

'Barber, don't hang up. Just listen. From the time I decided I was going to use you, I've had you under surveillance. I know what happened on Saturday night.'

Steve almost dropped the phone, his palms suddenly slippery with sweat.

'Meet me on the Embankment in an hour. Wait near the *Discovery*,' Carmichael said, and hung up.

Barber stood there for several moments, the dialling tone buzzing in his ear. Then he hung up slowly. Although he was shocked, his mind was working with ice cold clarity.

⋆　⋆　⋆

The two men met, nodded and fell into step alongside each other, strolling along the Embankment for a few minutes in silence, two friends enjoying the evening sun after a hard day at the office.

'Read the papers today?' Carmichael enquired presently.

Steve shrugged. 'No – and I don't intend to. Like the proverbial ostrich, I'd rather not know what's being written.'

'They weren't very flattering. Mind you, they described the victims as innocent young men, not vicious thugs responsible for muggings, beatings, terrorising of pubs – and of course putting your brother in hospital.'

'You seem to know a hell of a lot.'

'It's amazing how facts hang together when the key is known. So now, you see, you have no choice ... well no – that's not strictly true. You do have a choice, naturally; you either do as I say, or spend the next ten years in jail on charges of murder and attempted murder.'

'Hobson's choice, isn't it?' Steve commented grimly. 'All right supposing I do do as you say. What then? Are all charges dropped? Is the shadow of prosecution removed for ever?'

Carmichael chucked. 'Quite poetic, aren't you? Shadow of prosecution ... shall we worry about that when it's over? After all, we can't be sure what the situation will be then, can we?'

Barber halted so abruptly that Carmichael stopped too.

'Look,' he said, 'I'm not a fool. I've already worked out why you really want me, and what's in it for me at the end.' He thrust his hand into his pocket and withdrew the envelope with the details of their meeting. 'This is only one of the photostat copies I made. By tomorrow they'll be where you can't touch them ... I needn't tell you the circumstances required to ensure they'll be opened. Instructions on what to do are contained in each one.'

For a second Carmichael's bland equanimity was shaken. 'My word,' he said, 'you have been a busy little bee, haven't you? It still doesn't alter the fact that you'll work for me. If you don't Barber, I shall place all the information I have in the hands of the investigating officers, and let justice take its course. I'll deny your story of our meeting, and arrest the Secretary of State, regardless of the political consequences. I'll have nothing to lose – but you will lose at least ten years of your life, and the ability to earn the money you require for your brother. By the time you get out, your life will be ruined and your brother a permanent cripple. Do you get the picture?'

'I hate to disappoint you, Chief Superintendent, but your reasoning was totally predictable. I'd already made up my mind to do as you asked. 'That', Steve gestured at the envelope in the other man's hand, 'is to ensure I stay alive at the end of it. You see, once I carry out my part of the bargain my hold over you will become greater. We'll be able to trade, my freedom for my silence. But I'm sure you've already managed to work that one out for yourself.'

Carmichael nodded. 'I hate to admit it, but I'm developing a certain grudging respect for your abilities. I think I'm going to enjoy working with you.'

'I doubt whether the feeling will be reciprocated,' Barber reported.

'You never know. You may actually come to like me in the end,' Carmichael countered good humouredly.

'Sure, and pigs might fly.' Barber paused, then went on, 'Look, let's get one thing straight right from the start. I don't particularly like you now, and I don't think anything you do or say will make me change my mind. I'll do the job as best I can, and I'll co-operate in every way. As soon as it's over I don't expect ever to see you again.'

All right, Barber, if that's the way you want it,' the Chief Superintendent said, all pretence of friendship gone. 'It would have made working together easier; as it is, I don't give a damn. Tomorrow, report to this address; it's a house in South Wales, in the Vale of Glamorgan. Here's fifty quid for travelling expenses. Be there between 1700 and 1800 hours. Take nothing with you – not even a toothbrush. You'll be supplied with everything you need. Have you got that?'

Barber nodded. 'Anything else?'

'I suggest you tell your brother you'll be busy on Government business for the next two weeks, or so; what sort of business it's up to you to decide. I'll be there to meet and brief you.'

By now they had continued their strolling. Big Ben was visible in the distance, and presently the chimes of seven o'clock came distinctly to them.

'I leave you here,' Carmichael said. 'I suggest you get to

81

the hospital and see your brother. After that, go back to your digs, pack your gear and be ready to leave first thing in the morning. Put the stuff in a left luggage locker when you go to catch the ten o'clock train for Wales. You can collect it when you return; you won't be going back to your digs.'

He nodded and walked off.

By the time Barber arrived at the hospital he'd decided what he was going to tell his brother. 'What brings you back so early?' Phil enquired, looking anxious. 'Trouble?'

'Of a sort – but nothing to worry about. Listen, and I'll tell you what's happened and the precautions I've taken.' He told Phil everything down to the last detail, finishing with the meeting he'd just had with Carmichael.

'Christ,' Phil groaned. 'It's hard to believe. The trouble is, it's so incredible it must be true. How do you know this Carmichael is who he says he is? How do you know this whole thing isn't some sort of enemy play, with you as patsy?'

The words struck a chord in Steve's guts. He just hadn't thought of it that way.

'It . . . it's possible I suppose. My God, I've just . . . On the Embankment he said that secrecy was everything. Or was that last night? I can't remember. Anyway, he said secrecy was everything – yet his surveillance teams will know what I've done. They must have seen me, so why didn't they stop me? Surely just because they're watching somebody doesn't mean they wouldn't prevent a crime, especially a . . . what I did.' He paused. 'I wonder. Suppose they'd been following me and then lost me. After all, I went to ground in a pretty desolate spot, and I remember seeing a chap rushing up and down the path a few times just after I'd hidden myself. So that's it. No proof. He assumed and I fell for it.'

'Don't you think,' Philip said, 'bearing in mind what you've told me, that he'd probably be able to find the proof, if he has the head start he appears to have? The only trouble is, if he's arrived at the conclusion he has, then there's no reason to believe the others in the team won't as well. That might prove difficult for him – assuming, of course, he's who he says he is.'

★ ★ ★

'Sergeant Harris rang, dear,' Joan Carmichael greeted her husband when he arrived home. 'He said it was urgent, and would you ring him at home, no matter what time you got in.'

He kissed her absently, his mind working on the problem of the sergeant in charge of the surveillance team. Originally there had been two purposes to the surveillance; the first to ensure Barber was available immediately he was wanted, and to give Carmichael his present background, the second for use at the end of the operation. With Barber dead, killed by him, he could have reported the fact that a rumour had been put about, but insufficient evidence hadn't warranted any further action. It was regrettable, but a mistake had been made . . . etc., etc. He could have covered, used the facts to his advantage. Now it was different. He didn't dare kill Barber until he got his hands on the letters Barber had sent, and somehow he doubted he would be able to do that. Therefore, not only did he now have to keep Barber alive, he also had to get him off the hook for the railway murders.

Carmichael's temperament allowed him to accept any upset or change in his plans with equanimity. Calmly dialling Harris's number, he identified himself and went on.

'I know what you're going to say. Barber and the murders, right?' he waited for the sergeant to agree. 'I'd already come to the same conclusion. I've seen Barber and checked out his story. He was shacked up with a married bird all night, and the reason he vanished the way he did was because he slipped into her place by the back way, so the neighbours wouldn't see. Her old man was on night shift.'

'I see. That's it then is it sir?' said Harris, unable to conceal his disappointment.

'Never mind, sergeant – it was a good thought. If there's nothing else . . . Goodnight to you too.' He hung up thankfully. 'What's for supper, love?' he called to his wife in the kitchen.

Chapter 7

After an almost sleepless night, Barber was lulled to sleep by the clackity clack of the train wheels bearing him towards Cardiff. He'd spent most of his wakeful hours trying to think how he could discover for certain that Carmichael was who he claimed to be. Philip's suggestion had been distinctly disturbing. In most of the spy stories he had read, it had been the other side using the 'good guy' to commit some treacherous act. In this case, this real life case, it was the good guys using him – and he was cast in the role of the not so good guy; not black, exactly, but certainly a shade of grey. But suppose they, whoever they were, were the bad guys, using him to commit an act that would have serious repercussions? The resultant publicity, correctly handled, could plant the blame on the ultra right faction in Britain, and cause havoc in the political system.

Steve knew the Russians were capable of issuing misleading press reports, turning half truths into lies and forcing politicians, albeit unwittingly, to take the wrong decisions. The enemy commanded a powerful weapon in its manipulation of the media, a manipulation not available to the relatively democratic West, whose ability to affect Soviet reporting of the news was negligible.

Some time towards morning, the idea had occurred to Steve that it might be the right wing faction in Britain that was actually using him. He was appalled by the possibility. The enemy, in his eyes, had always been the Communists and left wing of the Labour party. The thought that he was being manipulated by the very faction he himself supported was quite horrifying. He was more unsure than ever, too, about Carmichael; the possibilities suddenly seemed endless, and he almost wanted to believe the original story. It made a certain amount of sense, he could accept it and, most importantly, it put him on the side of the law ... more or less. At least it wasn't as bad as operating completely outside it, with all the final ramifications it would mean to him.

The smoothness of the Inter-City 125 let him sleep until Newport. With ten minutes to go to Cardiff, he made his way to the buffet car and consumed half a stale bread roll and a cup of warm brown liquid euphemistically called coffee. As the train drew in to Cardiff General station, the rain clouds cleared, blown away by a strong wind, and the sun came out.

At just after 1300 hours he was sitting in the bus station waiting for the bus to take him to his final destination. Carmichael's instructions had been to wait in the city, and to catch a bus that would get him in half an hour before the 1700–1800 hours arrival bracket; a half hour's walk would see him there on time. The only way Steve could think of to discover any proof as to who Carmichael really worked for was to arrive early and nose around.

He quite enjoyed the ride through lovely countryside, passing through villages with unpronounceable names. All the road signs were in English and Welsh, but on some the English name had been crudely erased, presumably by Welsh Nationalists.

At the village of Pentyrch he got off the bus and, following his instructions, set off on foot along the small country lane skirting the Garth mountain and leading to another unpronounceable village – Efail Isaf.

After an initial short climb the road led continuously down hill, winding through woods and farm land, with high hedges on each side and only the occasional gap to reveal the heavily populated area on the other side of the valley, the scene dominated by the Cwm colliery and its coal tips.

Steve caught a glimpse of the house before he reached the gate leading into the drive. From there the house could no

86

longer be seen, but as there was no other building in the vicinity, it was safe to assume that the place he'd seen was the one he was heading for.

He looked up and down the road, saw it was clear and vaulted over the low wall alongside the gate. Pulling the hood of his anorak over his head, he made his way as quietly as he could through the thick, wet undergrowth, pausing every few moments to listen. Progress was slow, for he had to ensure there were no trip wires or alarm circuits for him to break. The place could be honeycombed with alarms for all he knew – but he was needed by Carmichael, so it shouldn't matter if he did set one off. Nevertheless, he preferred to arrive unnoticed.

Through breaks in the foliage he caught glimpses of the house. Arriving at the edge of a large lawn sweeping in three levels to the building, he stayed there for over twenty minutes, studying the terrain and his objective.

The three storey house was built of ugly red brick, hideous amid the splendour of the grounds. There were no lights visible, no smoke issuing from any of the three chimneys. The place had a desolate, empty look. Cautiously Barber made his way round the edge of the lawn to the side of the building. In contrast to the three rows of seven windows along the front, there was only a side door, with a small window alongside it. At the back was a large patio, served by double French doors and windows which stretched the length of the house. The place still looked empty.

Barber returned to the corner between the side and back, the closest point to the house and still nearly forty yards away. The lawns and gardens at the rear of the house were, if it were possible, even more magnificent than those at the front. Pausing, he quickly scanned the area, satisfied himself no one was watching and darted across to the wall, standing with his back to it at the corner, whence he could step either way and be out of sight if somebody approached from either direction. More importantly, if that somebody began shooting in his direction, the wall made a comfortable shield.

He grinned wryly at his own sense of melodrama, then reminded himself of the favourite peroration of the staff sergeant in charge of his initial SBS training:

'There are two categories of homo sapiens more likely than the rest to die in this game; the first is the foolish, the second those who feel foolish. If you always do as I tell you, and remember the lessons, you may live to collect your pensions – assuming, that is, and heaven forbid that you ever find yourselves involved in another war. No matter how stupid the precautions seem – and believe me, sometimes they appear very stupid – just carry them out. You may feel a little stupid a lot of the time, but it's a damn' sight better than feeling very stupid once, and for the last time.'

It was one lesson Steve Barber never forgot.

It took him half an hour to look into every window and check that the house was empty and securely locked. He had no burglary skills, which left only one course open to him. Finding a fist-sized stone in the garden, he took a deep breath, smashed the window next to the handle of the French doors with the stone and waited, tense as a coiled spring, for the raucous sound of alarm bells. So tense was he indeed that the silence came as quite a shock. Puffing out his cheeks in a sigh of relief, he undid the latch and opened the door. Silence still. His watch told him that there was still an hour and a half to go before his initial arrival time, which meant that Carmichael couldn't be far behind him.

Hurriedly he searched the house. In general the furniture was old, solid and well cared for. Downstairs, in addition to the large lounge by which he had entered, there was a separate TV room, a large dining room with a long table running almost the length of it, and an ultra modern kitchen in light contrast to the rest of the ground floor rooms.

The second floor bedrooms, eight in all, were airy and pleasantly decorated. The third floor was given over to offices. Drawing his finger along a polished surface, he realised the place had recently been cleaned. Every drawer in every desk was locked, as was every cupboard. The one safe he could find, situated at the end of the top floor corridor, had its lock securely scrambled, and though he fiddled with the tumblers there was no way he could open it. There was not a scrap of paper, not a single clue as to the identity of the occupants of the house.

Frustrated, Barber descended the stairs to the ground floor. He had just reached it when he heard the car arriving, and moved quickly to a window in time to see Carmichael getting out, a briefcase in his left hand. Barber returned to the lounge, poured himself a drink at the well stocked bar there and seated himself by the window. He'd taken his first sip of whisky when the door opened.

'Hullo, Carmichael,' he greeted the Chief Superintendent, and then blinked rapidly as he found himself looking down the barrel of a revolver.

'Bloody hell!' exclaimed Carmichael, slowly lowering the gun. 'Carry on like that and you'll be dead within a week. How did you get in?'

Barber gestured at the French doors, maintaining with difficulty his outward calm. He was sure Carmichael hadn't been holding the gun he was now returning to a shoulder holster, and the speed of the bulky man was quite startling.

'Why?' Carmichael went on. 'No – don't tell me. I know why. In fact I half expected this; if you hadn't been here I'd have been disappointed in you. You came here looking for evidence that I'm who I claim to be, right? The possibility of your doubt had occurred to me. No, that's not true. Again I'd be disappointed in you if you hadn't doubted.'

While he was talking Carmichael had moved across to the bar and helped himself to a can of beer from the fridge below the counter. 'As you rightly surmised,' he went on, 'the original plan, if carried out, would have ended in your death . . . at my hands. As it is now, I can't afford for that to happen. I hadn't counted on your covering yourself the way you have; a serious error of judgement on my part, but one that can't now be helped.' He settled himself comfortably on a bar stool. 'Where was I? Oh yes. Originally I was going to show you the kind of proof you require. The secrets of this house would have been known to you, and they would have died with you too. I now need to keep you alive, but the problem still remains of how to convince you . . . Right?' He paused while Barber nodded. 'It leaves me in a dilemma, and I can see only one solution. You still have to be shown the house.' He drained the can and set it down on the bar. 'Come on – no time like the present. I take it you've seen all the rooms?'

He moved towards the door, Barber trailing behind.

'A Welsh couple look after it for us,' he went on chattily. 'They keep the place clean and the grounds in order – with extra help of course – and ensure that the larder and bar are well stocked. Before coming down here we always telephone and tell them our time of arrival and expected departure, and while we're here they stay out of the way. During our stay we cater for ourselves, do our own cleaning and so on. We only ever come here for two purposes; one is defector interrogations, the other agent briefing and sometimes training.'

They were on the top floor, and Carmichael, his bulk shielding the tumblers, was unlocking the safe. He opened it to reveal rows of bunches of keys. Taking out three lots, he led the way into the nearest office, having first relocked the safe.

Handing a bunch of keys to Barber, the Superintendent said: 'Don't imagine for one moment we're paranoid about secrecy. It's become all too necessary, as has changing houses every eighteen months or so, along with house-keepers. Three years ago we lost four defectors in a row, before they could tell us very much.'

'A bit careless, weren't you, misplacing them like that?' commented Steve, deadpan.

'Not really. Three were poisoned, one was shot by long range rifle. Since then our precautions have bordered on the ludicrous, but we haven't lost a single person.'

'That's a hell of a lot of people trying to get out of Russia, isn't it?'

"Who said anything about Russia? Add on East Germany, Poland, Hungary, Yugoslavia, Czechoslovakia and Rumania, as well as the East, and it isn't that many. Most of them believe they have useful information they can sell to us, but unfortunately that's rarely the case. The four that were taken out were the best we'd had in a long time, and that fact alone convinced us of the necessity for these extreme precautions. We've had two top defectors through our hands since then, and didn't lose either.'

'Congratulations,' Barber said sarcastically. 'What happens now?'

'Help yourself. Read what you like, see what you like.'

Barber spent half an hour in the office. Although most of what he read meant little or nothing to him, the inter-office memos, the filing system and the stationery all added up to a Civil Service type of organisation, similar to that used in the armed forces.

'Here are the keys to another office,' Carmichael said, when Steve had finished his survey. 'It's the second on the right.'

'No thanks. I'd like you to reopen the safe, and I'll choose the keys and the office.'

The Superintendent shrugged, and led the way back into the corridor. This time Barber carried out only a cursory examination.

'Okay,' he said. 'I'm convinced that you're either real or very thorough. Or maybe both.'

'I hope for both our sakes it's both. There's one more room to show you, and then we'll go down to the kitchen and find some food.'

The windowless room next to the safe was a small, specialised armoury.

'You'll recognise some of the weapons, others will be new to you, which is hardly surprising considering they're one off guns. One of them you'll be using.'

Barber was impressed in spite of himself. He knew the Ruger Security Six, the FNO.38, the Webley and the Luger

.22, all hand guns. Amongst the Sterling 9mm machine guns he was surprised to see a Russian 7.62mm PPS42 and a Czech 9mm VZ23.

'Souvenirs of enemy action gone wrong,' Carmichael said, jerking his chin towards them. 'For them, that is,' he added with a grin.

As they turned to leave, a Belgian FN rifle and a Lee Enfield caught Steve's eye. The remainder in the rack of ten rifles were unknown to him.

As Carmichael locked the door he said, 'Some old, some new but all good – all with a special purpose. Now let's eat.'

The well stocked larder yielded a liver paté, sirloin steak and salad, followed by cheese cake. Because Barber preferred a dry wine and Carmichael sweet, they'd compromised with a rosé, which neither enjoyed very much. As they ate Carmichael expounded his ideas.

'I believe,' he said, 'that time is getting short. Sooner or later the Russians will move. I see them trying to get Parker to an Eastern country and capitalising as much as possible on the resulting scandal; assuming, that is, that we don't arrest him first. The scandal will be the same either way. Agreed? Good. If he's killed we can prevent that happening. Now . . .'

'Wait a minute. If the Russians think we're going to arrest him, why bother trying to get him out?'

'Two possible reasons. One, the way he came to our attention will be made public, and other agents in the field, knowing that their masters are capable of sacrificing such an important agent, will feel even less secure than they do now – which, believe me, is saying something. Morale would plummet; no bad thing from our point of view, of course. Two, we've had bad security leaks in the past. Why should now be any different despite all the precautions we've taken? Let's assume they know of our intentions. If we succeed, they lose a valuable propaganda weapon and the ability to inflict a stunning blow to our morale – plus all the other arguments you've already heard. Nobody except you and I will know when we strike – not even the committee I report to. In fact they think I don't intend using you until after Parker returns from his holiday in Copenhagen, but in my opinion that'll be too late. He won't be coming back. That is obvious. So you'll get him as he gets off the ferry in Holland.' They'd finished eating and were now sitting at the bar, drinking malt whisky. Barber made no comment and asked no questions, sensing the other man wanted to tell him his plan in his own time and in his own way.

'Wednesday I shall report to the Deputy Leader as his bodyguard, necessary because of intelligence gathered and so on. If he becomes awkward, the Prime Minister and the Opposition Leader will tell him to behave. Parker will be in a quandary. His reason for going to Copenhagen is to meet his parents, and he obviously won't want me around. I'll allow him to think I'm the soul of discretion and not averse to a holiday myself. I'll also imply that he may be going to meet a lady friend – if he doesn't do so first – and I'll suggest if he wants to lose me for a few days it's okay by me. When we get to Rotterdam I shall lead him into a certain position. You'll be in a building three quarters of a mile away. I'll stop, take out a handkerchief to blow my nose and you fire. It's corny, but it works.'

The two men went on to discuss further details of the actual killing and Barber's escape.

What about the Russians in all this?' the latter enquired. 'Presumably they'll be working out the ... er ... ramifications of this defection.'

'Oh, undoubtedly. One thing I've learnt about the Soviets is that they're incapable of reacting quickly. Their bureaucracy is so ponderously slow, checking, double checking and covering themselves, we should have sufficient breathing space in which to operate.'

'We hope. Or should I say, you hope?'

'We,' Carmichael supplied blandly. 'As I see it,' he went on, 'the Russians will start by checking the defector's access

93

to information. Once that's established they'll need highest approval to move. Whatever they decide will have vast political ramifications. It isn't a decision they'll take lightly, and it will require Politburo clearance. There's the strong possibility they may let British justice take its course. They'd be expecting us to arrest Parker, and still could achieve maximum embarrassment of this country.'

Barber nodded. 'Another drink?' He picked up the bottle standing between them and poured a liberal measure into each glass. 'It makes sense – but then, if I thought about it long enough I'm sure I could come up with another equally plausible theory.'

'Yes, I'm certain you could – but there's one difference. I have a good idea of how they work, how they think. I've studied the psychology, which is an important factor when trying to outguess them. That's why I'm taking this route. I may be wrong, but if so that's just too bad. I have to work on something, so we'll work on my assumptions. Okay?'

'Oh, that's fine with me. I was just making a general observation.'

'It's one that's occurred to me more than once.'

The effects of the wine at dinner and the three quarters of a bottle of whisky they'd drunk so far were beginning to show. Their speech was not slurred because they were taking care not to allow it to be so, but their responses were slower, and concentration difficult.

'Did I ... hic ... did I tell you why I left the Marines?' Barber asked presently.

Carmichael shook his head, reaching for the whisky bottle.

'Then I will...'

★ ★ ★

It was coming up to four in the morning when they eventually went up to bed. As he kicked off his shoes and crawled between the sheets, Barber had a brief, rational thought. Not only did he no longer feel any animosity towards Carmichael, he positively liked the fellow.

Barber's hangover wasn't severe; a dull throb behind his right eye was the only reminder of his over-indulgence, and even that subsided after a shave and a tepid shower. Carmichael was already sitting in the kitchen with a pot of coffee when he went down, looking considerably the worse for wear.

'Morning,' Barber greeted him cheerfully, not noticing his lack of response. 'It's a beautiful day. What would you like for breakfast? Bacon and eggs?' Carmichael looked up at him with the eyes of a mournful bloodhound. 'Oh. Toast, then?'

'I don't think I could stand the crunching. Do you mind stirring your coffee a little more quietly?'

Barber laughed. 'Oh dear. Suffering, are you? What I suggest is a raw egg in a glass, with plenty of Worcester sauce, vinegar and a dash of oil, seasoned with salt and pepper.'

'What will that do? Cure my hangover?'

'I doubt it. It'll probably make you sick. My steward in Singapore used to recommend it to me, but I never had the courage to try it.'

'I'm not surprised. I've taken a couple of codeine and I intend to just sit here quietly unil they take effect.'

'Okay. I'll just make myself some breakfast while I'm waiting.'

He'd put the bacon under the grill and the smell was beginning to waft across the room when he heard a grunt from Carmichael, and turned to see him stumbling through the door. He had finished eating and was enjoying a third cup of coffee when the Superintendent reappeared, looking rather better and ready to nibble a slice of toast.

'Today we'll see some film of the man,' the latter said, as they cleared up the kitchen. 'I know you'd recognise him and so on, but I just want to make absolutely certain. I'd hate you to mistake me for him at the wrong moment. After that we'll have some gun practice. By the way, keep the toilet gear you found in your room, along with the clothes. They're untraceable, should fit well and will make you look like a prosperous businessman – the last person anyone would associate with a killer ... Sorry,' he added hastily, seeing Barber's pained expression. 'I meant political assassin.'

'H'm. Er – listen, before we start, do you think we could discuss payment?'

'I thought you'd never ask.' Putting his hand into his pocket, Carmichael withdrew a fat envelope. 'There you are. Twenty thousand quid, cash, instead of a Swiss account, as you wanted. Count it if you like.'

'No thanks – I'll assume it's correct. Okay, now you have my undivided attention.' He put his envelope in his pocket, wondering. Carmichael was very sure of himself. What was to stop him running now he had the money? Even as he thought it, the answer occurred to him. It was simple really. There was nowhere to run to.

'Let's go and see the films, then.'

In the lounge, having spent a few minutes preparing the projector, Carmichael said, 'This first film shows Parker leaving his house in Hull with his wife and son. His wife, by the way, believes his trips to Copenhagen are connected with government business. She doesn't know he goes to see his Russian parents; in fact it's fair to assume that she doesn't know about his true birth place. We've had her carefully investigated and she's definitely of good British stock. We can trace her family back three generations.' Their film changed. 'This one was taken by the BBC. Parker was talking strongly about leaving the EEC and dropping strong hints we ought to leave NATO ... Here he is with his assistant secretary. She's a nice girl, and as far as we can tell, only his secretary.'

'Lucky fellow. I wouldn't mind dictating a few letters to her myself,' observed Barber, looking admiringly at the attractive blonde who, even on silent film, gave an impression of sensuality.

'Keep your mind above your navel. You will be attending a cocktail party on Thursday to enable you to observe Parker in the flesh. You may see the girl there at the same time. Take the leer off your face. There's a very good reason for all this. If things go wrong in Holland you'll have to continue, picking your own time and place. I'll be there and try to make things easier for you, but there'll be little I can do. At some stage there might only be time for a fleeting glimpse of the man, and immediate recognition is called for. By studying these films, noting his mannerisms, his way of walking, the way he holds his head, that immediate response should come more easily. It may make the difference between your getting him and missing. Useful though these films are, there's no doubt that seeing the man in the flesh, even for a short time, can make all the difference.'

For an hour they watched the films, Carmichael pointing out some of the man's subconscious quirks, like rubbing the side of his nose when thinking, or the lobe of his ear when agitated. When the reel had finished he rewound it, and they sat through it for a second time. Then Carmichael switched off the projector and drew the curtains, saying:

'We'll see it again later. I think we'll take a break now, and find you a suitable gun.'

He led the way upstairs and into the small armoury. The smell of clean gun oil brought Barber poignant memories of the Marines, but he pushed them resolutely away.

'This is the pride of our collection,' Carmichael said, lifting down an odd shaped gun from the rack. 'It was specially made for a one off job by Carlos ... the man they call "The Jackal". Although we got his stake out we arrived too early, found an accomplice and this,' he hefted the rifle, 'and missed Carlos. Still, that was of secondary importance under the circumstances. He didn't get his target.'

'Who was he?' Barber asked, intrigued.

'It wasn't a he, it was a she. Her Majesty, the Queen.'

'You must be joking! There was nothing in the papers about an attempt on her life. Anyway, what would be the point?'

'Correct. It wasn't in the papers; it never got out. The

point? You tell me the point of these maniacs. In Carlos' case it's for money. He'll kill anybody, anywhere. As for the Queen . . .' He shrugged. 'Think of the uproar, worldwide; the suspicion created, the accusations that would be flying back and forth.' He shook his head slowly. 'I'm not articulate enough to paint a picture of how bad things could be if anything happened to such a universally loved person. Dallas and Kennedy would be a minor incident by comparison.'

Steve nodded. 'I suppose you're right. Anyway, it looks an interesting gun.'

'Here, take it. See how it feels.'

He took the gun, rested it on his shoulder, looked through the telescopic sight. 'What a beauty,' he said. 'It's so well balanced you hardly feel the weight. Is that a silencer on the end?'

'Yes – part of the gun. It's accurate to less than two inches at three miles – and we got ten rounds of special ammunition along with it. We duplicated the ammo, and now have one hundred rounds for practice and ten for the operation. We've been keeping it for a special job.' Carmichael nodded slowly. 'I think this is the job. When you've used it, you'll have to take it with you. If the police found it and it was shown or described by the press, some of the men who use this place would undoubtedly recognise it, and that could create a problem. As you'll be so far from the scene you'll have plenty of time to dismantle it, and ditch it when it's convenient. We can discuss that later this afternoon.'

From another rack he took a Walther PPK, silencer and holster.

'Try this on for size, and we'll see how you get on with it. If things go wrong and you do end up operating alone, you may have to come in close. Let's hope not, but you can't be too sure.'

'What about you? Why don't you take him, if I don't?'

'Because my chances of ending up in jail are that much greater, especially if I kept my mouth shut. I don't really want to lose years of my life. However, having said that, if all else fails I will be back stop. But only if all else fails.'

'Hmmmmmm,' was Barber's response. 'Shall we go and shoot up a few targets?'

Outside, Carmichael led the way across the back lawns and into the woods. A short way in a firing range had been laid but in a shallow depression – though Barber did not recognise it as such until it was pointed out by the Chief Superintendent.

'Down the far end,' the latter went on, 'that natural looking ridge is in fact earth and grass covered reinforced concrete, with an initial double layer of railway sleepers. There are three firing points at one, two and three hundred yards. Further range alterations are achieved by differing target sizes.'

'What about noise?'

'We take care of that in two ways. Either we use silenced guns, or special ammunition with only 20% of the firing power. We've found that any less over this range affects the trajectory of the bullet, and the gun can't be properly zeroed in. Of course, this place absorbs a deal of the noise. All in all, nothing can be heard more than 50 yards away and no one except our own people is ever that close. Come on.'

At the other end of the range Carmichael unlocked the door of a small, windowless shed, filled with different size man-like targets. Barber had seen many similar, except that there'd been one important difference: military targets were of camouflaged, weapon-carrying soldiers; these were of bowler-hatted, unarmed civilians.

They set up four targets of varying sizes and slowly walked the length of the range back to the firing point at 300 yards.

'The target on the left represents a man standing half a mile from you. The next is at one mile and the other two at two miles. Try this,' Carmichael said, handing Barber the rifle.

The telescopic sight brought the target so close Barber felt he could reach out and touch it. Even the furthest target appeared less than 50 yards away.

'Remarkable. It's like trying to hit the side of a barn at ten paces,' he commented.

A few feet away, Carmichael was pulling at a piece of wood hidden in the undergrowth. It came clear to show a H configuration, which he then fixed upright in the ground, saying, 'This represents a window ledge. I want you to kneel with the tip of the gun on your side of the cross member, as though you were in a room.'

Barber tried it for size. By resting his left elbow on his knee, the silencer cleared the 'window' by a couple of inches.

'You'll be firing from the window of an empty office block of a similar height.' He handed Barber five rounds. 'Press that catch there, release the magazine and load with five rounds. That's the maximum it will take. Now, in your own time, fire one sighter at the left hand target, and if satisfied, fire a group of four.'

Barber sighted, held his breath and gently squeezed the trigger. The kick of the recoil was more than he'd expected, the force belied by the muted 'phut' of the silencer. He could see clearly through the sight where the bullet had hit the nose of the target. He'd shot slightly high, he'd been aiming at the mouth. Adjusting his aim, he filled the grinning mouth with his next four shots, like a row of blackened teeth.

'This is one hell of a gun,' he remarked, reloading quickly.

Carmichael, binoculars glued to his eyes, replied, 'And you're one hell of a shot. I assume that's where you were aiming?' he added, lowering the glasses and looking at Steve with a broad grin.

The latter nodded. 'Anyone could do it with a gun like this.' He stood, held the rifle loosely in his hands, suddenly brought it up to sight and fired three quick rounds into the second target. The mouth lost three of its teeth.

'Very impressive' Carmichael said dryly. 'Now try the right hand two targets.'

By the end of twenty rounds he was convinced no further practice was required. By this time too, each shot was becoming markedly louder than the previous one.

100

'We'll change the silencer when you practise dismantling and assembling the rifle later this afternoon,' he said. 'We'll use the same targets for the hand gun. Come on – we need to be much closer. But first help me throw this thing back into the undergrowth.'

As they made their way back down the range Carmichael said, 'What do you know about the Walther?'

'Nothing. I never came into contact with it in the Marines.'

'The PPK, which stands for Polizei Pistole Kriminal, was first made by Walther of Ulm in Germany in 1931. It holds seven rounds of 7.65mm in a detachable box.' As he was talking Carmichael displayed the gun, showing its mechanism to Barber. 'Its operation is blowback with a double action trigger, and it can fire 30 rounds in a minute. It's 15½ centimetres long and weighs .6 kg. In a fast draw the external hammer has been known to catch on loose clothing, but so far I haven't heard of any fatalities through this. It's still in use by the armed forces of France, Germany, Hungary and Turkey.'

They stopped twenty yards short of the target. 'With the silencer the gun is an extra six centimetres in length and .2 kg heavier. Its effective range is forty yards – provided one can hit the target at that range. Here – try it.'

Barber loosed off all seven shots and clipped the top right hand corner of the left hand target only once. With the target representing a man at ten yards, he managed to hit it often enough for Carmichael to remark: 'With a bit of luck he should bleed to death. Let's wrap up here. Help me pick up the rest of the empty shells and put away the targets, and then we'll get some lunch.'

After the meal, consisting of a cottage pie taken from the freezer, some fruit and coffee, the Superintendent showed Barber the special suitcase into which the dismantled rifle neatly fitted. Barber then practised taking the weapon apart and putting it back together again until he could do the operation in under a minute. After that he sat through two more showings of the film, at the end of which he was quite sure he'd be dreaming about Parker.

101

'Once you've carried out your mission, take the train for the Hague, and then on to Calais,' Carmichael instructed him. 'Catch the night boat for England, and on your way throw the gun away, piece by piece. It'll never be found, scattered across the Channel. The suitcase is specially weighted; once holed it will sink quite quickly, so after you've got rid of the gun, ditch that as well. Change the clothes you wear for the shooting and leave them in the suitcase. That way no traces of gun oil will be found on you. Okay?'

Barber nodded. 'Clear so far, and very thorough. But what about the gun being missed from here?'

'A duplicate is being made by a contact in Germany right now. It will be in place the day after tomorrow so no one will be any the wiser.'

'You seem to have thought of everything. When do I go to Holland?'

'On the Friday before; we're sure Parker won't be travelling earlier than Sunday. There's just one more point. If you have to contact me urgently, I'll be wherever Parker is. If you can't talk to me direct use the word "operation" in your message, and give a telephone number. I'll get back to you as soon as possible. That's really a back up I can't envisage us having to use, but we must cover for every eventuality. Find yourself some decent digs, and stay out all day, every day. Act the part of a bank clerk or insurance salesman. Once you're installed in the digs, ring this number and leave your address and 'phone number on the answering machine.' He paused. 'Any questions?'

'I don't think so. Only one point. The money you've paid me is for the job. What about operating expenses?'

'You really want to have your cake and eat it, don't you? Here's another thousand quid.' Carmichael threw him an envelope. 'Make it last.'

'You were expecting it. What if I hadn't asked?'

Carmichael grunted. 'You wouldn't have received.'

'I thought as much. Well – if that's all, when do we leave here and when do I see you again?'

'We leave in an hour; at least you do. I'll follow. There's a bus into Cardiff, where you can stay the night, and travel up to London by train in the morning. I'll see you at the cocktail party on Thursday. You'll get a written invitation by post at your new address on Thursday morning; that's why you need to find a place as soon as you get to the city, and let me know where you are.'

'What sort of party is it? Do I need a cover?'

'It's a Civil Service farewell party for a couple of senior people in Parker's department. Say you're from the Ministry of Health or something. One of the people leaving is a chap called Stuart Owen; just suggest you've known him for some time if anyone asks, though I doubt if they will. By the way, you won't know me nor I you. Okay?'

A little while later Steve Barber left, his suitcase containing the rifle in his left hand and the Walther an uncomfortable weight on his left side. Little did either of them know that almost all of their preparations had been a waste of time. Almost all. Some of the more minor points discussed would provide the difference they'd need.

Chapter 8

Enis Baum had naturally assumed the role of leader, having inspired the rest to go on. Her hard core of fanaticism, the result of the relationship with Jemel Varak, made her an obvious choice. There were ten members of the group, and this was to be their final meeting before they carried out their plan, its culmination to be the freedom of their friends in prison, and the issue of Palestine ringing around the world again.

'You all have sufficient knowledge and training of the pistols but I have received a new gun which we must familiarise ourselves with. I have been unable to get hold of the Uzi but this will take it's place.' Enis hefted a British Sterling Machine Gun in her hand. 'We will receive another three guns next Monday. At the same time we take delivery of ten kilos of plastic plus three remote controlled fuses. We will also get four Beretta 38/49s and two Beretta 12s. We have four Swedish Husqvana pistols, all of which take the same 9mm Parabellum rounds. Ammunition will therefore not be a problem as it is interchangeable.'

'How many rounds will we have?'

'Enough,' was the short reply. 'Let us carry on. I shall start with the 38/49, known as the Model 4. Unloaded it weighs 3.2 kilos, holds 20 or 40 rounds, depending on the magazine used, and will fire at 550 rounds per minute. Its effective range is 200 metres, though in long bursts it pushes to the right; therefore you should fire a few rounds at a time if you hope to hit what you're aiming at. The 12 can be fired in single shots at 40 per minute, automatic at 120 per minute or, like this one, in cyclic at 550 per minute.'

She carried on in the same vein, demonstrating how to take the gun apart and put it back together again, firing questions as she did so on facts she'd just stated. Her pupils learnt well and quickly. After they'd all practised with the weapon she turned to the plan of action.

'This Friday we shall hire two cars, one in my name, the other in Nuri's.' Khatun, on her right, nodded agreement. 'The fact that they'll be in our own names is immaterial. We'll be known soon enough as it is.' There was a small burst of nervous laughter. 'The first half will drive to Calais to catch the ferry on Monday morning. My half will leave on Tuesday, after I've collected the remainder of the guns. Group A will have all the ammunition, pistols and explosives, broken down into units as small as possible and concealed throughout the car. Group B will have the SMGs, all broken down in the same way. I don't foresee any problems with customs; after all, what could be more innocent than five French passport carrying citizens sharing a large car for a tour of Britain? We'll meet at the motorway restaurant, Nuri knows where, and return on the Wednesday ferry. The journey lasts all night, and should give us plenty of time to get ready. Our strike time will be 2.00 a.m.'

Enis paused, and looked gravely round at the attentive faces of her listeners.

'Remember, this is going to be a short term operation. For maximum effect we have to not only appear ruthless but BE ruthless. If for one minute they don't believe we'll carry out our threats, then all will be lost; therefore, there must be no hesitation, no reluctance to pull the trigger when you have to. Furthermore . . .' she paused again, then went on deliberately, 'we must not be afraid of the supreme sacrifice. It is better to die for the cause than to lose it.'

The intensity of her words elicited a fervent response of nods and 'yesses', as she had hoped.

'Right,' she concluded. 'While Nasima, Amie and I see about some food, you men play amongst yourselves.'

Nasima Karami, at the back, giggled loudly.

105

'That's Nasima's dirty mind for you. I meant with the gun, of course.'

Amid laughter she led the other two girls into her small kitchen where she had laid out cold meats, bread and lager.

The rest of the evening would pass in discussion of the fine details of the plan in small groups, and any problems arising would then be aired and resolved by the group as a whole.

* * *

Andrea Bolkovsky settled himself into the chair with its ornately carved arms and called the meeting to order. As Number 2 in the KGB he was used to chairing such meetings, but this time there was a slight exception. Slight? That was a joke. It was probably the most important meeting of his career so far. Once the action was decided upon there was nothing else for him to do except wait and see the results. The other three men would help him in the planning, but the final responsibility would be his.

Bolkovsky was a child of the revolution, the son of a Ukranian father and Siberian mother. His father had been banished to Siberia during the bad Lenin days of 1920; he'd been a butcher in a small town called Yansk, and had made the error of lending an acquaintance a small sum of money. Unfortunately, when the time came for the money to be repaid, the man hadn't got it. Instead, he'd reported Bolkovsky's father to the new Communist authorities who, unused to exercising any power and thus now abusing what they had, put on a show trial.

It hadn't even been that. In court, with so many similar cases to be heard, all that was required was for someone to accuse a man of not supporting the Reds and he was done for. He could deny it as much as he liked, but unless he had a lot of money and could bribe his way out, or had friends in high places, he was lost. No defence witnesses could be called; it was just one man's word against the other, and the outcome was always the same. Sven Bolkovsky had been sent to Siberia for five years and all his possessions confiscated; he had arrived in Siberia with only the clothes he stood up in, more dead than alive.

Bolkovsky knew the story well. His father had been on a train for six weeks. They'd been fed once a day – if they were lucky; more often it was only every other day. The food was watery soup made of potato peelings and ham bones already picked clean by the guards.

The prisoners had travelled in cattle trucks, twenty in each, huddled together for warmth as temperatures frequently fell ten degrees below zero during the night. In their carriage they'd been lucky. A section of the floor in one corner could be lifted away, allowing them to squat over the hole to defecate. Some of the others were less fortunate, and when they were allowed out at their infrequent stops, the stench gradually became overpowering. Those who lived in it failed to notice, and often couldn't understand why the others, at meal queues, tried to keep away from them.

Andrea's father had also had another advantage in having a doctor in his truck. After the first week the doctor had insisted that they all cut their hair as short as possible to enable them to deal with head lice, and that they do their utmost to keep clean. One woman, whose hair had reached her waist, fought like a tiger when the rest of the women held her down and cut her hair close to her scalp, and she'd cried for two days afterwards.

Bolkovsky knew every horror his father had seen or experienced. Thanks to the doctor, twice as many survived in their truck as in the others; fourteen of the original twenty got through to the end. Their destination was an unnamed village deep in Siberia, where they'd climbed out of their trucks and stood huddled together, their rags no protection against the icy wind of early spring.

The train had pulled out before they'd realised there were no guards and no one to meet them. The huge, snow-covered wastes stretched all around them as far as the eye could see in any direction. As one they turned towards the huddle of houses, the first less than a hundred yards away.

As they approached, Bolkovsky's father and the doctor found themselves in front of the remaining 208 men, women and children. Four fur-clad men emerged from the house and hurried towards them, welcoming them and leading them into a hall just big enough to hold them all. There they'd been given hot soup, thick with potatoes and ham; a positive feast. They had quickly discovered that everyone there was a prisoner, unable to escape because there was nowhere to go. The welcoming committee had been expecting only fifty people; the additional numbers would prove a serious burden on the community. If they could last just one month, however, until the spring really arrived, they'd have a chance of survival.

Spring had been late. By the time the snow had melted, and it was possible to go out and hunt the deer and boar which abounded on the plains, and collect the roots and shrubs they used as part of their staple diet, another 32 people had died.

For the next four months they laboured like maniacs, building houses, hunting and collecting food. Bolkovsky, being a butcher by trade, spent all his time cutting up the animals and curing the meat. Thanks to his skill, it lasted better that winter than it had ever done before.

More people arrived. The village was growing into a town and families were settling down in private houses, no longer having to live communal lives. Within three years, only the newcomers needed to live together, and that for rarely longer than one winter. Businesses were set up, buying and selling by barter. The old and infirm were cared for properly, food and medical care given freely. By the beginning of their fifth year in exile the people had created an ideal socialist state, and he was Mayor of the town council. It was in that year that he met and fell in love with a Siberian girl, whom he married. Two years later Andrea was born.

Prisoners were no longer sent to the town. It became respectable, and indeed forgotten by the Soviet leaders until World War II. Then young men were called up, including

Andrea, on his eighteenth birthday. On the day that he finished his initial training, the war ended. He didn't return
home. His father, who had become an important person,
wielding power and patronage throughout his area, arranged
for his son to go to Moscow University; Andrea never knew
how his father managed it.

During his final year at the university, fire swept through
the town of Andrea's birth. The wooden buildings went up
like tinder; only a dozen people survived to tell the tale.
Andrea's parents perished in the fire, and their death affec-
ted him badly. His father had taught him all his life to be
strong and just; to be afraid of no one, but not to bully.
When his father died, Bolkovsky reacted strongly. He joined
the KGB, where his utter ruthlessness gained him respect
and promotion – and the hatred of many.

One day, something inexplicable happened. The teach-
ings of Andrea's father came back to him; he remembered
how his father had forgiven the man who'd wronged him,
who'd been responsible for his banishment. He remembered
a lot of things, and he changed.

He remained in the KGB and continued to work hard, but
there was one difference. Now he used his new found hu-
manity to help others. He became a paradox. Offenders
were given a proper trial, sentencing was correct, punishment severe but not harsh. Somehow, Andrea made
Number 2 – and now here he was at the crossroads of his
career. If he succeeded in bringing Parker back to the USSR
he would eventually reach the top. If he failed, then his
assistant, Number 3 in the KGB, could well oust him.

The latter, he knew, was a thoroughly evil man, promoted
despite his, Bolkovsky's objections. There were those in the
politburo who considered Andrea too soft. He was in too
powerful a position for them to harm him directly; instead
they worked from the inside, using Karloff Bitov.

Bitov was Number 3, and wanted desperately to be
Number 2. His father had been an important member of the
government in Stalin's day, surviving all the political purges

of that unhappy era and moving ever upwards in his career. By the time he was twenty, Bitov expected to go to Moscow University by right. His ability was unquestionable, but not his character.

At the age of seventeen he'd escaped being sent to a labour camp by the intervention of his father. A young girl of thirteen had been savagely attacked and raped. Her older brother had found her, and had claimed in court that she had named Bitov as her attacker. However, the girl had died from her injuries before anyone else could hear her accusation.

Even Bitov's father couldn't prevent his son's arrest. What he could and did do was to persuade the doctor carrying out the forensic tests on Bitov to falsify the evidence. His acquittal was automatic, but his innocence remained suspect, and was confirmed, as far as the local people were concerned, when during yet another purge, the girl's family disappeared. The rumours intensified, and in the end Bitov's father sent him to Moscow for his final year before entering university.

During that time, under threat of no further help from his father, Bitov kept out of trouble. He became involved in minor skirmishes during his student years, and came to the attention of the authorities, but fortunately for him he was on the winning side, advocating greater state control, particularly of university campuses, and harsher punishment for dissidents. His answer to the Jewish problem was simple . . . Hitler, in his opinion, had set a good example. Needless to say he was not popular with other students, but it didn't matter to him.

By his third and final year at university Karloff Bitov was working for the KGB. A great number of students suddenly discovered that things they had said in private were being used against them in public. They were never brought to trial, but were either sent down without explanation before they took their degrees, or did far worse than expected, and were able only to find employment in the outer reaches of Eastern Russia.

Luckily for Bitov, he'd completed his final exams before the other students discovered who the traitor was. When five of them, friends of others whose lives had been blighted by Bitov, finished with him, they'd left him with a limp for life and no appetite for sex. His pleasure came from inflicting pain, and once he'd suitably recovered and became a full member of the KGB, those responsible for crippling him were among his first victims. He had taken his revenge three years after he'd been declared fit for training as a KGB agent. Bitov prided himself on his long memory. He rarely forgot a favour, and never a wrong.

His ambition was to change the KGB back to its former ways of absolute terror and power, but in order to do so he needed a reason for removing Bolkovsky from the scene. A major cock up in this operation was just what he was looking for; provided, of course, the blame could be placed squarely at Bolkovsky's door.

'Gentlemen, shall we begin? Time is short and we have a lot of ground to cover.' Bolkovsky's thick, guttural speech betrayed his place of origin. 'You know the purpose of this meeting, which is to decide what to do about the British Member of Parliament, Parker. Comrade Bitov,' he indicated the latter with a nod of the head, concealing his dislike, 'knew who Parker really was, as you'd expect of Number 3, but it must have come as a bit of a surprise to the remainder of you.'

The other three men present nodded agreement. Nikita Rinski, liaison secretary between the KGB and the Politburo, raised a finger to catch Bolkovsky's attention. 'Why is this information now being passed to us?' he asked, his fat jowls wobbling loosely as he talked. 'I see no reason why we should have become involved at all.'

No, you wouldn't, you fat chicken, thought Bolkovsky. Aloud, he said: 'It's quite simple, my dear Minister. The decision we have to reach today is too important for the Bureau alone to decide upon. It requires full backing from your people.' He didn't add 'In case it goes wrong,' or that if his

111

head went, many others would roll too. Rinski appreciated that fact. It had been the modus operandi of Russian officials for as long as any of them could remember.

Joseph Kolotoff sat impassive at the end of the table. He was an adviser on the Premier's staff, and as such would contribute very little to the meeting. Once it was over, however, he would report immediately and directly to the top. That way, if their masters decided not to go ahead with the plan it could be cancelled quickly and discreetly, before it went too far. Otherwise, the slow, ponderous machinery of Russian bureaucracy would ensure that they received the information too late to act upon it.

The fifth man was Stephen Kuybyshevski, Bolkovsky's loyal aide and good friend. The two men had risen through the ranks together, Bolkovsky always one step ahead; at least, until they reached the hierachy. There Kuybyshevski's limitations were realised, and while Bolkovsky had gone on he had been content to remain as special aide to his friend. Between them they had been responsible for the new humaneness of their organisation, spending many leisure hours together playing chess and discussing KGB policy.

All of the men at the table knew that the real power of the KGB lay with Bolkovsky, the number one position having become more of a figurehead. They were all also aware however, that once Bolkovsky moved up, he intended taking that power with him. Of the four, only Bitov was opposed to the idea.

'As I see it,' Bolkovsky was saying, 'there are three alternatives open to us. One, we do nothing, two, we get him out, and three, we kill him. I propose we weigh the pros and cons of each, and then decide which to follow. After that, Comrade Bitov, Stephen and I will plan the method. First; doing nothing. What's your view on that, Comrade?' He nodded at Bitov.

Bitov, who had expected to be called on first to voice an opinion, chain lit another cigarette and puffed for a few seconds before replying. 'If we do nothing, then we know the

British will kill him. We received full details of their plan only yesterday from "Bronze Wing". Incidentally, he's beginning to panic. He thinks that if the British can find out about Parker, they can find out about him. He says he wants out; he wants money, a new identity and the safety of a friendly country. As he isn't one of us, merely a traitor to the British, I suggest we leave him to their tender mercies. It's true the source of the Britishers' present information didn't have access to the file on "Bronze Wing", but he may have acquired it without our knowing, to increase his bargaining power with them. I've passed this back to "Bronze" . . .'

'Comrade Bitov, can we forget Bronze Wing for now and concentrate on the matter in hand?' Bolkovsky interrupted impatiently.

Bitov's thin mouth tightened. 'By all means,' he replied, concealing his anger. 'The British action cancels out our third option; that is, elimination; therefore I see no point in discussing it. If we do nothing, then all advantage we may have gained from this man will be lost. After all, although he's been able to supply us with useful information in the past, we have for some time ceased to use him in that capacity, in case we jeopardised his position. For your information, gentlemen,' he added, turning to the non-members of the KGB, 'that decision was taken when we realised Parker was really in with a chance of reaching the top of British politics.' He paused to light another cigarette. 'Our use for him now is to embarrass the West as much as possible. To do that he has to be alive, to expose himself to the Western press. Once dead, even if we do declare who he really was, the West will be able to prove otherwise; so we need him alive, and we need to get him out of Britain and back to Russia as quickly as possible.'

No one spoke, or gave any sign of agreement. They simply waited for him to finish, knowing Bolkovsy would either see it the same way or veto his ideas and put forward suggestions of his own. In the final analysis the decisions of the meeting would be taken by Bolkovsky. The KGB would then act upon them, and if their political masters agreed, all well and good. If they didn't . . .

The silence became oppressive.

'I see it the same way,' Bolkovsky finally said. 'As always, Comrade Bitov's appreciation of the situation is accurate; in my opinion, that is.' He picked up the phone in front of him. 'Natya, send in some coffee, please. Oh, and those biscuits we received yesterday.' He replaced the receiver, and asked abruptly, 'How do you three see this matter?'

Surprisingly, it was Kolotoff who answered. 'I don't think I'll be giving away any secrets if I tell you that's how "he" sees it. He also told me to tell you that he regrets that this has happened, but appreciates there's nothing else to be done, particularly in view of the British reaction.'

In spite of himself, Bolkovsky was impressed by the speed with which the Chairman had been informed of the latest situation.

'Ah, coffee,' he said, as his dowdy, grey haired secretary pushed open the door and deposited the tray on the table. 'You must try these biscuits, gentlemen. Butter Osborne from the famous store of Marks and Spencer in England. I think you'll enjoy them with your coffee.' His secretary fussed around for a few minutes, handing out the cups and passing the sugar and cream. All except Bitov helped themselves to the biscuits.

'What's the matter, Comrade? Too bourgeoise for your taste?' joked Bolkovsky, relieved by what Kolotoff had said.

'Not at all. I happen not to like sweet things,' Bitov replied coldly.

Shortly afterwards, the non KGB men left. Bolkovsky could hardly believe things had gone so smoothly and easily. He put it down to the fact that not only were they of one accord, but that speed of execution of operation was paramount.

Pouring himself another cup of coffee, he said: 'Stephen here will outline the plan as far as we've got, and then I think we'll discuss it further before . . . you, Number 3, start the ball rolling.'

'We propose to send in a team of three, led by Uri Sta-wizcki,' began Kuybyshevski.

Here it comes, thought Bolkovsky, the first objection.

'No, I don't believe he's the right man for this operation,' said Bitov, right on cue. 'I propose we send Wilhelm Henken. He would make a far superior leader for this oper-ation.'

'I don't agree,' Bolkovsky argued. 'Henken has his uses, it's true, but not for this. He's a killer; that has always been his primary role, and it will continue to be so. When it's time for him to leave, Parker is going to be as nervous as a cat on hot bricks. That's why he needs someone like Stawizcki around, to hold his hand and lead him quietly away. Henken wouldn't be capable of that.'

'You may be right, but I don't see his role in that way. Parker will be told of – what's his name? – Carmichael's true role in this affair. He'll be frightened. He'll want someone strong like Henken to instil confidence in him, knowing he'll kill if he has to, to get him out. Your man's an old woman. He just won't do.'

There it was, out in the open. Your man. In the same way that Henken was Bitov's, Stawizcki was Bolkovsky's – and each man reflected the personality of his boss.

Stawizcki, a happily married man with two children, lived quietly outside Moscow. He drove to the office every morn-ing, just like other middle management civil servants. Some-times he was called upon to go abroad on a mission. When he did he always told his wife he was accompanying a trade mission somewhere, and never forgot to bring back a small souvenir of the visit for his family. His speciality was the col-lection of information and the passing of agents in and out of Communist countries and he excelled at operations like the one concerning Parker. Furthermore, beneath his mild and friendly manner lay a tough, ruthless streak, well concealed but present just the same.

Henken, on the other hand, lived up to his nickname 'Die Henker – The Hangman'. Utterly cold and unfeeling, he was worse than a man who enjoyed killing because the act caused him to feel no emotion whatsoever. He could kill, maim or torture men, women and children without an atom of compunction. So far he'd carried out seven assassinations for the KGB, and had helped to kill hundreds in various trouble spots around the world, acting as 'adviser' to so-called Marxist representatives of the people whose sole interest lay in their own position and the power that could go with it.

Andrea Bolkovsky realised that men like Henken had their uses, but he also believed they had to be closely controlled and not allowed into positions of responsibility. Indeed he thought of them as wild animals that should be caged, let loose only when needed and afterwards herded back to their cages until the next time.

Bitov, on the other hand, wanted to create elitist groups led by trained and tested killers for use in all forms of espionage, believing that their killer instincts were capable of bringing them through any situation. If he could get The Hangman leading this team, he'd be that much nearer the achievement of his ambitions. If not, at least he'd get him included in the team.

The argument finally became so heated Bolkovsky had to agree to allow Henken to accompany Stawizcki as the team's Number 2. The third man was Bolkovsky's choice. Gerhard Karpov would be the odd job, courier man of the party. His duties being to take care of all logistic and movement problems, leaving the other two free to look after Parker, in case the British changed their plans unexpectedly.

'How quickly can we mobilise?' Bolkovsky asked Kuybyshevski.

His aide cleared his throat. 'Stawizcki and Karpov can be ready for briefing first thing in the morning. I don't know about Henken.' He looked enquiringly at Bitov.

'I can have him here by late tomorrow evening. He's taking a well earned rest at Sochici, in Georgia. You know – at the rest farm we have near the Caucasus.'

The other two men nodded. Of course they knew it; they'd

both been there to recuperate at one stage or another in their careers.

'Is he fit?'

Bitov regarded Bolkovsky almost long enough for the look to become insolent. Almost, but not quite. 'Naturally he's fit, otherwise I wouldn't have suggested using him. I can arrange a special pick up, and get him here by about 1900 hours.' He did not smile at this small victory. He knew how much Bolkovsky hated wasting funds on that kind of transport, especially when an adequate regular flight covered the area, but all three knew that to get the Hangman there on time it would be necessary to use a helicopter and military aircraft. Bolkovsky nodded agreement, giving his authorisation for the flight.

'You, Comrade, and Stephen here will brief the men tomorrow night,' he went on. 'We must get them mobilised on Friday morning – and even then they won't reach Finland until Saturday afternoon. Arrange for them to pick up Finnish passports from our Embassy there, get them on the first available flight to Sweden, arrange for them to change identities once more and then fly them on to London. Do we have someone reliable who can contact Parker and let him know what's happening?'

Bitov answered. 'Yes. We have a man in London who's proved useful in the past . . .'

'No, no. I only want to use our own people for this one. It's far too important to allow amateurs anywhere near it.'

'We do have what you want, sir,' said Kuybyshevski. 'One of my men is suitably placed. I can get the information to him in tomorrow's bag, and he can contact Parker; if not during the week-end, then by Monday at the latest.'

'Fair enough,' said Bitov, adding, 'We'll have to work out very carefully what we tell your man. We don't want Parker to panic at this stage, and do something stupid.'

Bolkovsky fixed him with a cold stare. 'Parker has been living in Britain for years. He's kept his identity secret from his family, as well as the authorities – no mean task. It takes a very special man to do that, one who's not likely to panic under any circumstances. Therefore we shall tell him exactly what the situation is. Do I make myself clear, Number 3?'

'If you say so,' Bitov replied sullenly.

'Good. Now, shall we get on and finish discussing this in detail before lunch? Then you can start getting the team together.'

Chapter 9

On Thursday morning Steve Barber arrived at the hospital to see his brother. Knocking on the door of Phil's private ward, he went in, a determinedly cheerful smile on his face.

'Hi. How're you feeling this morning?'

'Oh – not too bad. How are you?'

Phil's appearance belied his words; he looked terrible.

'I'm O.K. It's you we have to worry about.' Steve said.

'Rubbish. I'm being well taken care of – but you, you dumb bastard, are on the way to getting yourself killed.' He bit his lip anxiously. 'Steve – I've been thinking about what you told me. They've really got you in a cleft stick, haven't they?'

Typical of his brother, Barber thought, to worry about him, Steve, and not himself. What a great guy. His problems were all his, Steve's fault, and now all he could do was add to them by telling Phil all that was going on. Perhaps he should have kept his mouth shut in the first place – but it was too late now. Phil would want to know the rest, of that he had no doubt.

'And up the creek without the proverbial,' he said, grinning.

'Also by the short and curlies. So what's happened?'

Steve told his brother everything, bringing him right up to date. By the time he had finished it was obvious that the effort of concentrating was too much for Phil, whose eyelids had begun to droop.

'Now listen – nothing will happen until after the weekend now, so I'll be in tomorrow and you can tell me all your

news,' Steve said softly. 'And don't worry. You know me –
I'm an orthodox survivor. I'm going up to see Sue; I'll give
her your love. Okay?'

Phil nodded drowsily. 'Okay,' he whispered. 'Thanks . . .
for coming.'

Phil was asleep by the time Barber reached the door. He
stayed with Sue for only a short while, discussing what to call
the baby and admiring the tiny clothes she had knitted. Not
until he stood up to leave did she ask him if the doctor had
said anything to him.

He shook his head. 'Nothing special. Why?'

'Oh . . .' She shrugged. 'It's just that . . . well, they won't
tell me anything. You know what doctors are like. They
make reassuring noises, and that's about all.'

'You are talking about Phil, aren't you?'

'Who else?' Sue said, surprised. 'Certainly not me. All I'm
doing is having a baby, and that's as easy as falling off a log.
Or at least so the nurses keep telling me. The pregnancy's
going exactly as it should . . . If only . . . if only it wasn't for
Phil.'

'I know, love,' Barber said gently. 'I can't tell you how
sorry I am. It's all my stupid bloody fault. The trouble is,
regrets and "if onlies" don't help.'

'True.' She didn't try to assuage his guilt, and in a strange
way he was glad. It would have been too much, if they'd both
forgiven him; he felt he deserved some form of punishment.
Sue's acknowledgement of his responsibility went some way
towards administering that punishment.

'I know it's easy, trite even to say don't worry,' he said,
taking her hand in both of his. 'He'll be as right as rain – the
doctors have assured me of that. What you have to do is try
to relax and present him with a bonny, bouncing baby.
That'll be the best tonic in the world for him. It'll certainly do
more good than all the medicines and all the operations the
doctors can administer.'

She squeezed his hand and tried to smile. 'I'm sure you're
right. Tomorrow, after they've done a sonic test, or what-

ever they call it, I'll know whether it's a boy or girl. That should cheer him up . . . take away the uncertainty of it all.'

'What the hell's a sonic test?'

'Oh – they put a scan thing on my tummy, send sound waves into me, and that projects an image of the baby onto a screen. Apparently they use it to check to see how the baby is laying. They then take out some fluid and check for Down's Syndrome. At the same time they can tell whether it's a boy or girl.'

Steve grinned. 'The wonders of modern science. In that case I'll look in tomorrow and find out.' He kissed her cheek. ' 'Bye now – and take care.'

'You too, Steve.' Her usual warm affection was once more in evidence, the excitement of talking about the baby making her forget the damage he'd caused to her husband.

Trying to dispel his guilty, gloomy thoughts, Barber walked the streets for a long time before returning to his newly acquired, fully furnished flat. He'd been incredibly lucky in getting the place, having walked into one of the many bureaux specialising in flat and bed-sit letting to find someone just on the verge of moving out. Within a couple of hours he'd installed himself in the small but ultra modern apartment. The bedroom and living room, with a kitchenette partitioned off at one end, were done out in Scandinavian style which he found very pleasing. He used some of his expense money to buy a continental quilt, and an assortment of kitchen ware. Half a dozen bottles of assorted wines and a couple of glasses completed his household purchases.

He had a leisurely bath, shaved and dressed in a smart dark blue, pin-striped suit, the waistcoat having been specially designed to hide the shoulder straps of his gun holster, and the jacket to conceal the bulge of the gun itself. When he'd finished he stood before the mirror, opening and closing the jacket. Either way, he couldn't detect the pistol.

Suddenly the whole thing seemed farcical. Here he was acting like some thriller super spy, when in fact all he was was a shit-scared amateur, playing games. But it wasn't a game. It was mind bogglingly real, and within a week he was going to be responsible for yet another man's death. This time though, he tried to persuade himself, he was going to enjoy it. He was going to eliminate one of the most serious Communist threats to the country since World War II. He was going to kill the enemy.

No – he wasn't. He was going to kill another human being – but Christ Almighty, it was happening all the time, all over the world, so why have qualms? He knew the answer. If he hadn't done what he did to those punks, he wouldn't feel so bad about it. As it was . . .

He'd heard from Carmichael that one of them was dead and the other critically ill. If he survived, he would probably be completely insane, and spend the rest of his life in a mental hospital. No matter how Steve tried, he couldn't justify what he'd done. His brother had been right; he should have left them to the courts. And now Parker. He knew, understood and endorsed the reasons for requiring Parker's death, but even so . . . wouldn't it be better for a judge and jury to convict and condemn? After all, what if he was innocent? What if Carmichael and the rest of them were wrong? Shit! He'd spent enough years in the Marines taking and issuing orders not to start questioning his superiors at this stage. They HAD to be right. If he didn't believe that, he might as well give up altogether . . .

He hesitated, took the gun out of its holster, placed it in the drawer of the bedside table and let himself out of the flat. He hailed a prowling taxi and gave the driver the address printed on the cocktail party invitation card. It turned out to be a large, terraced house in Hammersmith, and he arrived to find the party in full swing.

There must have been upwards of 200 people standing in small groups, all with a glass of something in their hands. A few of the men wore dinner jackets, their ladies in long evening dresses, but the majority were, like him, in business suits.

He wandered between the spacious sitting and dining

room, a glass of very weak whisky in his hand, looking for Parker. Before he found him he spotted Chief Superintendent Carmichael who looked through him as he gazed around the room and then looked back. Parker was standing beside Carmichael.

The Minister looked exactly as he did in the photos and films Barber had been watching – which really wasn't surprising. After a few seconds, realising he was staring, he turned abruptly away, bumping into someone's back, as he did so. She turned and looked at him as he apologised, and smiled. She was beautiful. The photographs Barber had seen had not done justice to her striking sensuality. Parker was even luckier than he'd thought.

'I'm terribly sorry. That was very clumsy of me,' he said.

She laughed. 'That's quite all right. I was just wondering who knew me well enough to greet me so heartily.'

She wore her straight blonde hair shoulder length, in a gleaming bob. Her blue eyes were large, almost almond shaped, her mouth generous, her lips red, moist and inviting. For the second time in a few seconds, Barber found himself staring.

'Do you come here often?' he enquired, straight faced, and thought how delightfully her nose crinkled when she laughed.

'Only when I'm so bored I need to prove to myself I wasn't really bored after all. At least not by comparison with this,' she added, moving a hand in a disparaging gesture.

'I know what you mean. If you're alone, let me get you a drink and at least try to remove some of the tedium. I may not succeed, of course . . .'

'I'm quite sure you will.' She slipped an arm through his. 'I'd love a drink, and I'm sure I won't be bored again tonight.'

Barber was elated. Don't count your chickens, he told himself. After all, she only wants a drink. There's many a slip twixt bar and bed. He got her a gin and tonic, and this time helped himself to a stronger whisky and water.

'Here's looking at you,' she said, raising her glass and smiling at him over the rim.

123

'And you. Which is something I could do all night,' he added, looking boldly into her eyes.

'My mother always told me not to go to bed with strange men, especially on first dates,' she replied.

'I have a certificate proving I'm not strange,' he replied, enjoying himself hugely, 'so I hope first dates don't count.'

'Let me see it, and I promise to give it some thought.'

'Ah, but there's a problem. It's back in my flat. You'll have to come with me before I can show it to you.'

She laughed. 'At least that's more original than inviting me to see your etchings.'

'I hope you don't have a similar certificate?' Steve enquired.

She shook her head.

'That's good – because I make it a rule always to go to bed with strange girls on first dates. Well, that covers all the necessary qualifications, all we need to do now is decide upon time and venue.'

'Uh – uh.' Again she shook her head. 'One qualification is missing; we aren't on a first date. I just happened to meet you, briefly and in passing, and as I'm a civil servant, and I guess you are too, you'll know as well as I do that under no circumstances whatsoever can we break a rule.'

'Absolutely correct, of course. Therefore, as I totally agree with you, I suggest we find our way, like all good civil servants, around the problem. The solution is obvious. When this boring do is over, you and I have dinner together. Thus all objections will be suitably overcome.'

'Unless, of course, any more arise during the evening.'

'There is always that possibility. However, having undergone training courses so brilliant, uncomplicated and logical that only the mandarins of Whitehall can understand them, I'm sure between us we can find a way around any objection.'

She looked up at him, and blushed faintly. 'There are one or two objections not even we can overcome. However,' she added quickly, not giving him time to respond, 'I accept your invitation. Where shall we go?'

'I'm not sure – I don't know London all that well. Do you have any suggestions?'

'Not really. Shall we just sally forth and find some new, exciting, hitherto undiscovered bistro or trattoria, deep in the heart of the concrete jungle known as the West End?'

'Great. How soon can we leave?'

'We-ell . . . certainly before the farewell speeches. I can't stand these poignant leave-takings of senior people, all of whom are retiring early to take up directorships of some prestigious company, or to return to Whitehall to serve on a Government committee, collecting their inflation-proof pensions at the same time. Before we go though, I must tell my boss I'm leaving.'

'Oh? I thought you were alone. Who is your boss?' Barber asked innocently.

'His lordship over there,' she nodded towards Parker. 'The one surrounded by fawning admirers. In case you don't recognise him, he's the deputy leader of the Labour party.'

'Sounds as if you don't care for him.'

'Sorry, I didn't mean to give that impression. Actually, my feeling is mainly one of indifference. I've been secretary to quite a few politicians and I'd say he's fairly average. Better than some, of course; worse than others. In fact I could tell you quite a few stories I've heard from other secretaries about some of our so-called leaders. They'd make you realise what a bunch of useless . . .' She paused. 'No, I won't say what I think; I'll let you decide for yourself. Contrary to popular belief, though, they're all as bad as each other.'

'I'm fascinated,' said Steve truthfully. 'But tell me – if they're so awful, why don't we read more about it in the press?'

She shrugged. 'I suppose so much of it is mere hearsay. The thing is, even allowing for exaggeration, some pretty awful things do go on. And they're supposed to command our respect . . .' She broke off, bit her lip and laughed. 'Oh dear – there I go, riding my hobby horse again. You should never have let me get started ... Oh, oh – I think the speeches are about to start. I'll hurry over and say cheerio, then we can sneak away.'

Barber threaded his way through the throng which was now crowding into one room to listen to the flattering tributes about to be paid to their colleague. He waited at the door for her, and was just beginning to wonder whether she'd been trapped by the crowd or changed her mind when she arrived, somewhat breathless.

'We'll take a taxi. It's starting to drizzle,' Barber said, opening the door for her. While they waited, he introduced himself and learnt that the girl's name was Janet Walker.

Ten minutes later they were still waiting.

'Shall we walk?' Janet suggested. 'It's not far to the tube station.'

'I'm willing if you are. After all, if Gene Kelly could sing and dance in the rain, I'm sure we can manage a stroll.'

Arm in arm they whistled 'Singing in the Rain,' slightly off key as they walked quickly towards the Underground. Half an hour later they were sitting in a small restaurant called 'Mario's', off the beaten track, and about ten minutes from Piccadilly Station.

'I hope the food will be all right,' murmured Barber, glancing round. 'I always think if a place isn't crowded, especially by this time of night, there must be something wrong with it.'

She smiled. 'You may be right, or on the other hand, you may be wrong.'

'Typical civil servant,' he teased. 'Unwilling to commit yourself.'

'And quite rightly; how else will I get my damehood? It could be nobody's found this place yet, and the meal will be excellent. Let's wait and see.'

They did have to wait, and the food when it came was mediocre. Over a starter of a few prawns on a bed of soggy lettuce, liberally doused with a shocking pink dressing out of a bottle, Steve learned that Janet came from a well-to-do

126

family living in Hertfordshire. She'd been to grammar school, taken 'A' levels and then spent three years at Bristol University, emerging with a second class honours degree in English and History and a determination to become a teacher. After six months of trying she'd given up, declared the Labour Government the winners and enrolled for a year's bi-lingual course at a secretarial college. After that, her father having used his influence, she'd obtained a job in the Treasury, and had had four Civil Service appointments since then.

At that point, fifteen minutes after they'd finished the first course, their steak arrived, supposedly cooked in a delicious red wine sauce, but in fact virtually tasteless.

During the main course, Barber heard how Janet had fallen madly in love, only to discover that not only was her boyfriend two-timing her, but also his other girlfriend was six months pregnant. She gave him up, and swore off men forever. Three weeks later she found herself another man; married, this time, to ensure she didn't get too involved. A few months after their affair started his wife found out, and gave him an ultimatum; either he stopped seeing Janet, or she left him. He stopped seeing Janet.

'That was last month,' she added, with a smile.

'That's good. I mean,' Barber added hastily, 'that's good from my point of view, because presumably you haven't had time to find anyone else. From your point of view it's a very sad story.'

She grimaced. 'Not really. I'd say a very ordinary one – it's happening all the time. Now that's enough about me. What about you?'

Before Barber could reply the waiter appeared and asked if they wanted anything else. Janet shook her head.

'No thanks,' said Barber. 'Just the bill, please.' He drained his glass. 'At least the Chianti wasn't too bad.'

'Very nice.' Janet pulled a comical face. 'Better than the food.'

He grinned. 'Sorry about that.'

127

'Not your fault – we both chose the place. And the company was excellent,' she added, with a mocking little bow.

'Ditto, ditto. Now when can I make amends by dining you properly?'

The waiter came back just then with the bill. Steve paid, and they departed without leaving a tip.

'I know a little bar not far from here that serves drinks to friends at all hours,' Janet said. 'Shall we try it?'

'Why not? And thank goodness it's stopped raining!' Taking her hand, and wanting to keep the conversation away from himself, he added, 'By the way, you promised to regale me with stories about our glorious leaders.'

'So I did – I'd forgotten. Let me see now. Did you know that the previous Minister for Agriculture in the Labour Party was an alcoholic? He used to get through a bottle and a half of gin a day. One of his assistants, a back bencher, often had to put him to bed – so what do they do with him? Make him a lord and boot him off upstairs!'

'That doesn't really surprise me. I thought drinking was almost an occupational hazard.'

'So it is – but not true alcoholism.'

'I see. And what other little nuggets of gossip are you going to fascinate me with?'

'We . . . ell.' She pondered, then went on, 'You know Sylvia Cready?'

'Not personally.'

'Clot!' She dug him in the ribs. 'I didn't mean personally. She was a member of a working committee investigating the viability of a scheme to build cycle tracks around London streets. To help the committee, a secretary was assigned to them; a very attractive girl and also, as it happens, AC/DC. I've met Cready, and honestly, she's even uglier than the photographs of her. To cut a long story short, she made a pass at my friend, who told her to get lost in no uncertain terms. She, Cready that is, obviously wanted it badly, and offered my friend money. My friend blew up and asked her what the hell sort of girl did she think she was – so Cready told her. You see, Sylvia Cready knew that my friend had been away for a weekend with Joyce Pearson.'

'Joyce Pearson? You mean the Minister for Education?'

'The very same.'

'But she's married! She's got a couple of kids, hasn't she?'

'She is and she has; just goes to show, doesn't it? In fact she paid my friend £100 to go away with her. They spent two days and nights in bed in a cottage in mid Wales. My friend didn't mind. Like I said, she enjoys sex with either sex, as it were – and the extra money came in useful. However, under no circumstances was she going with Sylvia Cready.' She broke off. 'Here we are. Knock on the door and give my name.'

A few minutes later they were sitting at a quiet table in a dark, smoked filled room. A bar ran the length of the room, and at the far end a group of three black men and a white girl played and sang pleasant ballads, not too loudly. About three quarters of the seats were taken, and half a dozen or so people stood at the bar.

Barber ordered a bottle of white wine, and when it came, urged Janet to carry on with her story.

'Well,' she continued, 'this friend of mine is a bit of a bitch. She could see Sylvia Cready had the hots for her, and played up to her like mad; you know – touching her hand, brushing against her, apparently not minding when Sylvia rubbed the back of her hand against her thigh.'

Barber laughed. 'Poor cow. She must have been going up the wall with frustration.

'Oh, she was,' agreed Janet. 'After about a month she apparently accosted my friend in the ladies' loo, took hold of her hands and kissed her. My friend was outraged; told her never to do that again. Within a week Cready had offered my friend £100 to go away with her. A week later she upped it to £200 and ... well ...' She shrugged. 'My friend could use the money. As you men say, I believe – who looks at the mantlepiece when you're stoking the fire?'

'True. One could always put a pillow over her face as well.'

'Hmm. Might be a bit difficult in this situation.'

'So they went away together?'

'Yes – but the joke is this. Sylvia took my friend to the same cottage as Joyce Pearson had, and it transpired that she and Pearson had been lovers off and on for years; had often shared a third woman, in fact.'

'Good God! But they belong to different parties. One Labour . . .'

Exactly. Interesting, don't you think?'

'Fascinating.' His mind raced with the political implications, though where they would lead if generally known was impossible to imagine. 'Er . . . shall we dance?' he asked, indicating the few couples that were gyrating slowly around the tiny dance space between the tables and band.

'Yes, I'd like to.'

He held her close, her head against his shoulder. He could feel the pressure of her breasts against his chest, the warmth of her breath on his neck. His response was obvious. He squirmed slightly but Janet just held him tighter. He was rock hard pressing against her. She lifted her head and he kissed her, slowly and gently at first and then with more passion.

'I think it's time we left,' Barber said, looking down into her eyes.

'Where to?' she smiled.

'My place if you like – or yours. I don't mind.'

'A bit late for coffee, isn't it?' she teased.

'First of all it's never too late for coffee and secondly who said anything about coffee in the first place?'

By way of an answer she took his hand and led him back to their table. She picked up her handbag and turned to face him. 'Shall we?' She gestured to the door.

★   ★   ★

Barber lit the gas fire and made coffee for both of them. Now they knew what was to happen, they didn't intend rushing anything. They sat on the floor, backs against the settee, and sipped their hot drinks.

'I never expected to end up here with a girl from a party like that one,' Barber said quietly.

'Me neither,' Janet replied – 'with a boy, that is.'

He kissed her and placed his hand on her left breast. Massaging her nipple, he felt it harden again. After a few moments he moved his hand down to her waist under her jumper and back to her breast. He felt her hand moving on his leg. Tantalisingly she brought it up his thigh to his erection, then let it rest there.

Barber slipped his hand around her back and undid her bra. Her heavy breasts filled his hand. He pushed up her jumper and, in the reflection of the fire, brought his mouth down to suck her nipples. She moaned and squeezed him tightly. As he shifted his hand down to her knee and along her leg under her skirt, she began undoing his shirt buttons and rubbing her hand across his chest.

He sat up, then knelt in front of her. She lifted herself to let him pull off her panties and tights and then, settling alongside her once more, he gently rubbed her clitoris until she moaned again.

'It's not fair,' she whispered, 'you still have too much on,' and with that she pushed his shirt off his shoulders and then began undoing his belt. He interrupted her and pulled her jumper over her head. Slipping off her bra, he began kissing each of her nipples in turn. Janet continued undoing his belt and then unzipped his fly.

They now lay full length on the floor, a cushion under Janet's head. His hand continued rubbing her and from time to time he half put two fingers inside her.

Her hand wormed itself under his pants and slowly she began to massage him.

'Let me get your trousers off: it'll be easier.'

She sat up and knelt in front of him. Barber lifted himself and Janet peeled off his trousers and pants together. She leant forward and gripped his shaft, then brought her head

131

down to engulf him, sucking and moving her hand quite rapidly. This time it was Barber who moaned.

'If you don't stop I'll come soon – ' He put his hand on the side of her face and lifted her head away. 'That's not fair. Let me do the same for you – let me get your skirt off.'

Obediently she moved around and Barber undid her skirt, throwing it to one side. Then he lay back, his head on the cushion, and Janet straddled him. Her mouth firmly wrapped around him, she began sucking hard and moving her hand first slowly and then more quickly.

Barber began by pressing his tongue against her vagina and then licking her clitoris. She pressed down harder and he took hold of her buttocks and spread her cheeks, partly massaging them but controlling the force he used against her. The eroticism of it brought him to the verge of coming and because he wanted them to come together he thought of anything which might distract him – cold showers, cars, even his time in the Marines. When Janet's sudden sense of urgency told him she was on the verge of orgasm, he let his mind return to what she was doing.

'I'm about to come,' he warned her.

Instead of pulling away she moved her hand faster and pressed down even harder on his face. He began ejaculating as she started to shudder in climax.

When every drop had been drained from him she lifted her mouth away, then turned to snuggle against him.

'I hope that was as nice for you as it was for me.'

'It was – thank you.'

'The pleasure was all mine.'

Her hand was once more between his legs manipulating his already half hard penis.

'What a greedy boy he is,' she murmured, kissing him. 'Doesn't know when he's had enough ...' Again he was fully erect as she pushed his foreskin back and forth. 'Shall we go to bed before you get on top of me? This floor is getting hard.'

He grinned back. 'Of course. Come on, I'll show you the way.'

'I've already found it.'

They stood up and Janet, holding on to his erection, led him towards the bedroom. Barber flung back the quilt and they climbed onto the bed.

'Brrr, it's cold. Get on top and warm me up.' She guided him into the moist warmth of her.

Chapter 10

The next morning, after Janet left, Barber wandered around the city for a while until it was time to visit the hospital.

Phil was looking worse than ever when he got to the ward.

'What's up?' Barber asked, concerned.

Phil shrugged. 'I heard this morning I'll probably be a cripple for life.' He spoke so quietly Barber had to lean forward to hear. 'What a stinking mess.'

'No listen, Phil – that's not true.' Barber sat down beside the bed and went on eagerly, 'The doctors told me about it. They said there's a guy in Switzerland who can fix you up.'

'Yes, I know – and at what a cost! I can't afford that kind of money. I had good prospects, before this happened, but things were pretty tight short term. I've a hefty mortgage, an old banger of a car and very little capital.'

'Ah – but I've got this,' Barber told him triumphantly. 'Look.' He took the fat envelope out of his pocket and put it in his brother's hands. 'Ten thousand quid; exactly what you need for the operation – and don't worry about a thing while you're away. I'll look after Sue, the baby and the bills.'

'But . . .' Phil's face was a study. 'Where on earth . . . Did you rob a bank or something?'

'Nothing so mundane,' Barber said, adding with a forced grin. 'It's the Parker blood money.'

'I see,' Phil said quietly. 'Thanks Steve – I appreciate it. I'll let you have it back one day.'

'Oh no. There's no question of paying back, so forget it.

134

It's my fault you're here, and this goes just a little way towards making amends. It's a gift, not a loan. O.K?'

'Well . . . thanks. But don't blame yourself, Steve. It was circumstances that put me here; call it fate, if you like. It certainly wasn't you.'

Barber smiled wanly. 'Thanks kid.' He squeezed his brother's hand. 'Thanks a million.'

They grinned at each other, then Phil, revitalised, exclaimed, 'Hey, let's change the subject. So what's new with you?'

'Ah. I told you I was going to a crummy cocktail party? Well, I met the most gorgeous bird you ever saw . . .' He briefly related the events of the previous evening.

'And to cap it all, we're going away for the weekend to Dartmouth. In fact I must be on my way. By the time I see Sue I'll be fairly late checking on our arrangements. By the way, there's nothing further about the other business,' he added, getting to his feet.

'Steve, this job,' Phil said, putting out his right hand. 'Don't think of it in the terms you are. Parker is an enemy agent. What he's doing . . . he doesn't deserve to live. Remember, he's a Commie bastard and an enemy of all free people. Just think of the human rights business going on at the moment in Russia; how they're hounding the Helsinki Group, and the way they're being treated. The Russians are turds. Not the people – they're like people everywhere – but their leaders. You know what's going on. We must prevent the same thing happening here at all costs. Don't forget that.'

'I won't, and you're right. I'll keep reminding myself of the fact. See you next week, probably after this business is over. Okay?'

'Okay, big brother. Take care, you hear?'

'Will do. See you. Bye.'

Sue was up on the next floor, in fine form and getting ready to go down to see her husband.

'The doctor said it's definitely a boy,' she said. 'I can't wait

135

to tell Phil, he'll be so pleased. Although he didn't really mind either way I think he was secretly hoping for a son and heir.'

'That's great. It'll cheer him up no end. When do they think he'll be arriving?'

'Next Friday, or thereabouts. I must go – I can't wait to see Phil. See you soon.' She kissed him quickly, and left.

Back in his flat, Barber 'phoned Janet and confirmed their plans. He'd hire a car, they'd share the cost and drive down that evening; she was to be at the flat by six o'clock. There was no time for more because she was busy. When she'd rung off, he contacted a local car hire firm and arranged for a Sierra 1.6GL, unlimited mileage, at special weekend rates. He walked round and collected the car, packed a holdall and settled down to wait, impatiently, for Janet to arrive.

Around five o'clock the phone rang. It was Carmichael. Barber told him of his plans for the weekend.

'That's fine. It's good for you to stay loose before something like this. Do you have a number I can contact if I need you in a hurry?'

Barber had obtained the number from Janet for that very purpose, and passed on the information.

'I'm now with Parker full time,' the Chief Superintendent told him, 'so don't forget, if you need me in a hurry and I'm not available, use the word "operation" in any message you leave. Anything else? No? Good. See you in Holland. At least, I won't see you but you'll see me.'

Janet arrived shortly after six, looking radiant. She was smiling and obviously reflecting the excitement Barber was feeling.

By seven-thirty they were well out of London and driving along the M4 towards the Bristol and the West. The skies had cleared and the wind had dropped; conditions were perfect for a pleasant drive. The car handled well, and cruised effortlessly along in the outside lane at a steady seventy miles an hour. It was then that Janet began pinning Barber down on what exactly he did in the civil service.

Having thought about it, he'd decided on a better story than the one Carmichael had suggested about the Health Authority.

'After serving so long in the Marines,' he told her, 'the powers that be decided that my specialist knowledge was too valuable to lose, and offered me a job with the M.o.D. So here I am – and quite enjoying it, too. A lot of the work is hush-hush, of course, so I keep my mouth shut about most of it. That way I reduce the risk of making a cock-up by talking about something I shouldn't.'

'Very wise. Let's make a pact; neither of us talk shop. Okay?'

'Fine with me. Shall we stop the other side of Bristol for something to eat, or would you rather press on and finish the journey?'

'Let's go on. I've brought some paté and wine and French bread, so we shan't starve when we get there.'

On the outskirts of Taunton Janet fell into a light doze and did not stir until they were past Totnes with only a few more miles to go.

'Where are we?' she asked sleepily.

'Almost there. We pass the College's aerodrome in a few minutes.' He opened the window for air as a wave of tiredness swept over him. 'You'll have to direct me from there.'

'Down the hill, follow along the front and past the Floatel.'

He followed her directions. 'Straight on here past the lower ferry and around to the left. If you park here we can walk up to the house, it's at the top of these steps.'

She led the way into the house. It was quite small, two up and two down, with a kitchenette and bathroom. It was tastefully furnished in a modern style, all smokey glass and dark wood, with a white, long pile carpet throughout.

'Some weekend retreat,' commented Barber, standing in the doorway to the kitchenette while Janet prepared them a snack. She nodded. 'Not bad, is it? The sort of place I'd like one day along this coast.'

'You and me both,' he said, envy in his voice.

The light snack they had was excellent. The second bottle of wine they took to bed with them. The night was all they had each hoped for.

★　★　★

It was Saturday, and the Right Honourable Edward Parker, MP, was deeply perturbed. He was in the study-cum-office of his large house, situated on the outskirts of Hull, his constituency seat, angrily pacing up and down the room. As if he hadn't enough to contend with, without this! The fools – the bloody idiots. Didn't they realise how close he was to the ultimate goal? And now to jeopardize everything by arranging a meeting between himself and a KGB man. . .

Words failed him. For the first time in his life he couldn't find adequate expression for what he was thinking. He'd told them on the 'phone about Carmichael, but they hadn't seemed surprised. On the contrary, they had appeared to know in advance, and had issued strict instructions on how to deal with the situation.

Parker clenched his hands behind his back, trying to stop them shaking. He didn't understand it, that was the trouble. If only he knew what was going on. It had all started with that oaf of a Chief Superintendent insisting on acting as his bodyguard. He'd protested vehemently, and had finally 'phoned Neil. He had said it was important and only temporary.

Damn it! This meeting . . . He'd been going round and round on this same track since Friday, when he'd received the call. It had been a long time since he'd last heard the cold, anonymous, voice but he'd recognised it at once. He wondered if this was just a reminder of who he was; of his background and his real bosses. Did he need reminding? Guiltily he tried to remember when he had last thought of Russia as the motherland. Not for a long time.

Even his meetings with his parents didn't mean as much as they used to. It wasn't that he no longer loved them; far from it. It was just that he'd out-grown them, not in years, but in status and lifestyle. They were still peasants, with peasant attitudes. It had been all right in previous years, because they'd always stayed in a self-catering cabin, near a lake or in a forest, occasionally on a Russian owned island (purchased through an anonymous front, of course), but more often in some remote part of the beautiful Danish countryside. Last year he'd taken them to a hotel for a few days; a dreadful mistake. Two nights had been more than enough. He'd cut his holiday short, then made the excuse of too much work and returned to England three days earlier than planned. This year he wasn't looking forward to the holiday at all.

There was another problem; of course. The Soviet Union believed that keeping him in touch with his parents would deter him from doing his own thing, if such a thought ever crossed his mind. What they didn't know was that he was already drawing up plans to exclude the USSR from interfering in Britain. He and he alone would lead the country to a real Socialist state.

His day dreaming took hold once more. He would become Prime Minister after Neil's death. That was the final use he would make of the USSR. After that he would pay lip service but be his own master. Perhaps the first British President, after abolishing the House of Lords and the monarchy.

This time he was so taken up with his own plans and dreams that his return to reality was even more painful. It was there, he knew it. Time, which was on his side, could see him fulfil his dream . . . No – it was more than a dream, it was destiny. He needed only to survive this small crisis that now faced him, and in due time his patience would be fully rewarded.

Plans had been made for Parker to meet his parents in one week's time. He had to go, in case the Soviets realised they no longer had that hold over him. He must continue to appear to play ball with them, until he was too powerful for them to harm him. Once that day came . . .

Firmly putting the recurring daydream from his mind, Parker concentrated once more on the issues at hand. First

139

the meeting. He considered carefully what he had to do, then turned his thoughts to an even more pressing problem. He was due to go abroad in seven days. Suppose he cancelled it? After all, with Carmichael practically following him to the shithouse, how on earth could he get to see his parents for the best part of a week, without him finding out? The more he thought about it, the more impossible it seemed – and then, quite suddenly, an alternative solution suggested itself. Eagerly he sat down, picked up pen and paper and began to work out the problem.

When he'd finished he had before him what would, he hoped, be the ideal answer. It was risky, of course, but it could work. He'd go to Copenhagen as arranged. Once there, he'd have a man-to-man talk with Carmichael, explain he wanted privacy for his meeting with his mistress. Parker could play the 'we're all boys together' bit as well as the next man. He'd give Carmichael expense money and get rid of him for a few days. No – not even that. He'd see his parents for just a couple of nights and then return. The Soviets would be able to understand that; after all, they wouldn't want to run stupid risks, just for the sake of renewing their hold on him.

It was ideal. The KGB would be happy, he'd have the minimum time to spend with his parents, so he'd be happy ... and Carmichael? If he agreed to it, then presumably he'd be happy too. Who wouldn't be, with a two day holiday in a fun city like Copenhagen, especially if you're spending someone else's money?

The more Parker thought about it, the more he liked it. Even if Carmichael didn't agree to two days, he surely wouldn't object to leaving him, Parker, alone for a few hours, to give him time to see his parents. He didn't want that. He wanted to spend a little time with them, but if he couldn't ... well, there was always next year.

The unease he'd been experiencing since Carmichael turned up, compounded with his worry about the meeting with the KGB, began to recede. He sat back in his chair, and once more allowed his dreams to dominate his thoughts. As he did so, he slowly shredded the notes he'd been making into little pieces, then burned them in the large, heavy onyx ash tray, the only article remaining on his desk.

Chapter 11

After a long and lazy day Barber and Janet went out into the town in the early evening, strolling along the front as far as the upper ferry.

'This place has hardly changed at all since I was last here, over five years ago,' Barber said.

'Not surprising really,' said Janet. 'Places rarely change, only people. What were you doing here then?'

'Playing rugby against the Naval college. I know what you mean about change. It's just that after so long one somehow expects things to be different.'

This early in the season there were few holiday-makers about, and at the pub next to the ferry landing point they were the only customers.

They had been sitting there for about an hour before Barber brought the conversation around to work and the personalities of their respective bosses. Having made a few comments about his own purely fictitious superior, he enquired casually:

'What's Parker like to work for?'

'Not bad, as I've told you before. Better than some and not as good as others.'

'Is he a moody chap? Ever fly off the handle – things like that?'

'Not really. Why are you so interested in him anyway?' Janet added, glancing at him curiously.

'No particular reason. It's just that I don't get the chance to hear the lowdown on an important person, especially one I dislike intensely.'

'Hmmm, I see. I admit I'm not in agreement with him politically, but he's difficult to dislike as a person, once you get to know him. He genuinely believes in what he's trying to do for Britain. At least, that's the way he comes across, even in private.'

Janet my love, if only you knew, thought Barber. Aloud he said. 'What about extra-marital affairs? Any hints of that?'

'None whatsoever. He seems to love his wife, and though his son is a true blue, they appear to have an affectionate respect for each other. I don't think they discuss politics much.'

'What an unblemished life he leads,' commented Barber.

Janet smiled. 'True.' She paused. 'Actually, it's funny you should suggest an affair, because I did wonder about that only the other day. Probably my dirty mind working overtime again,' she added with a grin.

'Probably,' agreed Barber smiling, 'but what made you think it?'

'Oh, it's nothing really. I just overheard him say something on the telephone about a meeting on Tuesday, but it's not in his diary. I'm usually the one who makes his appointments.'

'Aha! Not so pure after all. Who was he talking to? A female?'

'I've no idea. Anyway, I'm sure we're barking up the wrong tree. No doubt it's to do with some political meeting which he'll tell me about on Monday.'

'No doubt,' Barber said, wondering if in fact the answer was as innocent as that. Still, he didn't need to worry. Carmichael was there to see nothing went wrong. He was just over-reacting, now that the time was getting so near for him to remove Parker permanently from the political scene; from any scene, in fact.

Resolutely pushing thoughts of Parker from his mind, he suggested moving on, adding that the place was getting too full of naval types for his liking. About a dozen fresh faced, short back and sides young men had arrived, and all with only one exception, were badly dressed. The clothes themselves were in good condition, obviously of excellent quality, but the style was totally out of date. The sight of these youngsters reminded Barber of himself when he'd first joined the Marines, and the thought inexplicably depressed him.

They went from pub to pub, mixing their drinks with increasing abandon. At closing time they found themselves in a dingy restaurant not far from the promenade. It was the only place open at that time of night, and though the decor left much to be desired, the food was excellent. Barber had frequented it during his rugby days, and knew something of the history of the place. The owner, a Rumanian exile who'd settled in Dartmouth some twenty five years earlier, was also the chef. Originally a fisherman, he had lost a leg in an accident and had to quit the sea. He was an excellent cook, at his best when drunk – and his food was more often than not of the best.

A bottle of red wine finished what the earlier drinks had begun, and when they left the restaurant at some time after three a.m., Janet and Barber cheerfully supported each other in their meandering walk back to the house.

'Thish – hic, beg pardon,' said Janet, leaning on Barber's shoulder, 'thish hash been – hic – one – hic. Blasted hippucs, I mean hiccups. Ash I wash shaying, one of the mosht enjoyable dish, dish ... dish'pated weeken's of my life, an' I've loved every minute of it,' she concluded, in a concentrated rush of words.

'My shentimentsh 'ntirely,' agreed Barber. 'You ... you are a truly wunnerful girl. Sexy, gor ... gorshush ... lovely girl ... Oops!' They tripped on the steps in front of the house, and ascended the last half dozen on their knees.

'Thish ... thish is dishgushting,' declared Janet, leaning against the door, while Barber fumbled with the key, trying to get it into the lock. 'Wha' would my bosh say if he saw me

'– hic – now? Washamarra? Don . . . doesh, . . . doeshn't the key fit?'

'Dunno,' replied Barber. 'Bloody lock won't shtay shtill long enough for me to – hic – blast – now I've got 'em too. Won't shtay shtill long enough for me t' try it.'

'Here, lemme have a go.' Janet took the key from him, inserted it into the lock and turned. Unfortunately she was leaning against the door as it flew open, and she was precipated into the room, landing on her hands and knees. Giggling, she picked herself up, clapped a hand over her mouth and made for the bathroom.

Barber closed the door and somehow made it up the stairs to the bedroom and flopped down onto the bed. Vaguely, as he passed out, he heard Janet being sick.

★   ★   ★

'Pass the roast spuds, please, Dad,' Simon Parker said to his father, holding out his hand for the platter. 'Thanks. Hey, what's up? You don't look too good.'

Parker forced a smile. He thoroughly enjoyed his son's Sunday visits. Being at opposite ends of the political spectrum, they had tacitly agreed to avoid the subject of politics when they were together, and thus managed to maintain a good, fond relationship.

'It's nothing,' Parker replied, his mind on the forthcoming meeting with his Russian "comrades". 'Just a few constituency problems. You know the sort of thing; bad landlords, management upsetting unions, council harassment of a tenant. The boring stuff people rarely hear about.'

'Don't you mean bad tenants, pig headed and stupid unions and a council trying to recover a bad debt?' Replied Simon, adding hastily, 'Sorry – only joking. By the way, have you seen that new play in the West End? The black farce about Ireland today?' He knew his father had a passion for the theatre; it was an area in which they could have enjoyable discussions and arguments.

'No, I haven't had time. I will though, if you think it's

worth it,' Parker said, wondering how the hell he could broach the subject he most wanted to discuss. 'Er . . . how's Queens?'

'Fine, thanks. We've just started a gourmet club; I'm to be secretary. It should be good. We're restricting membership to twenty, and having one meal a month.'

'Sounds like fun, but I don't know how you do it. If I ate like you I'd weigh twenty stone. How do you manage to eat like a horse and yet stay slim and keep fit?'

'Simple, Dad. No exercise, plenty of beer and making it a rule never to stand when I can sit down,' joked his son.

Parker laughed aloud. 'Well – that's one way.' An idea suddenly came to him. 'Listen,' he went on, 'to change the subject completely, how would you fancy a holiday in Russia? I'm thinking of going there myself, and . . .'

'Thanks, Dad,' Simon interrupted, politely but firmly, 'but I think not. You know my views on that place.'

'I know, son. All I'm suggesting is that you go there, see for yourself what it's like. I'm sure you'll be pleasantly surprised.'

'I'm sorry, but I can't believe that. I think I'd only see what they wanted me to see – nothing more. In my view, the only way of finding out what's really going on is by reading all the various newspapers and comparing stories. Once one has done that one can make up one's own mind as to what one should believe – and so far, everything I've read has convinced me that the Russian people are oppressed prisoners in their own country. Look at what they're doing to the so-called dissidents . . .'

★ ★ ★

God, he felt sick. He couldn't remember the last time he'd had a hangover like this one. Painfully he turned his head to look at Janet, but he wasn't focusing too clearly; his eyeballs felt as if they were being pierced with red hot skewers. With a groan he closed his eyes tightly again.

'Are you awake?' Janet asked digging him gently in the ribs.

'No,' he groaned again. 'I'm dying, and death will be a relief. What time is it?'

'Three o'clock, and it's a beautiful day. We should be out enjoying the sunshine,' she told him cheerfully.

'Ohhh. You go, and if I'm not there in an hour's time go on enjoying it without me. Aren't you suffering?'

'Not particularly. I think being sick last night helped. I got rid of some of the alcohol instead of absorbing it. Gosh – I'm starving. Do you fancy breakfast?'

'Ugh!' Barber replied with feeling.

'Some nice greasy bacon and a fried egg, with some fried bread,' she added mischievously.

'If you don't shut up,' Barber muttered, 'I'll puke all over you. I could use some fruit juice and a couple of aspirin, though. I feel completely dehydrated.'

'Right. One gallon of orange juice coming up.'

She got out of bed, and Barber dozed off again uneasily. Next moment, it seemed, Janet was shaking his shoulder and telling him to sit up. With a superhuman effort, accompanied by loud groans, he struggled up on one elbow.

'There's no justice,' he said bitterly. 'Look at you . . .'

'Ahh . . . diddums. Come on now – drink this, take the aspirin and you'll feel better. I've made you some toast as well.'

Barber swallowed half a tumbler of juice, and then forced down three aspirins. 'Is the toast soggy?' he asked pathetically.

'No, it's nice and crisp, just the way toast should be.'

'I don't think I could stand the noise. How about a cup of coffee to dunk in it? I might be able to manage then.'

'Dunk toast? You pleb!' she kissed him lightly. 'Very well, O Master – to hear is to obey.'

'Good. At last you've learned your station in life,' he replied, smiling, his eyes still shut against the sunlight filtering through the curtains.

147

She chuckled. 'It's only because I want you to keep your strength up,' she said impishly.

'Not tonight, Josephine,' he quipped. The aspirin was taking effect – or perhaps it was purely psychological.

It was two in the morning when they arrived in London. Barber stopped the car outside Janet's flat and turned to kiss her goodnight.

'Aren't you coming up for a nightcap?' she asked.

'Sorry darling – no. I've got a busy day tomorrow and I need some rest.'

'Oh. All right.' She paused, her hand on the door handle: then when he did not speak she went on, 'Is that it, then? Just goodbye?' The tremor in her voice made Barber's heart melt. He reached out and laid a palm against her cheek, turning her face towards him. 'Don't be silly love. I'll 'phone you. All right?'

She shrugged. 'I was beginning to wonder. You've hardly said a thing on the way here, and now . . . I was starting to think that . . . well, having had everything, you're ready to move on.'

'Nothing of the kind.' He kissed her gently. 'Look, I've got a few things to do this week but with a little bit of luck I'll be free for the weekend. Let's go somewhere. Not for a return match; you can't repeat a good thing. Let's try for something different.'

'Okay,' she replied brightly. 'How about my flat, playing Scrabble for two days?'

'You're on – provided there's a prize for the winner.'

'There is – for you. For me there's only a fate worse than death.'

He gave her cheek a little pat, and then released her. 'Good night. Be good.'

'And you,' she said, opening the door and stepping out. ''Night.'

Barber drove away, leaving unspoken words hanging between them. Their parting had been far from satisfactory, but it would have to do for the time being. Somehow he doubted whether she'd want to see him the next weekend. She'd be too shaken up over her boss's death . . .

★ ★ ★

Parker had slept badly, and now he found it difficult to concentrate on what he was trying to dictate to his secretary. When he made the fifth mistake in less than a couple of minutes he broke off, saying irritably:

'Oh – blast! Sylvia, go and get me a cup of strong black coffee, will you, and a couple of aspirins. I've got a filthy headache.'

'I thought there was something wrong,' Sylvia Henshaw replied. 'You don't usually dictate so badly. I won't be a moment.'

Parker's only reply was a grunt. Normally when Sylvia criticised him, even gently rebuked him, he took it in good part. She was an excellent person, efficient and unflappable; that was why he allowed her to say the things she sometimes did. She kept him on his toes. Today, though, was different. Today he had too much on his mind.

As the door closed behind her he bent down, opened the bottom drawer of his desk and stopped the tape recorder. He rewound it a few feet and listened. The mistakes in his diction came through clearly, but not as loudly as he'd hoped, even with the speaker volume turned right up. Quickly he readjusted the recording volume, checked that the microphone hadn't been disturbed and sat back in his chair, just as Sylvia walked in carrying a tray. She was a true socialist, regarding it as her natural right to have coffee with her boss, using the same sort of crockery and sharing his biscuits. Her socialism never took her quite as far as buying the biscuits herself however.

For two hours, his mind cleared by the coffee and tablets, Parker dictated letters in reply to questions and complaints from his constituents. Finally he sat back with a sigh. 'That's it, I think,' he said, wearily rubbing his eyes with his hand.

That blasted headache was back. 'When's Janet arriving from town?'

'Tonight, sir. About nine o'clock.'

Parker nodded absently. 'Good. Well, that's all for now. Get those typed and we'll do some more this afternoon. I suppose that blasted policeman is still outside?'

'He was when I went for the coffee. He's a very patient man, is Chief Superintendent Carmichael. Mind you, I think he must be a bit brainless as well, just sitting there and not doing anything.'

'Keep your voice down, Sylvia,' Parker said, instinctively lowering his own voice. 'You know anyone outside can hear us in here.'

'Rubbish,' retorted his secretary – though herself following his example. 'He can only hear an indistinct mumble. He can't tell what we're saying.' She got up to go. 'Anyway,' she added. 'I don't care if he does hear me,' and with a toss of her head she marched out of the room.

Her greeting of, 'You still here, Inspector?' brought a smile to Parker's lips, but only fleetingly. His problems pressed in on him once more, and he rested his head wearily in his hands, trying to think. What was the next thing he had to do? Oh yes, ring the jeweller. He replaced the receiver and lifted it immediately, the dialling tone burring in his ear. He'd left the receiver off the hook while he was dictating, not only to prevent interruptions but also so that there'd be no recording of the telephone being used. When he went out that afternoon he intended leaving the receiver off again; that way, his instruction that he wasn't to be disturbed under any circumstances made more sense. It had worked throughout the morning, there was no reason why it shouldn't work that afternoon.

'Hullo?' he said, when a voice answered the other end. 'Samson's? Edward Parker here. I'm sending my secretary to you this afternoon to collect the brooch I chose the other day. Yes. Yes – that's the one. Good. Thank you. Goodbye.'

He hung up, walked to the door which led directly to his garage and then paused irritably. Hesitating for a moment, he retraced his steps across the room to the other door, opened it and put his head out.

'Ah, Chief Superintendent. I'm just going into the garage for a few minutes. If someone attacks me, I'll scream at the top of my voice. All right?'

The sarcasm was apparently lost on Carmichael, who merely grunted in reply. Inwardly he was seething. If there was any attacking to do it would be him, strangling the supercilious bastard. He and Parker had taken an instant and instinctive dislike to each other. Carmichael didn't hate Parker for what he was, nor for what he'd accomplished; that was all part of the game. No – his dislike was personal, as was Parker's for him. Inside the garage, Parker opened the bonnet of his Maestro and pulled off the distribution cap. He slipped off the rotor arm and dropped it into his pocket, replaced the cap and closed the bonnet; then he went back into the house for his lunch.

At just after 2.00 p.m. he and his secretary settled down for some further dictation. He'd issued instructions that under no circumstances was he to be disturbed, and felt fairly confident his orders would be obeyed. He was about to lift the receiver to disconnect the telephone when it rang. Irritably he answered.

Two minutes later he dismissed Sylvia, and spent the next hour on the 'phone, talking on a three-line link up with Kinnock and the Labour Chief Whip. At first he'd been inattentive, wanting only to end the conversation, but the more he became involved the more his personal problems receded. His meeting that afternoon with the KGB was forgotten in the myriad problems of running the party. He had no idea that the Leader of the Opposition found it almost impossible to be civil to him, and that he'd only been contacted because of the insistence of the Chief Whip who knew nothing about the situation.

He'd only just hung up and was sitting back, satisfied with

151

the way things had gone, when the 'phone rang again. The voice on the other end brought him back to reality with a jolt. It was with the greatest difficulty that he managed to persuade the caller to postpone their meeting until the following day, and his hand was shaking as he replaced the receiver once again.

It took a great effort of will to force himself to ring the jeweller and make fresh arrangements for the next afternoon, and an even greater effort to return to the garage and replace the rotor arm. He didn't even bother to inform Carmichael. By now he felt so washed out he was past caring about anything.

★   ★   ★

In a controlled voice Uri Stawizcki told the other two what had been said. As he expected, Wilhelm Henken exploded into anger.

'The stupid fool! After all our efforts to gain a day, he can't manage a meeting. Give me the number. By the time I've finished with him he'll be begging to see us!'

'No, Willy. We'll do things my way. I understood his reasons. Nothing is lost; it only means we didn't gain after all. We simply revert to our original time table, that's all.'

'That's all?' The Hangman's contemptuous dislike for their team leader was obvious. 'It isn't all. There's a lot more. It means an extra 24 hours in enemy territory. It means giving the British Secret Service extra time to perfect their plan to take care of Parker. It means . . .'

'Enough.' Although Stawizcki spoke quietly the word cut through Henken's tirade. 'I am the leader, and as such I make all decisions. Furthermore, the British Secret Service is not involved. Any first year student knows that it's the British Special Branch we're up against, albeit a select section of that august body. And,' he continued, rubbing salt in the wound, 'you should also know that the British Secret Service is connected only with world wide espionage, not counter espionage.'

'All right, all right. Semantics, that's all that is. Just fucking semantics. And you,' he whirled on the third member of the team, Gerhard Karpov, 'can wipe that stupid grin off your face.'

Karpov's smile vanished, but he couldn't keep the amusement from his eyes. He knew the Hangman for what he was – a cold blooded killer – but the knowledge didn't unduly perturb him. He hated the man, and the knowledge that he could do nothing about it made him hate all the more.

With a disdainful shrug he lay down on the bed and continued reading an Agatha Christie whodunnit; she was one of his favourite English authors. Meanwhile Stawizcki and Henken glared at one another for a few more seconds until the latter, with a grunt of disgust, turned away and sat down on the edge of his bed. Stawizcki left, returning to his own room. He didn't like the extra waiting any more than Henken, but there was nothing he could do about it. It was essential to act with caution; no point in rushing into things, just to gain a few hours. Yet again he regretted having the Hangman forced on him as a member of his team – but he understood the reasons, and knew there was nothing to be done about it. He'd have to try harder than usual to get along with him, that was all. The bastard.

★   ★   ★

Barber spent a lonely day sitting morosely in his flat. He couldn't settle to anything. The radio only irritated him. He started to read a book, but threw it aside. Pacing up and down the room, hands thrust deep in his pockets, he made himself face the fact that it was not the coming operation that was distracting him, but Janet. The more he thought about it, the more certain he became that he was about to fall in love with her. He tried to conjure up a picture of Louise, but his inner eye insisted on showing him Janet instead. Towards evening he was becoming desperate. Surely there was no harm in ringing her, just to say hullo, to hear her voice . . .

He was about to pick up the telephone when the front door

153

bell shrilled imperiously. Muttering, he threw open the door, the surly greeting dying on his lips.

'Hi. How about sharing this little old bottle of wine and a luscious sirloin steak with me?' Janet smiled. 'The sweet is standing before you.'

Grinning hugely, Barber pulled her across the threshold and into his arms. 'And what about starters?' he murmured, his fingers already busy with her zip.

Chapter 12

'Sylvia, I want you to go to Sampson's this afternoon and pick up Dorothy's birthday present. It'll be ready for collection at about one thirty. Okay?' Parker said to his secretary, as they sipped their morning coffee. She nodded and he continued, 'Don't tell anyone where you're going out at all. Let them think you'll be here all afternoon . . . if anyone says anything, that is,' he added hastily. 'That way there's less chance of my wife's surprise being spoilt.'

'Sylvia smiled. 'If you say so, not a word. Let me just get rid of these cups, then we can get on.' She placed the cups on a try and carried it to a side table.

'Where's Janet this morning? I thought she was due back last night,' Parker asked as they settled once more to deal with his backlog of mail.

'Oh, I forgot. She rang this morning to say she'd been delayed, and that she'd be here as soon as possible after lunch.'

Parker grunted. He knew very well that Sylvia Henshaw never forgot anything. He was also aware of the arrangement she had with Janet; cover if possible, give an explanation of the other's absenteeism only if asked. More often than not they got away with it – or so they thought. In fact, Parker invariably knew when one of them was missing, which wasn't very often. He appreciated their good qualities, however, and as long as they didn't abuse the liberties they took, was prepared to tolerate them. The small, normal white lie gave him a pang of nostalgia. Whatever was going to be required of him at the coming meeting, he felt an era of his life was about to end. The throbbing headache that had nagged at him all morning seemed to double in intensity. With a sigh he rubbed his hands across his face, then used the middle fingers to massage his temples.

'Get me another cup of strong coffee and two more aspirins, will you?' he said. As she left the room he tried desperately to relax, to lessen the strain of trying to appear normal, when his frayed nerves tautened with each passing hour as the time of the meeting approached, making him want to scream. It had been bad enough the day before, but all the tension of that day had been wasted. The letdown of not finding out what the hell was going on had been almost too much, and made today that much harder to bear.

When Sylvia returned he gulped the coffee, swallowed the aspirins and tried to concentrate on his work. The morning dragged on until finally, at a quarter to twelve, Parker could stand it no longer.

'Let's finish for now,' he said. 'Be back here at one.'

Alone at last, he poured himself a large whisky and settled down in one of the deep leather chairs that stood on either side of the fireplace. He closed his eyes and forced his mind to become temporarily and blissfully blank. Hearing the door creak slightly, he opened his eyes again. Carmichael put his head around, nodded amiably, said, 'Just checking,' and withdrew.

Parker looked at the half empty glass of neat whisky in his hand, made a grimace of disgust and threw the spirit on the fire, where it flared blue with a brief roar. This was no time to drink. He needed a clear brain for the coming afternoon.

Sylvia Henshaw, returning just before one o'clock found her boss fast asleep in his chair. Her first reaction was to leave him. After all, she was going out shortly, and there'd be no harm done if he slept until she returned. In fact it would probably do him a lot of good; he'd been under too much strain of late, and was obviously sleeping badly. She decided to leave him.

She was busily occupied in sorting the correspondence when the 'phone rang. She reached quickly to answer it and

156

as she put the receiver to her ear Parker's eyes flew open, the sudden hush as opposed to the noise waking him.

'I'm sorry, madam, but Mr Parker is not available at the moment ... Yes, he is here. No, I'm afraid that's impossible. You see,' she lowered her voice 'he's in conference with the Chief Whip and Mr Kinnock at the moment.' A few seconds later she hung up. 'It always works.' She grinned at her boss. 'Sorry it woke you. I was going to let you sleep until I got back.'

With an effort Parker swallowed the angry reprimand that had sprung to his lips, and with an even greater effort managed to summon up a smile. 'That's all right. It was a nice thought, anyway.' He glanced at his watch. 'Look – it's nearly twenty five past. Why don't you go out to the jewellers?'

'Okay. Where are the car keys?' Sylvia asked, getting to her feet.

'In the ignition.'

She picked up her handbag and went through the connecting door to the garage; it was an arrangement between them that if anyone had to go out on business, they took Parker's car. It was cheaper than taxis. He heard her trying to start the engine, and waited a few moments before following her.

'The wretched thing won't start,' Sylvia exclaimed, her face flushed with annoyance.

'Oh well – never mind. Leave it for now, and I'll get someone to see to it. You can go on the bus.'

'It'll take longer,' she warned, getting out of the car while he held the door open for her.

'Never mind. No hurry,' Parker replied easily.

When she had gone he hurried back into the study and across to the other door. Chief Superintendent Carmichael was sitting just outside, his arms folded. He looks like one of the fixtures, Parker thought, with intense irritation. Aloud he said, 'You can do something useful, Carmichael. Make sure nobody disturbs us until further notice.'

Ignoring the other's baleful look, he closed the door.

Back at his desk, he set the tape recorder to 'play' and waited for five minutes, listening to himself dictating to Sylvia. Then he removed the telephone receiver, crossed to the door leading to the garage, paused to cast an anxious glance at the other door and left.

★   ★   ★

Janet was sure she was in love. All the way in the train she thought about Barber. No other man in her life had ever turned her on the way he did. It wasn't just the love-making, though that was fantastic; no, it was more, far more than that. It was the way they could talk together, be silent together, laugh together. Yes, the laughing was important. Maybe that's what love's all about she thought. Laughing together.

She couldn't wait to see him again – and now, instead of having to wait until the weekend, he was changing his plans and coming to Hull for the night. She wondered what sort of job he had that allowed him to come and go as he pleased. Not that it mattered; she'd find out sooner or later. It was enough that he was coming for the evening.

Janet couldn't know that Barber was disobeying Carmichael's express instructions to stay in London and be ready at short notice to leave for Holland, just in case Parker changed his plans unexpectedly. Barber rationalised that the message recorder installed in his flat at Carmichael's insistence would suffice to tell the Chief Superintendent where he was.

When she arrived at Hull station, the last thing Janet felt like doing was going to work. May as well be hung for a sheep as a lamb, she thought and, her overnight case dangling from her hand, she strolled towards the gardens laid out in the town centre. Once she became accustomed to the stink of fish that pervaded the town she began to enjoy her walk.

She was sitting on a bench in front of a clump of rhododendrons, indulging in a happy daydream, when a voice penetrated her subconscious. Slowly she came back to her

158

surroundings, tender thoughts of Steve Barber fading as she recognised, or thought she recognised her boss's voice.

She looked around, the male voices having come from behind her, but the men were hidden behind the leafy shrubs. Another voice was speaking – a voice with a strong foreign accent – and then the first voice spoke again. Janet sat up with a jerk. That voice, for all the anguish in it, surely belonged to her boss.

She was about to walk around to the other side of the rhododendrons, casually, to see if it was him, when three men emerged and, without a glance in her direction, walked away. There was no doubt about it; the centre figure was that of Edward Parker.

Janet wondered what on earth he was doing there with a couple of foreigners. Could he be in any sort of trouble? But no – that was impossible. People like the Right Honourable Edward Parker were never in trouble; at least, nothing they couldn't handle. In fact more often than not it was they who were causing problems for other people. Still, there had been no mistaking the worry in his voice.

Now what was it he'd said? She thought hard, but couldn't remember. Something about tomorrow – but no. Really she hadn't been able to hear clearly enough.

Her mood altered, she found a taxi and went on out to Parker's place, ready to start work, though in Hull there was very little for her to do. Sylvia took care of all the local stuff while she dealt with the London end and some of his more important meetings. It was rather a wasteful system, in her opinion, but it seemed to suit Parker, so neither she nor Sylvia minded. She had a bed-sit in Parker's house for use when she was in Hull, with its own private fire escape, so she could come and go as she pleased. Barber would be spending the night there, but would have to leave before dawn the next day.

The irony of being in the same house as Carmichael and Parker had not been lost on Barber, and though he found it

159

amusing it also worried him more than a little. Janet, of course, knew nothing about that.

*   *   *

Parker was back in his study fifty minutes after leaving. He was relieved to find everything as he had left it. His own and Sylvia's voices were still talking on tape as he closed the door behind him and sat down wearily at his desk. He replaced the telephone receiver and switched off the tape, the silence a relief to his shattered nerves. So – it had finally happened. His worst fears were realised; it was all over.

Suddenly the door opened and Carmichael looked in. 'The silence,' he said, by way of explaining his intrusion. 'Where's Sylvia?'

'What?' barked Parker, startled by the interruption.

'I said, where's Sylvia?'

'Oh . . . she's gone out on an errand. She won't be long.' Parker replied irritably. 'I thought I told you I didn't want to be disturbed. Close the door.'

Unperturbed, Carmichael did as he was bid. Arrogant louse, he thought as he returned to his seat. In all his years in the force the one thing he'd become used to was waiting. Now he could sit for hours, planning in his mind the sort of retirement cottage he and Joan would buy when he finally got out of the game. Only seven years to go until he was fifty five; the earliest when he could finish with a comfortable pension, provided they didn't go mad with their money. He was looking forward to it immensely, and was sure his wife was too . . .

This time, Parker didn't throw half the whisky away. He drank it in two large gulps and then, with a second glass in his hand, sat down beside the fire and thought about the meeting he'd just had. All over, it was all over. All the work, all the effort – gone.

The meeting played back slowly through his mind. What was his name? Stawizcki? He was a humane man; he understood his, Parker's feelings, his objections. No – not objec-

160

tions; false hope, simply a hope quickly and apparently gleefully shattered by the other man, Henken. The most devastating blow was the revelation of Carmichael's real reason for being there. He, Parker, was being set up to be killed, and ... AND, according to them the Prime Minister knew about it. Had actually sanctioned it. The old cow. But Neil as well? God, it was hard to take.

He shuddered. Perhaps the Welsh Wonder wasn't such a pushover as the left wing thought. Perhaps under that bland exterior there really was a core of steel. If there was, it wasn't often in evidence.

His mind wandered off on a different tack, into politics and personalities but then returned abruptly to his own predicament. His first reaction had been to go to the police, confess everything, tell them about the plot to kill him; let justice prevail. All right – if he proved his story he'd end up in jail, but there would be an exchange in a few months, and he'd be out and in Russia. Meanwhile Britain and NATO would have suffered extreme embarrassment.

It hadn't taken much persuasion, though, to convince him that all aspects of the situation had been considered, and theirs was the only way. If he tried his plan, he'd probably end up in a mental home for the remainder of his days. With a sickening feeling he knew they spoke the truth. There was nothing to gain by trying things his way, and a lot to lose. For one thing, Special Branch would want to know how he had come by the information. The ones that mattered would know it to be true, for all the official denials. They'd start asking the right questions, and pretty soon they would come up with the right answers. One of the top Soviet sources of information ever received from a traitor would probably dry up.

At that point Sylvia Henshaw returned with his wife's birthday present. Parker told her abruptly to finish for the evening and to be in first thing in the morning. She noticed the half empty glass by his chair, but sensing his mood, refrained from comment. For the first time since she'd started working for him she realised that the thing that was worrying him far outweighed any problem he had had to deal with over the past three years. Murmuring her thanks and goodbye, she left him to his brooding.

Parker hardly noticed she had gone. He picked up the small parcel and fingered it. Thursday was Dorothy's birthday; he'd planned a special surprise. His eyes filled with tears of self pity. God, but he loved his wife. How many men could say that, after all these years together? Sure, they'd had their ups and downs – which two people didn't, but their marriage was basically a completely happy one. Could he persuade her to live with him in Russia? He had to. He needed her, always had done – and now he needed her more than ever. Could he make her understand why he'd done it – convince her that he'd had no choice? It was true. Once he'd been forced to start, the only thing to do was to carry on as best he could – and look where it had got him. He had been Secretary of State for Energy, was now Deputy Leader of the Opposition and with the distinct possibility of becoming Prime Minister one day. But that was all over now. There'd be no Socialist government, run along proper lines. Not like Wilson and his cronies, where only lip service was paid to the concept of Socialism. Would her love for him be stronger than her love for her country? He thought so . . . or maybe that was just wishful thinking? Whether it was or not, he clung to the idea like a drowning man clutching at straws.

Thinking of his wife, he remembered the instructions he'd been given. He'd send her away for the day, and leave a letter explaining everything to her. He prayed to God she'd understand. The second stunning blow that day was to be told he had to leave the next day. His first thought when he'd heard had been for his son. Would he ever understand? Certainly he would never join them in Russia. Them? It might only be himself. He shook his head. No, Dorothy would come after him; he was sure of that. Last Sunday was probably the last time he'd see his son, though. Heartache, he now knew, was a real physical pain.

162

When he'd tried to argue about the abruptness of his departure, they'd told him about Carmichael's true role. Carmichael. The dislike he'd felt for the man had hardened instantly into hatred. All his problems, the collapse of his world as he knew it were manifested in Carmichael. Given the chance, he would kill the man without a moment's hesitation.

Mixed with his anger Parker felt a bitter disappointment. He was not afraid for his life, though he knew he was in danger; one false move, indeed, and he'd be dead. The knowledge didn't particularly bother him; what did bother him, what stuck in his throat more than anything was the lost opportunity. The premiership – so near, and now dashed away. The thought tortured him. The injustice of it . . . the unfairness. All his dreams, all the plans. Once the knowledge of his real identity became public it would set the left wing back ten, no, twenty years. The Tribune group, of which he was undisputed leader, would be in disarray. People he'd known as friends for many years would begin to despise and then hate him as their power and influence in the party inevitably waned. The press, even their own left wing papers, would crucify them – and the Tory rags would have a field day.

He conveniently forgot that in order for him to achieve his ambitions, his goals, the Leader of the Party would have to die. As he had slid closer to his destination his megalomania had grown, slowly at first but even more strongly. Now he saw the death of Kinnock as just one more justifiable step. The true socialist dream was within his grasp. Only a few more years had been necessary. One more gigantic push. The daydream took hold for a few seconds and then was dashed away in the cold grip of reality.

He got up to pour himself another drink. He could hardly believe the situation in which he now so suddenly found himself. Not only was he not going to be Prime Minister, he was going back to Russia, a failed agent. But no – that was stupid. He hadn't failed. He'd done more, achieved more

163

than any other agent since the war, if not before it. The most audacious, most far reaching plan of the Soviets was about to fail, through no fault of his own.

The whisky was beginning to take effect. He was becoming maudlin, thinking, remembering. Thoughts of Simon crowded in; Simon as a small boy, growing up . . . Dropping the glass, heedless of the spilled whisky, he buried his face in his hands and wept.

An hour later, outwardly composed, Parker left his study, walked past Carmichael without so much as a glance in his direction and ascended the stairs to his bedroom. He needed to lie down, to arrange his thoughts and decide what he was going to tell his wife when she returned later. He had been told arrangements would be made for his family to follow, which was all well and good – but what about the meantime? How would Dorothy cope as the target of the country's hatred and contempt? Happy birthday my darling, he thought sadly.

*   *   *

The five of them were in high spirits as they turned off the M1 motorway into Boreham Wood Services. Everything had gone without a hitch, exactly as planned. The others were less than two minutes behind, on schedule. Emile Parri parked the car and amidst much laughter Enis Baum, Nasima Karami, Abdul Meuin and Ibrahim Bakr climbed out. The laughter was a more nervous than merry sound, but to a casual onlooker the group were what they were pretending to be . . . a bunch of French youngsters on holiday.

Deeply tanned, thin, an attractive group, obviously from the south or even with Algerian connections.

A second car drew up alongside, and five more joined the group. Their reunion was joyous, as though they hadn't seen each other for some days – which in fact was almost the case. Since Nuri Khatun, Amie Bustani, Rashid Yagir, Aman al-Baz and Maneka Kamal had left Holland a couple of days earlier, the car containing Enis and her companions had passed them on the motorway a few minutes earlier, but this was their first opportunity of communicating. They were all elated that they'd managed to make it, and had got through customs without a hitch.

The forged passports they were travelling on were of the very best. Supplied by the PLO in Beirut they were all originals with doctored photographs. Most passports stolen across the world now end up with one terrorist organisation or another. The operation was so sophisticated that the little books, identity card, driving licences and all the minutiae that goes to establish an identity was correlated and indexed. It was possible to go to the files and find a French caucasian, aged between 25 and 30, 5ft. 8 ins. tall, weighing 140 lbs. brown hair, brown eyes. The passports with that description were pulled out and the photograph closest to the subject was taken. A slight doctoring of the photo, the subject or both resulted in a passport that no customs or immigration man was going to look twice at. Terrorism on a world-wide scale had come a long way since the old days.

As the ten young people made their way to the restaurant, laughing and chattering, a police car drew up in front of them. Scared, they moved apart, each one on the verge of flight, but Enis, looking around, realised there was only one car and said sharply:

'Pull yourselves together. It's just one car containing two policemen; they're traffic cops, that's all, patrolling the motorway.'

'I wish I had a gun with me,' muttered Ibrahim Bakr and one of the others murmured agreement.

'And what would you do with it, stupid?' Enis retorted, in a savage undertone. 'Kill two policemen, and get us all arrested? Keep your heads, for God's sake. Come on – follow me.'

She marched on determinedly towards the restaurant, deliberately passing close to the stationary police car. On the spur of the moment she swerved, walked directly up to the vehicle and tapped on the window. The driver, a sergeant, wound it down.

'Yes miss? Can I help you?' he enquired, eyeing her admiringly.

'I hope you can,' she replied, with a dazzling smile, exaggerating her accent. 'Can you tell me please how far it is to Edinburgh from here?' The Scottish city was the first place that came to mind.

'It's a long way,' the policeman replied. 'About 350 miles, I reckon. What would you say, Bert?' he added, turning to his companion.

'Yeah, Alf, I guess it's about that,' the other policeman replied disinterestedly.

'Thank you, officer.' Enis straightened up and hurried to catch up with her companions. Emile Parri paused to wait for her just inside the door, and she smiled pleasantly as she joined him.

'What the hell did you do that for?' he demanded fiercely, speaking in a French dialect barely discernible to other Frenchmen.

'Because I felt like it,' she retorted. 'Just to show the others.'

'To show them what? All you did was scare them even more than they were already.'

'Serve them right. We've got a job to do, and I mean to do it. I just want Jemel out, and to hell with the rest. The cowards . . .'

'I wouldn't say too much, too loudly if I were you,' Bakr interrupted. 'We need them, and we need them completely and wholeheartedly on our side, so don't do anything else that might alienate them. We're all in this together, and don't you forget it.'

He turned on his heel and marched off towards the toilets, leaving Enis standing there feeling rather small, and already regretting her stupidity. She made her way into the eating area – it did not deserve the name of restaurant – and queued at the counter with a tray. The food looked unappetising, but she was hungry, and settled for soggy chips, burnt sausages and cold beans. As she sat at the table with a couple of the

166

others she was overcome with depression, her previous
elation having entirely disappeared. Having picked at the
mess on her plate, she laid down her knife and fork and
pushed the plate away with a grimace of disgust.

'Revolting, isn't it?' said Amie Bustani, also pushing her
plate away. 'The British have the palates of peasants.'

Enis forced a smile. 'I think you're right. Ugh! The coffee
is just as bad.'

After a few seconds' silence, Rashid Yagir, a slight, intelligent looking boy, asked: 'What did you say to the police,
Enis? You sure had us worried for a moment.'

She gave a brittle laugh. 'I only asked how far it was to
Edinburgh. If the pig remembers me – and from the way he
was looking I don't see how he can forget – he'll have one
hell of a thrill when he reads the papers in a couple of days
time. He'll be able to tell all his friends, assuming he has any,
that he actually spoke to me!'

Her companions exchanged glances, and began to smile.
All at once the tension eased and they began talking among
themselves, keeping their voices low, although the restaurant was virtually empty, and speaking in French. They
swapped stories about the journey and their passage through
British customs, making it all sound more dramatic than it
really was.

After half an hour, one or two of them began making nervous suggestions about moving on. Travelling in the cloi-
stered confines of a car had given them a feeling of security,
of invulnerability. Here, subject to the stares of strangers
and with nowhere to run to, nowhere to hide, they felt
exposed. Enis understood this, experiencing the same sensa-
tions herself.

'We'll go in a moment,' she said. 'Now you all know where
we'll meet next . . . on the boat. Don't forget to find a decent
hotel for tonight, and put together . . .' She broke off.
'Well, you all know what to do, so let's go. Good luck,' she
added, as the occupants of the second car rose and left the
table.

A few minutes later she and her group followed. Now there was no laughter, no attempt to lighten their feelings. They were on the final lap leading to only one of two possible endings; disaster and possible death, or glorious achievement. All were confident that the latter would be the case. Only Abdul Meuin had doubts – a premonition – but he dared not risk the ridicule of his companions by voicing them . . .

*   *   *

Janet met Barber at the station. The pleasant, warm after-noon had deteriorated into a wet evening, with a cold blustery wind. The weather did nothing to dampen Janet's spirits, however. She felt as giddy and breathless as a school-girl on her first heavy date; she wanted to skip and sing, but instead expressed her feelings only in a broad smile. Typi-cally the train was late, but even that didn't upset her as much as it usually did. I guess, she thought, I really am in love.

At last the train pulled in. She stood at the back of the dozen or so other people waiting to meet family, friends and lovers, content now that the moment was here to extend the period of waiting. She couldn't stop herself from waving though, as Barber walked up the platform towards her. He grinned in return.

'Bloody British Rail!' he greeted her, kissing her warmly.

'At least your here, and that's the main thing,' she replied. 'Come on. I'll buy you a drink, and afterwards I'll help you to forget the hassles of the journey.'

'What journey?' he said, squeezing her hand tightly.

Later, in the bed-sit, after a simple meal of steak and salad, they settled on the settee. Presently Barber said: 'What's wrong, love? You keep kind of withdrawing, as though you have something on your mind. It's not us, is it?'

'Should I worry about us?' She countered, and after a pause went on. 'No actually it's my boss. I saw him today in the park with two other men, and whatever they'd said certainly seemed to have upset him.'

'Oh? How so?' Barber asked, trying to appear casually interested, although his pulse was racing, wondering if one of the men was Carmichael.

She told him, adding that although she couldn't remember what Parker had said, she had a feeling it was the key to the problem, from the way he'd exclaimed.

'Try and think,' Barber urged. 'It may be something important.'

She shook her head. 'It's no good. I've been trying to remember all afternoon. Anyway,' she added, snuggling up to him, 'it doesn't matter. Let's forget about him and concentrate of us.'

Silence reigned for a few minutes as they kissed, Barber's hand stealing under her jumper and up to her bra. Damnation, it was no good, he thought. He had to know what the hell had been going on that afternoon. He wondered irrelevently how spies managed to cope, pretending to enjoy themselves while trying to extract information from their partners – and soon became aware that he knew the answer. In spite of his preoccupation he was getting an erection.

He cleared his throat. 'Excuse me love, I'll just pour some more wine.' Removing his hand, he leant forward to fill their glasses from the second bottle of rosé they'd opened that evening. He felt Janet stretch her arms and heard a rustle. When he turned back she was undoing her bra and discarding it. He lifted the glasses and handed her one.

'Cheers,' he said, his voice suddenly husky, all thoughts of Parker and his problem forgotten. As he looked at her breasts her nipples puckered. They clinked glasses, his other hand reached out to stroke her gently. Leaning forward, she put her hand in his lap and at the same time poured a little wine onto her left breast. Barber bent and licked up the wine, then slowly teased her nipple with his tongue and lips, feeling it harden as he did so.

'Hmmm, that's good,' she murmured. 'Come on, let's take the wine to bed with us.'

They both stood up, still clinging to each other. Janet unzipped him, wormed her hand inside his trousers, and giggled. 'Hang on – I'll show you how the sofa unfolds. You see? Living room and bedroom combined. That way I save time.'

Releasing him, she bent to pull the bottom of the sofa forward. As she did so Barber lifted her skirt, pulled her panties down past her knees and then off.

'Don't move,' he said, inserting himself from behind.

Later they made up the bed and lay with their arms wrapped around each other.

'I don't suppose you've thought what your boss said,' Barber murmured presently.

'You're joking! Anyway, if I said I did you'd be most upset, wouldn't you? Thinking about him instead of concentrating on all the nice things you were doing to me.'

He chuckled. 'I guess so.' How the hell, he wondered, was he supposed to find out what he wanted to know without explaining why he wanted to know it – which, of course, was out of the question.

Unexpectedly Janet said: 'I told you I thought about it this afternoon. I'm sure I heard him say 'tomorrow's ferry' but that doesn't make sense. If he was going anywhere I'd certainly know about it, because I always make his travel arrangements. I know he's going to Scandinavia at the weekend, because I made the bookings. Therefore his reference to the ferry, if that's what it was, is nonsensical.'

Barber's heart was hammering like a pile driver. She was wrong; there was sense to be made of it, assuming she had heard correctly. But where the hell was Carmichael during all this? He was supposed to stick close to Parker. Maybe one of the men was the Chief Superintendent. Maybe Parker's plans had changed for some unknown reason – but no, that didn't make sense. None of it made sense. He sighed. Nothing for it but to sit tight and wait to hear from

170

Carmichael. Or maybe 'phone him and let him know what he'd learned.

As he was looking at his watch, his mind registering the fact that it was one o'clock on Wednesday morning, Janet dropped her bombshell.

'There was another odd fact about this afternoon. My boss told me that he had a policeman trailing around to protect him or something and last week I saw him standing with Parker outside the House . . . Parliament, that is. I saw him quite clearly, and I'm pretty sure who it was. I'm equally sure that neither of the men with Parker today was that policeman. Of course,' she went on, furrowing her brow, 'they could be guarding him by roster or something – but somehow I didn't get that impression from him.' She laughed. 'Listen to me. I'm making a mystery where none exists. Guess I've been reading too many novels. Anyway, let's get some sleep.' She kissed him. ''Night, darling. Don't forget you have to be out of here before dawn, and I've got to go to work.'

'Goodnight love.' Barber responded, glad to have the opportunity to think about this latest bit of information . 'Sleep well.'

Chapter 13

Ironically, one floor and two rooms across, the subject of Barber's ponderings was spending a sleepless night. Parker and his wife had been to see an amateur production of Wilde's 'The Importance of Being Earnest' a play he normally enjoyed. That evening, though, his thoughts had, not unnaturally, been elsewhere, he had to talk to Dorothy, explain the situation to her – but how the hell was he to do it? All evening he'd looked for an opening, but none had occurred, and now, lying wakeful beside her, he sighed deeply. What had he been expecting? An opportunity to drop casually into the conversation the information that he was Russian by birth, and not the man he appeared to be at all? He was a coward, and he knew it – but he couldn't bring himself to hurt her. Fool! His conscience screamed at him. If you don't tell her, she'll suffer that much more when she does find out.

An involuntary groan escaped Parker's lips, and Dorothy stirred and slipped an arm around him.

'What is it, Edward?' she asked softly. 'Tell me what's wrong. Something's worrying you, I know. You've not been yourself for several days now.'

The bitter irony of her last words pierced him like a knife. 'All right,' he said, sighing heavily. 'I'll tell you. Let me switch on the light so I can see you.' He reached out and turned on the bedside lamp. His wife's face, pale against the white pillow, was creased with anxiety.

'I . . . I don't really know how to tell you this,' he began, then stopped as two large tears coursed down her cheeks. 'Darling – what's the matter? What have I said?'

She shook her head. 'I never dreamt . . . I thought we were so happy together . . .'

Parker felt the tears rise in his own eyes as he put his arms around her, saying, 'Darling, darling, Dorothy, it's not that. Don't you know yet it could never be that? I love you and only you. There'll never be anyone else, no matter what happens.'

She sighed. 'For a moment . . . I thought . . . another woman. Oh – thank God . . .'

Then, her own fear dispelled, she went on anxiously, 'What is it, Edward? Tell me.'

He dried his eyes on the sheet, then did the same for her.

'I . . . I'm not sure how to tell you this,' he began. 'It's going to come as a dreadful shock, and will upset you so much . . .'

'Then don't keep me in suspense,' she interrupted. 'Tell me, and let's get it over. As long as you never leave me I can stand any shock, believe me.'

Parker took a deep breath. 'I'm not an Englishman,' he said, watching her eyes grow wide with disbelief. 'I'm Russian.'

Once he'd admitted that much it was easy, or relatively so. He told her everything as he knew it, only omitted all reference to Carmichael and his role in the matter. He gave as his reason for returning to Russia imminent exposure by a Soviet defector. It was almost the truth, and he didn't see any need to worry her more than necessary.

When he'd finished there was silence in the room for a full minute; then Dorothy drew a deep breath.

'That's some confession. I'm not sure what to say.'

'Don't say anything for a moment. I'm going to ask you one question, and I want you to consider only that, and give me your answer in the morning.' He glanced at the alarm clock. 'Well – it's nearly five now. Perhaps I should say when you wake up. Dorothy – will you come and live with me in Russia?'

She looked startled. 'Think about it?' His heart sank; her

173

mind was made up without any need for reflection. 'Don't be silly. There's nothing to think about. Of course I'll come with you. What else would I do?'

He looked at her, his face transfigured. 'You mean that? You really mean it?'

'Of course.' She put her arms around him and hugged him. 'You're still my man, no matter what happens. There's only one problem.'

'Simon?'

She nodded.

'I know,' he said softly. 'I don't know what to do about it. Perhaps you could talk to him. Try and make him understand I had no choice – explain about my parents, his grandparents. Ask him to put himself in my shoes if he can. Tell him what my plans were had I been made Prime Minister. Try and make him understand, please Dot.'

'Of course I will.' She drew his head down on her breast and stroked his hair, like a mother comforting her distressed child.

*   *   *

At the same time that Edward Parker was making his confession to his wife, another couple were having a sleepless night. John Smith was a man as mediocre as his name. After a lifetime in the Civil Service he'd just retired from a middle grade post in the Inland Revenue, having opted for a small pension, and commuted the maximum he was allowed by the regulations. Instead of buying the dream cottage he and his wife had planned, he was spending every penny available on a world cruise for them both.

There was no point in buying the cottage. They had no children, and he didn't want to linger along until the end of his days, living out the dream he and Ida had shared. A lonely old age frightened him more than his wife would ever realise. It was better this way, to enjoy their last few months together as much as possible. Ida would be dead within three

174

months from leukemia; she'd had her final blood transfusion only two weeks previously, and the doctors were reluctantly convinced that nothing further could be done. There were drugs that would reduce the discomfort to a tolerable level. Tolerable? What a word to use. What was tolerable, with only three months to live?

John Smith, anguish tearing at him, turned to his wife lying beside him, and cuddled closer. She stirred, and he realised that she too was awake.

'Are we doing the right thing?' she asked softly. 'I mean, what are we doing staying in this posh hotel in Hull, waiting for a boat to take us to a liner to go on a world cruise? It's a waste of our savings, John. Don't you agree?'

'No I don't,' her husband replied quietly. 'We've done it, it's all paid for so we may as well enjoy ourselves.' Just in time he avoided adding, 'while we can.' Why us, God? he asked, for the millionth time since they'd learnt of Ida's condition nearly a year previously; why us? Of the two of them, Ida had taken the news the most stoically. Her immediate thought was for her husband. How could he manage without her? Who would make his breakfast, clean up, wash his clothes? These things worried her more than her own approaching death.

John Smith viewed the future with a sense of desolation. The loneliness would be unbearable without Ida. He simply could not envisage what his life would be like.

There was one factor that sustained them through their ordeal; they both had a deep and sincere belief in God, had no doubts that they would meet again one day in paradise. Only the prospect of the waiting time between was daunting.

'How about a cup of tea?' Ida said presently. 'There's a kettle over there on the side. Only powdered milk, I'm afraid, but it'll do.'

'Yes – good idea.' John groaned suddenly, and buried his face between her breasts. 'Oh, Ida – I do love you . . .'

★   ★   ★

Fear was keeping Simon Birdridge awake, that early Wednesday morning. He'd prayed for hours but it hadn't done any good; the fear was still there, a live animal gnawing away at his guts. He was deeply ashamed of his terror, because he knew that underlying it was a lack of faith. He just didn't have the courage to go to an outback missionary post in Rhodesia as a representative of the Pentecostal church.

Simon had been ordained in the church for five years, since just after his twenty first birthday, and during that time had worked and preached all over England and Wales. He had never been abroad, but after the mission Rhodesia had been attacked and horribly destroyed, volunteers had been called for, and he knew, from the way it was put to him, that he was expected to put his name forward. He did so, and, since his fear of flying was well known within the movement, it was arranged that he should go by ship. He'd be taking the ferry to Rotterdam, a liner from there to Cape Town and then travel by train through South Africa and up to Rhodesia. At the border he'd be met by a church member and taken to his destination, less than thirty miles from the place where the attack had been carried out – an attack that had caught the imagination of every newspaper in the free world.

Simon had read and seen so many of the newsclips covering the incident that the scene played around and around his mind every waking moment, nearly driving him mad. Now he tossed and turned, and then his alarm clock showed five-thirty, gave up trying to sleep. Getting up, he went into the kitchen of his small Bayswater flat to make a cup of coffee. Before he caught the train for Hull he'd have a long session in prayer. Perhaps it would help him, sustain him through the day. That was all he asked for; help to get through the day.

★   ★   ★

While Simon Birdridge was making coffee, Steve Barber was trying to sneak out of bed without disturbing Janet. He in-

176

tended catching the first train back to town, find out the times of flights to Holland and the time of the ferry from Hull. Once he'd done that he'd contact Carmichael and tell him what he knew. That way, he figured, they could hedge their bets to the maximum.

He shaved and dressed quietly, thinking about Janet. Once this is over, he told himself, I'll find a decent job, settle down and see if she'll make a go of it with me. He grimaced at his reflection. It would be over in a few days – and then what? He wasn't sure, but oddly enough he was feeling confident and lucky. As he knotted his tie he realised his mood was the result of a successful night of love making; it had left him with the feeling that he could take on the world and win. The trouble was, he knew it wouldn't last.

When he was ready to leave he crossed to the bed and stood looking down at Janet, peacefully sleeping. Then with a small sigh he left the room and quietly let himself out of the house via the fire escape.

Half an hour later, at a quarter past six, he was on the train for London, concentrating entirely now on the job he was to do for Carmichael.

The train was on time, arriving just after nine twenty. A lowering sky threatened rain, and people hurried about their business wearing light raincoats or carrying furled umbrellas. It took Barber twenty minutes to find a travel agency and another twenty to accumulate the information he required. Then he returned to his flat, checked there were no messages on his answering machine and picked up the telephone.

'Hullo?' said a female voice on the other end of the line, when he had dialled the number he had been given. Drat the girl – why couldn't she learn to answer the telephone properly, either with a number or a name?

'Hullo?' he said irritated. 'Who's that?'

There came a soft cough. 'Excuse me, sir – who's calling please?'

He only just stopped himself from giving his name. 'Let

177

me speak to Chief Superintendent Carmichael,' he said harshly.

'I'm sorry, the Chief Superintendent isn't here. May I take a message?'

'Look, before I say anything will you tell me who you are?' demanded Barber.

'Don't you know, sir? After all, you rang the number.'

'For God's sake, woman! If I knew I wouldn't have asked, would I? I don't mean your name but your organisation, your department, whatever.'

'I understood perfectly well what you meant.' The female voice was icy now. 'I'm the duty officer at Special Branch. I can't put you through to the Chief Superintendent, but I can relay a message.'

'How long will that take?' Barber asked, trying to make his tone more pacific.

'As long as it takes me to locate him, sir,' came the cool reply.

Biting back an angry retort, Barber said, 'Don't take too long, sweetheart, or there could be trouble. Tell him that Phil's operation is scheduled for next week. Have you got that?'

'I take it that the important word is operation?' she said tartly.

If ever there was a case of instant dislike between two people who'd never met, this was it. The girl shouldn't have said what she had, but she wanted to ruffle the caller. She had had a long and irritating night, and because her relief had been taken ill she was still on duty, three hours later than she should have been. She had to take it out on someone.

'No it's not,' lied Barber, 'it's scheduled. So just pass the message as I told you, and hope we never meet in the future.' He slammed down the receiver, then remembered he'd intended to let Carmichael know where he'd be. Stupid, bloody girl; it was all her fault. He was about to 'phone back, then decided against it. There wasn't any point really. Carmichael would know he'd be waiting for him to ring the flat, and the less conversation he had with that bitch the better.

The next few hours were amongst the longest in Barber's life, and when he eventually moved there had still been no 'phone call from Carmichael.

★   ★   ★

The Right Honourable Edward Parker had spent the morning putting his private affairs in order. Sylvia Henshaw, his secretary, and Janet Walker, his personal assistant, had both been given the day off, and he'd worked alone in his study until just before ten o'clock. He had then driven his wife to the station in his own car, Carmichael following behind in a taxi. Dorothy was going to spend the day and night with her sister before returning to Hull the next day. Probably by then the news would have broken; his true identity would be public knowledge. When that happened, Dorothy wanted to be alone, away from everybody. Parker understood how she felt; he'd want to do exactly the same.

On the way back from the station he called in at his bank, had a word with the manager and withdrew a large sum of money. Carmichael, by this time, was feeling distinctly alarmed. What the hell was going on? Only that morning he'd checked with the Walker girl and she'd assured him that Parker wasn't planning to leave the country until the weekend. Nevertheless he had a gut feeling that there was something amiss.

He'd been a policeman too long not to trust his instincts, but he analysed the day so far and found nothing particularly unusual about it. Parker had given his two girls the day off. Fine – so that made him a considerate boss. God knew they seemed to work hard enough. His wife had gone visiting relations, and he, Parker, had been to see his bank manager. Everything normal ... and yet. There was a kind of finality about it all ... The more he thought about it, the more convinced Carmichael became that Parker knew. Somehow they'd got to him; he was sure of it. The way the man had been behaving, his tenseness, the strain he appeared to be suffering – it all added up. Was it possible? Could the Russians have moved so quickly? Possible, in this game anything was possible.

For the trip back he was sitting in the passenger seat of Parker's Rover, and so had no chance to get to a 'phone before they arrived back at the house. He needed to make two calls, one to Branch and one to Barber to get him ready to move.

Carmichael spent a frustrating half hour trying to find a way to use the 'phone without alerting Parker. Finally, realising that any excuse to leave the house while the latter was still there would look suspicious, especially as he'd taken such pains to impress on him that he, Carmichael, had to be with him at all times, the Chief Superintendent decided to ring his office whether Parker was present or not.

Parker went into his study and left Carmichael in the hall. The Superintendent at once picked up the telephone standing on the hall table, wincing as the bell tinkled, and rang his office. He knew that the 'phone he was using was an extension of the one in the study, but that couldn't be helped. If Parker wanted to listen in there was little he could do about it. At least anything he, Carmichael, was told would be couched in such terms that only he would understand it.

'Carmichael here,' he said tersely. 'Give me the operations officer.'

'Just a moment, sir. I have a message for you. Anne took it and asked me to pass it on; she said you'd understand.' This time the voice was male. 'It reads, "Phil's operation is scheduled for next week". Does that make sense, sir?'

'Yes,' replied Carmichael gruffly. 'It's a family message about a ... er ... a cousin of mine. Er ... you can forget about the Ops officer for now. If there's anything ... No, never mind. I'll 'phone in tomorrow. Goodbye.' He waited until the line was clear, and then heard the distinct click of the extension being replaced. The dialling tone resumed; this was his chance to use the 'phone again without alerting Parker.

180

He'd dialled four of the nine digits when a voice behind him said: 'Put the 'phone down gently, Superintendent, and slowly turn around. One sudden move and you're a dead man.'

Carmichael did as he was told, and found himself facing three men, two of whom were levelling silenced guns directly at him.

'We meet at last, Chief Superintendent Carmichael,' the eldest of the three newcomers said pleasantly, his gun still steadily pointing. 'You must excuse me if I do not shake hands. It is difficult, you understand.' His voice had the faintest of accents.

'Perfectly, Stawizcki. How was the Middle East?'

Carmichael had given no hint of the shock he'd had when he saw who was behind him. He would have recognised their professionalism by the way they'd spread out and the way they had him covered, without needing to recognise the two with the guns. The third would come forward to disarm him, lacking the encumbrance of a gun himself and thus avoiding even the slim chance of Carmichael's grabbing him and his weapon. Even as Carmichael thought this, the man stepped forward. Expert hands quickly searched him and removed his .38 Special.

'The Middle East? Not quite as good as it might have been, as you well know, thanks to you and your organisation,' Stawizcki replied politely.

Carmichael shrugged modestly. 'We do our best . . .'

'Look, cut the crap,' Henken said harshly in Russian to Stawizcki. 'This isn't a social gathering.'

Carmichael grinned, pleased he'd nettled the Hangman. 'Wilhelm, you really should learn to curb your impatience, especially when your betters are talking,' he said softly in fluent Russian.

Henken looked startled for a second, then quickly recovered his poise. 'So you know me? I'm flattered but unimpressed.'

'Oh, I don't think you'd be flattered if you knew what I've been told,' said Carmichael needling him more.

Henken flushed a dark red and Stawizcki, fearing he might do something stupid, intervened. 'Enough. Please keep silent, Chief Superintendent. If you do as I say there's a distinct possibility you may live to see another day. If not . . .' He waggled his gun, grimacing at the same time. 'Now, kindly step into the study.'

A few minutes later Carmichael was securely tied to a chair. Ten seconds of surreptitiously flexing his muscles had been enough to convince him he could never get free.

Turning to Parker, who had been watching impassively, Uri Stawizcki said, 'I'm sure we could all do with some coffee. I suggest you go with Gerhard to the kitchen and make some and at the same time he can tell you about our travel arrangements.'

Parker hesitated for a moment, then walked away word-lessly, Gerhard Karpov following.

'I didn't think it wise for you to learn how we were travel-ling,' Stawizcki went on, smiling benignly at Carmichael. 'Now, provided we keep you incommunicado for at least 24 hours, I cannot really see any point in your . . . what is the word? Demise?'

In spite of the situation, Carmichael couldn't help smiling back at his adversary. They had been remotely connected for over ten years, each recognising the other's handiwork whenever he came in contact with it. During that time a mutual respect had grown up, between professionals. Neither killed nor ordered a killing if it could be avoided, and Carmichael thanked God now that they'd sent Stawizcki to get Parker out.

'The word is quite correct,' he said. 'I congratulate you on your command of the English language. It has improved con-siderably over the last five years.'

Intrigued, Stawizcki said: 'How do you know what my English was like five years ago?'

'Remember the cell we broke up in Paris? You had been running it for . . . what . . . two years?'

Stawizcki nodded.

'We realised they'd outgrown their usefulness; that was why you let us take them. After all, what's eighteen French traitors? It allowed at least six of your own men to get back to Russia with the minimum of effort. I've always been sure it was your voice on the tape you left for us.'

Stawizcki smiled. 'Your assumption was correct. In fact on that occasion eight of my men got away.'

'That doesn't surprise me. A pity I was two days too late in realising it. By the time I knew what was going on I'd lost you. Still, one can't win them all.'

'There is never a winner, Jim. We only manage to maintain some kind of status quo.'

Parker and Karpov returned, the latter carrying a tray with coffee and sandwiches. 'I thought you might be hungry. He says you haven't eaten yet,' Parker said, nodding at Karpov.

'Thank you, you are most considerate.'

Stawizcki watched as Henken grabbed a sandwich and began stuffing it in his mouth. Everything about him made Stawizcki wince, and as he turned away he caught Carmichael's eye. A spark flashed between the two men; they both knew if they hadn't been antagonists, they'd be friends.

Christ, thought Carmichael, not for the first time, what a lousy world. He kidded himself he was helping to maintain the peace, but sometimes he wondered; wondered too how many other men in his line of work thought the same way.

'Untie his left hand and give him coffee,' Stawizcki said to Karpov.

'There's no spare cup,' Parker told him, with satisfaction.

'Then give him mine. Gerhard, fetch me another please.'

Parker's face darkened with sullen resentment as Karpov did as he was told.

'Thank you, Uri,' Carmichael said softly, flexing his left hand before taking the cup Karpov offered him.

There was no need to explain what was going to happen next. Henken removed the telephone receiver and they all settled down. Sipping his coffee, Carmichael wondered how long they'd be waiting. Although he ate and drank as slowly as he could, he finished finally and Henken crossed to retie his arm to the chair. Just before he did so Carmichael managed to pull back his sleeve and look at his watch. Ten past two.

★   ★   ★

Barber finally threw the paperback across the room, gave up all pretence of trying to remain calm and began to pace the floor, every few seconds casting a glance at the telephone. Ring, damn you, ring, he ordered the instrument.

By one thirty he'd had enough, and rang the number again. He was thankful that a man answered, and not the girl he had spoken to earlier.

'Look, I wonder if you can help me. I've been expecting to hear from Chief Superintendent Carmichael for the last few hours. Can you tell me whether he received the information about . . . er . . . about an operation?'

'You mean the message that Phil's operation is next week, sir?'

'That's the one.'

'Oh – I passed it to him myself about an hour and a half ago. I'd been trying to get through earlier, but . . .'

'Yes, well – thanks. Now listen, I can't give you my name, but believe me it's vital that I contact the Chief as soon as possible. Can you give me the number where he is right now?'

'I'm sorry, sir . . .'

'Okay, okay,' interrupted Barber impatiently. 'I know the routine. Just tell me one thing, is it a Hull number? That's all I ask, and believe me it's very important.'

There was a moment of silence, then the man said reluctantly. 'Well, I can tell you that much, I suppose. It is a Hull number.'

'Thanks.'

Barber hung up, pulled his wallet from his hip pocket and

found the piece of paper Janet had given him with Parker's number on it, in case he wanted to ring her. He dialled quickly, glancing at the wall clock as he did so. 1.45 – engaged. Five minutes later, engaged. And again, and again, engaged. He waited until 2.30 and tried once more. Still engaged. His mind was made up.

Adjusting his shoulder holster, Barber put on his jacket and overcoat, grabbed his holdall with the sniper's rifle carefully hidden in the bottom and left the flat. He had to hurry; the next train for Hull left in twenty minutes. The taxi driver was delighted with the offer of an extra fiver, payable only if they made it in time. They did, with three minutes to spare.

★　★　★

It was three thirty. Henken and Stawizcki had gone upstairs to rest, leaving Parker and Karpov to watch Carmichael. Stawizcki had insisted on the arrangement because, as he said, the dangerous time would be when they left the house, and there would be little chance of much sleep for at least the next 24 hours. If there were any callers, Parker would have to deal with them while Karpov kept his eye and a gun on Carmichael.

'I regret leaving you like this, Jim,' Stawizcki said before departing. 'I would have enjoyed talking to you. Before I go, tell me one thing. Why do you keep up the pretence of being a Special Branch officer? Why not operate in your proper position as a member of the British Secret Service? I'd have thought you could wield more power that way.'

Parker's startled double take made the Chief Superintendent smile.

'You'd be surprised, Uri, how wrong you are,' he replied. 'By showing my SB warrant card I can get a certain amount of response from some people when I need it. If I showed even an ordinary policeman my Service ID he'd think it was a leg pull.'

'A . . . leg pull?'

'A joke. Also, of course, it means I can come and go at SB's headquarters as I please, and use their facilities at will – which, I may add, are in some areas infinitely better than the Service's. Budgets and all that.'

Stawizcki nodded understandingly. 'We have a similar problem, though I suspect not nearly as great as your own. We were surprised to hear you were the brains behind this case. We thought you could only act abroad.'

Carmichael showed no reaction to these words. Stawizcki had made a grave error, and if any of them there realised it then he, Carmichael, was a dead man; of that he had no doubt.

'That's true enough – but we do our ground work here. The plan was to be executed . . . I do beg your pardon.' He broke off to smile mockingly at Parker. 'An unfortunate choice of words. The plan, as I was saying, was to be carried out in Holland. Hence my involvement.'

'I see.' Stawizcki was moving towards the door. 'Keep a close watch on him,' he added to Karpov as he left.

Carmichael's brain was racing. They knew of his involvement in Russia; in other words they were aware of it only days after he'd started on the operation. They knew that he was the brains behind it. Not running it but behind it! Only six men – no, eight if one included the Prime Minister and the Leader of the Opposition knew what he was up to. Himself and Barber, and he'd stake his life Barber wasn't the traitor: his boss, Sir Joseph Stark, head of the Secret Service, and the three men at the original meeting. It had to be one of them, but which one? He occupied himself in pondering the problem, trying not to think what would happen if Stawizcki realised the mistake he had made.

The clock in the hall chimed four o'clock. Parker had nervously paced the study ever since the other two had left, while Karpov sat quietly watching Carmichael, noting him surreptitiously trying to flex his muscles, and strain at his bonds. Carmichael knew he'd noticed; he wasn't trying to escape, that was impossible. All he was doing was letting the blood flow in different areas of his body as he eased first one part and then another.

Another hour dragged by, during which Parker chain-smoked his way through an almost full packet of cigarettes, smoking only half and then stubbing the rest out in the over-flowing ash tray. A few minutes later Stawizcki and Henken rejoined them, having slept quiet well, or so they both claimed. They certainly looked fresh enough.

'Now James,' said Stawizcki, 'the time has come to say goodbye. I fear you'll spend a rather uncomfortable night, but I'm sure you will be found some time tomorrow.'

'I still say we should kill him,' grunted the Hangman. 'What's the point of letting him live?'

'One day, Wilhelm – and God help us when that day comes – you may be in charge of an operation where you have carte blanche to do as you see fit; instead of merely being pointed at a target and told to kill. Until that day comes I suggest you shut up and do as you're told.' The lack of emotion in Stawizcki's voice was more frightening than if he'd showed anger or disgust.

'I shall report this as soon as we get back,' Henken retorted sullenly. 'And I shall report you as well . . .'

'I've no doubt you will,' interrupted Stawizcki. 'Now shut up, for God's sake.' He turned to Karpov. 'Help me to get him into the cellar. Parker, you go ahead and show us the way.'

Carmichael, his hands now tied behind his back, was led down a flight of steps into a dank cellar lit by one 60 watt electric bulb. One half contained coal, the other bits and pieces of junk of the kind normally accumulated in any household. Along one wall was a pipe carrying central heating from a separate bricked off area, and Carmichael was tied to this, his back to the wall and his hands at shoulder height.

'I apologise once more for the discomfort, but you shouldn't have too much difficulty in staying awake all night,' said Stawizcki, pausing with one foot on the step.

'Thanks Uri,' replied Carmichael. 'Goodbye.'

As Stawizcki left he switched off the light and the cellar was plunged into darkness.

Before the light went out Carmichael had been examining the pipe to which he was secured. About seven feet away, one end vanished into the brickwork, and about five feet the other way a staple fixed the pipe to the wall. There was another staple a few feet further on, and then the pipe did an unexpected U turn, downwards and then back up into the ceiling.

Carmichael braced himself against the wall and pulled on the pipe. It didn't budge. He moved along until he was next to the staple, swung on the pipe again and felt it move a fraction. Encouraged, he took hold of the pipe on either side of the staple and tried moving it up and down.

The cement between the bricks was old, and gradually the staple loosened. The length of pipe allowed some play and suddenly, unexpectedly the staple came out. Panting with the exertion, Carmichael worked the rope along to the end and with a sigh of relief brought his hands down in the rook of the U to waist level. By now his eyes were becoming accustomed to the dark and he could make out shapes in the blackness of the cellar.

Suddenly the light flicked on, blinding him temporarily. He blinked and squinted, and then recognised Parker as he descended the steps.

'So,' Parker sneered, 'trying to escape, are you?' He walked forward, stopping an arm's length from Carmichael, who stood poised, unsure of the man's intentions. He was soon to learn.

'I wanted to attack you all afternoon,' Parker went on. 'No, not attack. That's the wrong word. I wanted to kill you, with my hands. I had an overwhelming desire . . . after all this trouble you caused me.'

He must be unhinged, thought Carmichael, the strain has been too much.

Without any warning, Parker swung the short metal bar

188

he'd been carrying hidden behind his leg, slamming it viciously into Carmichael's lower rib cage. The pain made him gasp. Parker lifted the bar in both hands. Preparing to strike again. The blow, if it connected, would either smash Carmichael's ribs or permanently damage a kidney.

Grabbing the pipe at shoulder height to support himself, Carmichael kicked out with all his strength at Parker's crutch. He missed the target, but his foot caught the other man a hard blow in the stomach. With a grunt Parker bent double, dropping the bar and clutching himself in agony, gasping for breath.

Carmichael braced himself for the next onslaught as Parker slowly straightened up. The MP looked around for his bar, but it had rolled out of sight under the household rubbish. He stood there for a few seconds, rubbing his stomach and watching Carmichael through narrowed eyes. Then he said: 'I intended beating you to death, but there's not time. I have to get back to the car, they're waiting for me. Instead . . .' He bent down by the furthest wall and turned on a gas connection tap. The hiss of escaping gas was loud in the quiet cellar. 'I leave you to asphyxiate, slowly, I hope.'

Still holding his midriff, Parker limped up the stairs, switched off the light and slammed the door behind him. Carmichael stood still in the dark. Conscious that he was more afraid than he had ever been before.

Chapter 14

Barber watched the four men leave the house. He had arrived at the corner of the road only seconds before, and had stood there irresolute, trying to decide what to do next. In the train, it had seemed simple; one more attempt to telephone the house, and if he still got the engaged signal he'd knock boldly on the door and ask if he could speak to Carmichael.

There were two basic flaws in this plan, if it could be so called; hence his doubt as he arrived at the house. The first was that everything might be going exactly as arranged, and Carmichael would blow his top if he, Barber, appeared. The second was that there might be no one at home. They may have gone out for some reason, and someone had carelessly omitted to replace the receiver properly. The closer Barber had got to Hull, the more unsure he had become.

Although the men had left the house quite openly and unhurriedly, Barber noticed how observant they were, their eyes darting in all directions. He recognised Parker immediately, at the same time noting Carmichael's absence. The thick-set man who looked older than the rest glanced in his direction, then looked again. Barber, realising he had both to move and appear disinterested in them, walked up to the door of the nearest house and rang the bell. Trying to appear nonchalant, he gazed about him, half of his mind concentrated on the car the men had just climbed into, the other half on what he was going to say when the door opened. If it opened. He hoped fervently that there was nobody at home.

The door did open, and a well dressed, elderly lady stood

looking at him enquiringly. In films, novels and on radio a man in Barber's position deals with the situation calmly, quickly and fluently. Barber stammered, blushed and could think of absolutely nothing to say. After a few seconds, the elderly lady, her eyes twinkling, said kindly: 'Take a deep breath, young man, and start again.'

Barber cleared his throat. 'Does ... er ... does a Miss Walker live here, please?'

'No young man, I'm afraid not,' the lady replied pleasantly. 'I'm afraid you have come to the wrong house. If you tell me the address you're looking for perhaps I can direct you?'

'Er ... I'm terribly sorry.' Suddenly Barber found his tongue. 'I seem to have made a mistake. I do apologise.' He started backing away. 'I'll find it. Sorry...'

He turned and walked rapidly away. Jesus, he thought, that's more difficult than it looks.

The car was still there, and Barber decided to walk past and have a look at the occupants. As he neared it he saw that Parker was missing. The three men inside were watching his progress as he drew closer, and it took a tremendous effort of will to walk straight past without staring back.

Feeling the eyes of at least one of them still on him, he continued along the street until he had turned a corner. Then he leaned against the wall and heaved a sigh of relief.

Presently he peeped cautiously back round the corner to see if the car was still there. It was. He watched it for a minute or two, then noticed that two teenage girls who were walking past were looking at him and giggling. He must look an absolute idiot, peering around the corner like some second rate private eye in a 'B' movie. Hastily straightening up, he looked around, and saw to his surprise that people were coming and going continuously. He'd been so immersed in his own little drama he just hadn't seen them – but he must avoid attracting attention. Squaring his shoulders, he set off purposefully down the street.

After a couple of hundred yards he crossed the road and

walked back. To his heartfelt relief there was no need to repeat the procedure, for when he turned the corner again the car had gone.

This time there was no hesitation, no doubt. Barber was extremely worried about Carmichael, convinced something had happened to him, and the only way to find out what was to go into the house and look. There may be a clue as to his whereabouts, but on the other hand he, Barber, not being Sherlock Holmes, had no idea what to look for. He wouldn't know a clue if it jumped out and bit him!

Walking up to the front door, he rang the bell. As he waited, his hand resting comfortingly on the butt of his gun, his holdall in his left hand, he examined the entrance. He had climbed four steps to a storm door which he realised did not have a lock, though it was closed. The door was of solid wood, and after glancing round to make sure no one was watching him, he opened it, stepped quickly into the porch and closed the door behind him. The front door itself was panelled with panes of opaque glass, and had an ordinary Yale lock. Barber took out his wallet, extracted his credit card, waited a few more seconds until he was sure no one was going to answer the door and then tried inserting the card behind the lock to spring it. He knew this to be a simple operation; he had seen it done dozens of times on television.

A few minutes later he slipped his gun from its holster, smashed the pane next to the lock, put his hand inside and opened the door. Who, he thought, needs brains when brute force will suffice?

He stepped over the fragments of broken glass, closed the door behind him and stood still to listen, his heart hammering. All remained silent. He made for the nearest door, noticing as he did so that the hands of the loudly ticking grandfather clock were pointing to eighteen minutes to six. He turned the handle of the door on his left, paused to gather himself and then flung it open, leaping in and crouching, his gun cocked and finger curled on the trigger. The empty room seemed to mock his antics. Sheepishly, now convinced the

192

house was empty, he put the gun away and walked over to the desk under the window.

He began with the drawers, finding nothing of interest except Parker's tape recorder. He played it for a few moments, had just decided it was Parker dictating letters for his secretary and was about to switch off when he heard what he assumed to be the secretary's voice answering. It seemed strange, but ... he shrugged, dismissing it as of no consequence.

A quick look around the room convinced him that there was no clue there as to Carmichael's whereabouts. Leaving the study, he walked across the hall to the only other door leading out of it. He never did discover that the door led to the kitchen, because as he started turning the handle he heard the storm door open.

Pulling out his gun, Barber stepped across to the door and stood ready. The figure seen in silhouette through the glass was wearing trousers, so he assumed it was Parker returning. He heard the key turn in the lock, the door opened and feet crunched on the broken glass. Barber realised the exclamation was familiar even as he stepped out, the gun pointing at Janet's head.

She gave a little scream of alarm, then cried out his name in astonishment. 'Steve! What are you doing here? And why are you pointing a gun at me?' She added sharply.

'I ... er ... I thought you were Parker when I saw you through the door,' Barber said, hastily putting the gun away. 'You know – wearing jeans.' he added lamely.

'So? that still doesn't explain what you're doing here, nor why you're carrying a gun. It is real I suppose. I mean – it's not a toy, a part of a childish fantasy world of yours I haven't seen before?'

'Shut up, Janet, and don't be so bloody stupid.' Barber had at last found himself. It was time to act positively, and he knew what he was going to do; find Carmichael, and kill Parker, in that order.

'Don't ask questions, just answer them,' he went on tersely. She looked at him half frightened and he knew he had to reassure her. Putting his arms around her, he gave her a quick kiss, saying, 'Don't worry, I'm one of the good guys. I also love you and won't hurt you. Now listen,' he went on, releasing her, 'I'm looking for Carmichael, and it's vital that I find him quickly. He's my boss.'

'Your boss?'

'Yes. And I'm asking the questions, remember? Where do you expect Parker to be right now?'

She shrugged, spreading her hands. 'I've no idea. He gave me and Sylvia, that's his secretary, the day off. I only came back to change before going out again. In fact I only came in this way to see if he was here, and to check if there was anything that needed doing first thing in the morning.'

'I saw him leave here with three other men. I don't suppose you know anything about that?'

She shook her head.

'What about Carmichael? Where did you expect him to be?'

'Why – with him, of course. Unless he's been called off.' She frowned. 'No, that's not possible, otherwise you wouldn't be here looking for him, would you?'

'True. Now where in the house could they hide a body ... I mean,' he added hastily seeing the worry flood back, 'a live body. At least, I hope he's still alive.'

'My God! You don't think someone's got to Parker after all, even with a Special Branch Chief Superintendent looking after him, do you?'

'No I don't,' Barber snapped. 'Just tell me where they could put somebody.'

'All right, all right, don't get shirty. If we're going to get married you'd better realise right now you can't talk to me like that,' Janet added tartly.

'For Christ's sake, Janet, this isn't a game. A man's life is at stake. Now, answer the question.'

'Sorry,' she replied. 'It's just hard to think in those terms. It's been a bit of a shock, all this. I guess,' she added quickly, noticing Barber's jaw tightening, 'the cellar must be the only place.'

'Where's the door?'

'Around the back of the stairs.' She led the way. 'Here it is.'

'All right, stay here,' Barber ordered, opening the door. A strong smell of gas wafted out, and Janet gave an exclamation of disgust.

'Pooh! There must be a gas leak,' she said, and switched on the light.

'Stay here,' Barber said again, and filling his lungs with air, he dashed down the cellar steps. The first thing he saw was Carmichael's body slumped in a corner, his hands tied to a pipe over his head. Feeling the escaping gas blowing against his leg, Barber bent down, turned off the tap then moved over to the inert body.

Still holding his breath, he struggled to untie the knots. Before he was half done his lungs were aching. He let out half of the air, but by the time he'd untied Carmichael he couldn't hold his breath any longer. It came out in a loud 'whoosh' and he gasped in a lung full of gas-filled air. Coughing and spluttering he heaved the heavily-built Superintendent up and across his shoulders. He heard Janet calling to ask if he was all right, but didn't attempt to reply. Instead, staggering under his burden, he managed somehow to climb the steps back into fresh air. The last few paces were almost too much for him, but at last he was able to lay Carmichael down on the hall floor.

His own chest still heaving, he felt for a pulse. He couldn't find it at first, but after probing around the unconscious man's neck for a few seconds, he found the carotid artery and, through his fingertips, felt a faint, irregular drumming. Dragging the inert body into the study, he told Janet to open the window and set about administering the kiss of life.

He worked for about five minutes; then Carmichael gave a little gasp, groaned and stirred.

195

'Thank God,' said Barber, heaving a sigh of relief.

'He's going to be all right,' Janet said, 'but Steve, do you realise what this means?'

'Only too well.'

'My boss is in danger. They've got him.' She darted to the 'phone and snatched up the receiver.

'Put that down!' Barber's voice cracked like a whiplash. 'Put that damned 'phone down. There's nobody you need call. Leave everything to us.'

'But ...' She stood there, irresolute. 'I must call the police, tell him what's happened. They can put up road blocks. Find them before they get too far.'

Barber bent to examine Carmichael, ensured that his pulse was beating stronger and straightened up again. 'He's in no danger, love,' he began.

'I can see that,' she interrupted, 'but Edward Parker is.'

'I wasn't talking about Carmichael.'

Neither of them saw the latter open his eyes as they continued looking at each other. Janet's eyes began to widen.

'You mean ... Parker isn't in trouble? How can that be, when the man who was supposed to guard him is lying unconscious at your feet, and Parker is missing, having left with three other men?'

Carmichael, with a great effort, raised himself on one elbow.

'Never mind, Steve,' he said. 'I'll answer that all in good time. Where's Parker now? Any idea?' He pulled himself upright, gasped and put a hand to his side. 'Christ, between my head and this I feel like death.' He drew breath, and winced. 'I reckon he's cracked one of my ribs.'

'Who?' Barber asked, offering a hand to the Superintendent, who was clambering painfully to his feet.

'Parker. A farewell gift, the bastard.' He looked at Janet, who was staring at him aghast. 'Your Edward Parker isn't quite as honourable as you think, miss. Now,' turning back to Barber, 'why did you ring me with the operation message?'

'Eh? Oh . . . yes. Well, Janet here heard Parker talking to two men in the town park yesterday . . .'

He related what had been said, and when he'd finished Carmichael asked: 'what do you think?'

'In London, I checked on the times of ferries from Hull to the continent. One leaves for Rotterdam at twenty hundred.' Barber looked at his watch, 'In an hour's time, in fact. From what's happened here I'd say they've gone to catch it.'

'Hmmm, I agree. Miss Walker,' he snapped, 'don't stand there gaping. Go and fetch me some strong coffee, please, and a few pain killers.' He was already lifting the telephone receiver to send for a taxi.

Within a few minutes Janet had produced a pot of coffee and a bottle of codeine tablets. While she was out of the room the two men hurriedly discussed what to tell her.

As she was returning Barber said: 'She's highly intelligent and very astute. I don't think she'll believe any cock and bull story.'

They sipped their coffee for a few moments, and then Carmichael cleared his throat.

'Now, er, Miss Walker . . . Janet,' he began. 'I know this . . .'

'No,' she interrupted.

'Eh? What d'you mean, no?' For the first time ever Barber saw the Superintendent at a loss for words.

'In a few moment,' explained Janet, 'A taxi will be along to take you to the ferry. You think you're going without me, but I have news for you. You're not. In fact I'll spell it out for you; I'm coming with you.'

It was Barber who replied: 'No, you're not, love. It's too dangerous, you could get hurt. I won't allow it.'

Carmichael looked surprised at this choice of words, but understood a few seconds later.

197

'When we're married, Steve darling,' Janet's voice was pure honey, 'you can forbid all you like, but I'll still do as I think fit – provided I can persuade you to agree, naturally,' she added hastily. 'In the meantime . . .' She stopped, favouring him with a bland smile.

'No miss, I can't allow it,' Carmichael told her firmly. 'You'll stay here, and not contact anyone until you hear from us. Those are my orders . . .'

'Orders, Superintendent?' She broke in, not smiling now. 'Since when did you have the right to give me orders? Now let me tell you something. If you don't take me with you I'll do one of two things; I'll either call the police and tell them what's happened, or I'll send for another taxi and come anyway.' She paused, pretending to reflect. Then she went on brightly, 'I think I'll do the former, and then follow in the taxi. That way,' she added unnecessarily, 'I'll do both.'

Barber couldn't help smiling at her.

Carmichael, however, flushed with annoyance, and was about to make an angry retort when they heard the taxi tooting its horn outside.

'Shall we go?' said Janet, setting off towards the door. 'Luckily I have my passport and cheque book right here in my handbag. We'd better hurry, or we'll never catch that ferry. A real adventure,' she added to Barber, as they crossed the hall. 'I've always dreamed of being involved with one, now I can't wait to see what happens.'

He put his arm around her and closed the front door behind them. 'I don't think you're going to enjoy this one very much, darling, especially when you learn what it's all about.' He shook her gently. 'Now look – when we get there, you'll do exactly as you're told, no more and no less. I mean that. I'll have a quick word with Carmichael; I think there's a role for you to play. Now shut up,' he added, as they climbed into the taxi.

'How're you feeling?' Barber asked Carmichael, as they squeezed into the back of the taxi, Janet between them.

'Lousy,' was the terse reply. 'Driver, to the ferry, as fast as you like. There's an extra fiver for you if we get there in time for the seven-thirty sailing.'

'Yes sir,' said the young man, delighted that at last, after six months of taxi driving he'd been made such an offer. They went through three sets of traffic lights on amber and one that had just turned red. The three mile ride through the built-up town was done in six minutes, a record by anyone's standards.

They arrived with enough time to spare to enable them to walk casually to the booking office and arrange tickets. There was one cabin available with two bunks. Carmichael and Barber took it, Janet would have to manage in the main saloon.

'How the hell are we going to find them on board here if they just hole up in a cabin all night?' asked Barber.

They were standing at the entrance to the bar, speaking quietly to one another. Janet was already making herself comfortable in the lounge. After departure she would wander round the ship keeping an eye open for her boss. She had been given descriptions of the other three men but her chances of recognising them were not good. After all, she had already seen half a dozen people that would have fitted.

'After sailing the Purser will be given a copy of the cabin plan and the names of those occupying them. From the list he will know which cabins are still empty and announce to the passengers that berths are available. Some of the people here daunted by a whole night ahead without proper sleep will probably come forward and take a few. The others will just stay where they are, trying to sleep in the reclining seats available in the lounge. About an hour after departure the Purser will finish for the night and hopefully leave his office. If he does we go in and lift the list. It may tell us something.'

'And if he doesn't?'

'Then we do it the hard way.' Carmichael did not specify what that would be.

They did not enter the lounge or bar but wandered around

the upper deck keeping to the shadows as much as possible and their eyes open for any sign of the four men.

Shortly after came the announcement asking for all visitors to leave as the boat was about to depart, and the two men made their way down to their own cabin.

They sat in heavy silence for a few minutes until Barber said: 'This is a right bloody mess, isn't it?'

Carmichael pursed his lips, looked at Barber thoughtfully and then nodded. 'Are you talking about the girl?'

'That and everything else. She knows too much, and has seen too much. She'll be able to put two and two together and come up with some startling answers. They may be right or wrong. It won't matter. What does matter is that this whole operation is unravelling so fast we don't even have time to gather up the wool' Barber paused. 'Are we to kill all of them or just Parker? Then what? What was someone like Parker doing in the company of the KGB in the first place?'

'Who says they're the KGB?' asked Carmichael softly.

Barber thought for a moment and then said: 'True. So what is the story? Are we going to stop him or not?'

Carmichael scratched the side of his nose, thinking. 'As I see it,' he said after a few moments pause, 'we have no option but to stop him. We do that first and explain afterwards. It's going to be a long night and anything could happen.'

'That's not good enough,' expostulated Barber. 'Where and when is it to happen now? We can't follow the original plan, that's obvious. So now what?'

'Look, Barber,' Carmichael said wearily. 'My head hurts and I ache all over. Right now I don't care much what happens where or when. All I know is that the first thing we do is locate Parker and then decide. All right?'

Barber shrugged. There was nothing to say. He was desperately worried about Janet and had to admit to himself that in his heart of hearts he hoped they never saw Parker or the others. It would not be his fault if they failed. And he had the money. That was an error by Carmichael in hindsight.

But then if he had not been paid upfront and something had
have received the money for the operation. No, Carmichael
had had no choice. It had been his gamble which now may
not have paid off. Barber took some comfort in the thought.

★　★　★

Janet had settled in her corner alone. After a while she had
decided to take a walk around the public areas to see if she
could find anything. When she returned to her seat, after a
fruitless search, the other seats in her corner were taken.

She stepped over a few bags and outstretched legs, excus-
ing herself, ignoring the hostile glances from the young
people sitting there.

She suddenly caught herself listening to their conversation
and although she spoke French fluently and recognised the
language for what it was, the accent was so strange that she
only caught one word in three.

It would not have mattered if she had. Enis Baum and
Nasima Karami were only discussing the weather. They were
both hoping fervently for a calm crossing.

Chapter 15

Barber was standing at the porthole, watching the mouth of the Humber recede into the gathering dusk, wondering if he'd ever see England again. He thought fondly of his brother, offered up a silent prayer that the operation, when he had it, would be a success. He didn't realise Carmichael was standing beside him, and was mildly surprised when he spoke.

'It's a beautiful evening, isn't it? Just right for knocking off Soviet planted traitors.'

'Tell me something,' Barber replied, without looking round, 'do you hate him? Parker, I mean – or whatever his real name is.'

'Hate? Oh no. There's no room in this business for hate; it clouds the judgement. The best man I knew in this business was as cold as ice. He never got involved, felt nothing against or for Communists. He just saw it as a job to do.'

'You're talking about him in the past tense. What happened to him? Retired?'

Carmichael gave a mirthless bark of laughter. 'You could say that, I suppose – only he retired permanently. He broke his own most sacred rule, you see; he got involved. The girl he fell for turned out to be a Russian agent, and he was ordered to kill her. Of course, at the time nobody realised he was in love with her.' He lapsed into silence, remembering.

'What happened?' Barber asked, intrigued.

'He carried out his orders and then committed suicide.'

'My God!'

'Yes.' The Superintendent gave a small sigh. 'That just

202

about sums it up. Look,' he went on, 'we have a serious problem. There is practically no secrecy left in this operation. It's been a cock-up all the way through. So we have to play it out, at least as far as we can. That means we try for Parker if we can locate him, any ideas?'

'Plenty – but I don't know if they'll work. This sort of thing . . . er . . . is relatively new to me, and after all, you're the expert.'

Carmichael grinned wryly. 'Yeah, maybe. I'd still like to hear what you have to suggest, though.'

'Well,' Barber began thoughtfully, after a pause, 'It was drummed into us in the Marines that no matter what we tried, we should remember the objective. In this case, the primary objective is to kill Parker. The second is not only for us to avoid being accused of killing him, but for there not to be even a hint that we had anything to do with it.'

'An interesting choice of words, "to avoid being accused off". I take it they were chosen for a purpose?'

Barber nodded. 'It's obvious, isn't it? We have to kill him; there's no other way of achieving our primary objective. We also have to do it in such a way that we get away with it, so he must appear to die accidentally – but who shoots a man of that stature by accident? Answer, two dedicated men trying to rescue the said man of stature from his kidnappers.'

'Interesting. And how do you propose to do that?'

'They don't know we're here, right? We walk up to the door, if we know the right one, knock, when they open it we barge in, guns blazing, and shoot the lot. We then rig the stage to look like an O.K. Corral shoot-out with the goodies – that's us, for this plot – winning, and the baddies – that's them – losing. Parker, of course, regrettably gets killed in the cross fire. In the subsequent enquiry we get censured for not calling on the Dutch for help, we offer our abject apologies and our condolences to the widow.'

Barber stopped abruptly.

'Any more?'

'Only one tiny detail. I have no official standing. Remember the reasons you brought me into this in the first place?'

'Only too well,' replied Carmichael heavily. 'However, circumstances alter situations, and that one I can cope with. I can easily arrange for you to have been a member of the Branch for as long as I see fit. Actually,' he went on. 'I see things very much the way you do. I don't like it, but I can see no other way. My greatest regret is Uri Stawizcki.'

'Who the hell's he?'

Carmichael explained what had happened in Parker's house, hating the prospect of having to kill the man who had spared him. When he had finished he added: 'There's one thing I don't understand about all this. Miss Walker claims she saw Parker in the town gardens yesterday afternoon talking to two men, and that's what put you on to getting in touch with me. That's impossible, though, because I was sitting outside Parker's study all the time, and heard him and his secretary dealing with his correspondence.'

'Did you actually see him during that time?'

'No. He'd left instructions that under no circumstances whatsoever was he to be disturbed.'

The answer came to Barber in a flash of inspiration. He told Carmichael about the tape recording he'd found in Parker's desk, and the Superintendent nodded slowly. 'So that's how it was done. Simple, effective but risky. I may have looked in at any time, or someone may have arrived and insisted on seeing Parker immediately. Oh well – it worked, and anyway it's past history now. It's nice to have the full story though. I suppose it's time to go to the Purser's office.'

'It's a bit early, I think,' said Barber. 'Give it another half an hour. It's only just coming up to midnight now. I'll go and have a quick look and pick up some sandwiches and coffee.

'All right. That might not be such a bad idea at that. Here,' Carmichael took out his wallet and extracted a fiver. 'Try and get a receipt.'

Barber grinned to himself as he took the money. Typical Civil Servant after all. He could give away thousands unaccounted for, yet needed a receipt for a five pound snack. The thought was particularly amusing given the circumstances.

The grill to the Purser's office was closed and the shutter down. There was nobody about and Barber paused outside the door to tie his shoe lace. He could not see any light around the door and heard nothing from inside. He looked at the lock carefully. It seemed more like a vault door than an office door and he wondered how in hell Carmichael was going to get in there. Still, that was his problem. Right now he needed to get the coffee and sandwiches. He went into the bar, was served quickly, as many of the passengers were settling down for the night, stuffed the sandwiches in a pocket and balanced the two paper cups in one hand. A short while ago he would have laughed at the notion of instinctively keeping his shooting hand free. Today he was not laughing.

When he got back to the cabin he told Carmichael about the lock. Carmichael shrugged and said, 'Don't worry. I have the means to open any lock on this boat.'

Barber said nothing, just shrugged. Time passed painfully slowly. Finally he asked, 'When are we going?'

Carmichael looked at his watch. 'I'm going now. You follow in a few minutes. I don't want us to be seen together. It's occurred to me that the other lot don't know you're here nor if they saw you who you are. So it would be better not to be seen together. When we get to the Purser's office you stand back and keep watch while I open the door. I'll go inside, you stay put. When we leave you hang around for five minutes and follow me down.'

Barber nodded. 'Okay. Ready whenever you are.'

Carmichael left. As he walked along the corridor he did not notice the cabin door he had just passed open, nor did he see the man step from the cabin. At the sight of Carmichael the man stood stock still then turned his back and walked the other way. He glanced over his shoulder as Carmichael turned a corner of the corridor, now convinced that his eyes had not been playing tricks. He rushed back to the cabin to inform the others.

If it hadn't been for the lateness of the hour, the painkillers he had taken to bring his ribs from agony to a dull ache and the after effects of the gas Carmichael may have been more alert. As it was he was oblivious to all except his next task. At the Purser's office he looked about him and, like Barber before him, knelt at the door to tie his shoe lace. One look at the lock was all he needed. He straightened up and walked across the corridor to the gents' toilets along the way. Once inside he took out a rolled soft leather tool kit and picked out a long probe with an angled bend a few centimetres long at the end. He returned to the corridor, nodded at Barber who was stationed near some stairs up to the next deck, and went straight to the task of picking the lock. Although it only took Carmichael three minutes to unlock the door, to Barber it had seemed like an eternity. Probably due to the lateness of the hour nobody had appeared and Carmichael quickly swung the door open and stepped inside the office, shutting the door firmly behind him.

Less than two minutes later Carmichael reappeared, nodded at Barber, tapping his coat pocket at the same time, and quickly left. Barber, as nervous as a cat on a hot tin roof, heaved a sigh and went through the door onto the open deck. He stood there for a few moments savouring the fresh air and appreciating the stars. He would wait a bit longer before going back below. Anyway, he needed to use the heads after all the coffee he had been drinking.

⋆   ⋆   ⋆

Carmichael had quickly left the scene of his burglary, eager to get to the cabin and look at the plan of the cabins and compare it to the names. He prayed it would tell him something. He unlocked the cabin door and was pushing it open when there was an almighty shove in his back, he went sprawling through the doorway, a figure landed on his back and the unmistakable end of a gun prodded him in the back.

'Don't move Chief Superintendent, or you are a dead man,' said the voice in his ear.

206

It was all he could do not to scream out in agony. The effect of the painkillers he had taken earlier had been wearing off and his side was hurting more with every breath. The further punishment he was now receiving was agony.

'Stand up very slowly and turn around,' said the voice. He did as he was told and confronted the Hangman, leering at him. Karpov stood in the background, his face expressionless but the gun pointing at Carmichael was as unwavering as die Henker's.

'You should not have followed us,' said Karpov in a quiet voice. 'Now you leave us no choice.' He sighed as though with genuine regret, which he may have been feeling. 'Uri sends his regrets but you know how it is. Please go with this man. Goodbye Mr Carmichael.'

Carmichael was too shocked to react or do anything. He noticed with relief that the wrapping from the sandwiches and the cups he and Barber had used were nowhere in sight and Carmichael presumed that Barber had tidied them away before following him. There was still hope. He prayed Barber did not walk in right then because he would be totally unprepared and have two guns levelled against him.

Henken prodded the Chief Superintendent unnecessarily hard in the ribs, though luckily not on his injured side and said, 'Move, now. Outside. Turn right and along the corridor.'

Karpov followed them out, closing the door behind them.

★　★　★

'How much longer?' whispered Nasima to Nuri Khatun, her face taut, her hands nervously flexing.

'Ten minutes less than the last time you asked,' he replied impatiently. 'Now for God's sake don't ask me again or I'll scream.'

She turned away, now a stricken look on her face.

Enis Baum listened anxiously to this brief exchange. Tension was mounting; they were coming apart at the seams, and there was nothing she could do about it. She'd scheduled the move for three o'clock in the morning, when she counted on there being less awareness of what was going on, and therefore minimum resistance. After all, there were only ten of them, and they had much to do and a lot to cover.

When Aman el-Baz and Ibrahim Bakr also began bickering, she realised there was only one thing to do; bring it all forward – move, before they made such an error that somebody noticed something was amiss.

'All right,' she said tersely. 'We can't wait any longer. We move in,' she looked at her watch, 'in twelve minutes.'

Immediately the atmosphere changed. It suddenly became electric in its intensity; the squabbling stopped, fear became its place.

'It'll be one thirty,' Enis went on. 'Emile, you'll have half an hour, as we originally planned, before we start. Everything will be as before, except that it will all be brought forward one hour. Okay?'

Faces strained, the rest nodded agreement.

★　★　★

Barber saw Carmichael, closely followed by another man, walk away from him, towards the stern stairwell. The man behind Carmichael had one hand in his pocket, the other appeared, from the glimpse Barber had, to be on the Superintendent's right arm. Barber paused to give them time to get a few paces in front, then followed slowly.

He watched them turn the corner at the end of the corridor, sprinted after them and was in time to see them ascend the short flight of steps on to the upper deck. He followed quickly, silently. Something had gone wrong. The man had to be one of the Russians, probably Henken.

Pushing open the swing door, he stepped onto the deck. It was a dark night, clouds scudding across the sky, the wind blowing steadily from the starboard side at about fifteen knots. In the ship's wake, white caps reared up to about three feet before they broke. All this background impinged sharply on Barber's consciousness, even as he was concentrating on the two men stand at the rails. He ducked down by the side of a lifeboat to avoid being seen, its darker shadow hiding him from Carmichael's captor, who was now peering about him, presumably ensuring nobody was about.

Realising he only had seconds in which to act, Barber pulled his gun from its shoulder holster, inserted a silencer and quickly screwed it tight. With one fluid movement he took aim, even as the other man took his gun from his pocket and took a pace back from the Chief Superintendent, offering his back to Barber as he did so.

Steadying the gun with his left hand, Barber gently squeezed the trigger twice. The sound was like that of two bottles of flat champagne having their corks pulled simultaneously. The first shot hit the Hangman in his left shoulder, spinning him part of the way round as the second shot hit him on the top or his arm. The force hurled him over the side; it was so sudden he didn't even have time to scream.

As he emerged from behind the lifeboat Barber was unscrewing the silencer and slipping the gun back into its holster. Carmichael came forward to meet him, as calmly as though they were meeting for a quiet pint in a London pub.

'What's the time?' he asked unexpectedly.

Barber checked his watch. 'Half past one,' he said. Right, you cool bastard, he was thinking. If that's how you want it.

They returned to their cabin quickly and in silence. Once there Carmichael said, 'Thanks, that's two I owe you' – and nothing more was said on the subject, Barber being quite happy to play it that way.

'We haven't much time,' Carmichael went on. 'They'll be expecting Henken back any moment now – but we'll arrive instead. The one good thing is that we know where they are without having to go through the ship's plan. I saw them return to their cabin. There are only two of them and this changes things quite considerably. If we are fast we take them without bloodshed.'

Barber was puzzled. 'And then what? We shoot them in

209

cold blood? I know they're the enemy but . . . well, I can't do it.'

'Who said anything about cold blood? Or warm blood for that matter?' Carmichael looked grim. 'We'll take Parker from them.'

'And then what?'

'And then he follows Henken,' came the curt reply.

'And the others?'

'We leave them. We tie them up and simply leave them. I don't think that having failed in their objective they'll say too much to the police. In fact their best bet is to claim to have been robbed. We'll do that and relieve them of their money. But we'll leave their passports. That way they can make their statements to the police and will probably be allowed to leave. After that, of course, they'll vanish.'

'What if they don't? What if they start screaming blue murder and tell the truth? It would be easy enough to collaborate their story.'

Carmichael stroked the side of his nose. A gesture Barber was now aware meant that he was deep in thought. 'No, I don't think so. Nobody has Parker's name on board. Nobody knows where he is or what he's up to. When he goes over the side he'll have a weight on him to make sure he sinks. We remove all identification and leave him to the fishes. It's the best I can do at the moment.' Carmichael's admission worried Barber. What a mess. It could not have been better screwed up if it had been planned that way.

Barber followed Carmichael along the corridor. Risking that the Russians would leave the door unlocked ready for the Hangman's return, Carmichael grasped the handle turned it and pushed all in one move. The door flew open and they both sprang inside. Under different circumstances, the reactions of the three men to such an unexpected visitation would have been comical.

Parker opened his mouth and stared, Karpov froze where he sat and Stawizcki stood like a ballet dancer executing a particularly difficult movement, one leg forward, one hand

210

stretched towards the door, the other around his side almost on the butt of his gun.

Carmichael stepped forward, relieved Stawizcki of his weapon as Barber closed the door behind them, then motioned for Karpov to stand. Barber took Karpov's gun and gestured for him to sit again.

It was Stawizcki who broke the silence. 'I should not have underestimated you,' he said quietly. 'Where's Henken?'

'Over the side,' Carmichael replied. 'Don't feel too badly about it, Uri. It was sheer luck and Barber here that swung things in my favour.'

'Now what?' Parker had found his voice. 'What are you going to do now?'

'I regret to inform you, sir,' Barber told him sarcastically, 'that we're now going ahead with our original plan. We've just brought the arrangements forward a few hours, that's all – oh, and changed the rifle for a pistol. But don't worry, the effect will be the same.' Knowing that the man was both an important public figure and a Russian agent angered Barber beyond all reason, but only now he was face to face with him did it surface. He had always disliked the Labour party, despising the hypocrisy of their leaders, who wept crocodile tears over the poor while amassing wealth and possessions for themselves. Barber, like millions of others, would always believe Labour to be the most corrupt of political parties. The doubts he had entertained as to whether he could carry out the execution were dispelled. He would do it after all.

Parker's face had turned ashen, and he was trembling violently.

'You don't mean it,' he said hoarsely. 'You can't . . .' His voice trailed off when he saw the faces of the four men. The Russians, like the British, recognised the inevitable, understood the issues at stake. Even Barber, new to the game as he was, realised what went on, what was required of men in his position. This was the real world of sudden death and intrigue.

In Parker's world, the words 'sudden death' always meant a political demise, not the final one.

The fear he had felt in the past, when trying to get a private member's bill though Parliament, or when being cross examined by a Commons Select Committee – he remembered the inquiry about the British Steel losses – were nothing in comparison to this. Then, the fear had added spice to life, a chance to prove he could bear up under the most extreme pressure. But this – this was real fear that turned his legs to rubber and his bowels to water. He thought he had met hard men in politics, but looking at these implacable faces he realised that beside them politicians were merely children playing games.

There was no question of compassion, no point in appealing to their better instincts. They probably don't have any, he thought bitterly. He saw himself as a pawn between two groups of professionals, each trying to win the prize ... Parker's life or death. As long as he was alive the Russians wouldn't stop trying, provided the opportunity arose. If it didn't ... c'était la vie, or in this case ... la mort.

'I know what you're trying to achieve,' began Parker, in a nervous voice he hardly recognised as his own, 'but you ought to know that everything has been documented, and will reach the appropriate people in the event of my sudden death.'

'Really?' said Carmichael in a bored voice, concealing his alarm at the news.

'Don't you care?' cried Parker. 'Doesn't the fact that my death will be of no avail mean nothing to you?' He began sweating as the faces watching him remained impassive. 'It's not a bluff,' he said desperately.

Carmichael nodded. 'Let me tell you what will happen when the news breaks. Many people in Britain will rejoice and say good riddance, and others will ask who else in the Labour party is also a Russian agent, and probably ensure the party stays buried for a long time to come. I can speak for Barber as well as myself when I tell you that we'll be delighted with the outcome. If, however, nobody finds out, then this government will have a general election in the normal course of events, and we shall continue to see-saw between the two parties, keeping more or less in the middle of the road. Maybe. Or maybe the Alliance will get to power anyway.' He broke off, and shrugged. 'That's enough talk,' Carmichael said abruptly. 'Uri, turn around. And you, Karpov,' he added, jerking his gun at them.

As they obeyed, Barber cocked a listening ear. 'Hey!' he said. 'What's happening? We appear to be stopping.' He looked at his watch. 'That's funny, it's only two o'clock. What the hell's going on?'

'We'll wait and see. Nobody move. Stay facing the wall,' he added to the two Russian agents.

The minutes ticked by, tension mounting as the five men waited to hear the ship's engines start up again. As Barber looked at his watch, for the twelfth time in as many minutes, there was a knock on the door. It began to open before Barber or Carmichael could speak. Barber stepped quickly out of sight and Carmichael whipped his pistol away. Stawizcki turned, but saw they had the situation still well in hand. The only thing left was for Parker to call out – but if he did so, there was no doubt in the Russian's mind that both he and whoever was opening the door would die.

A steward put his head round the door, his scared expression changing to one of surprise at the sight of the frozen tableau.

'What do you want?' Carmichael demanded brusquely.

'Sir, you must all go to the saloon immediately. If you aren't there in ten minutes one of them will come after me, and they say they'll shoot anybody they find still here.'

The man was ashen faced, the words pouring out in a frightened torrent.

'What the hell are you talking about?' Carmichael snapped, glancing at Uri Stawizcki, who shook his head in equal bewilderment.

'The . . . the terrorists, sir,' stammered the steward. 'Th

213

... they've taken over the ferry and are ... are the ... threatening to ... to kill everyone on board and b ... b ... blow up the boat if their demands aren't met.'

'What terrorists? Who are they?' asked Carmichael, still suspecting the Russians of being involved, though how or why he didn't know.

'I don't know,' the man almost wailed. 'I was on the bridge when this woman arrived, and the Captain turned to tell her she had to leave, and suddenly some others pushed their way onto the bridge and the next thing we knew they were pointing guns at us and ordering us to stop the ferry. They told me to go around all the cabins and get the passengers and crew into the saloon and to tell them that anyone found outside the saloon afterwards would be shot.' The words had come out in a rush, but now terror made him begin to stammer again. 'They said if ... if I ... I was still here they'd sh ... shoot m ... me too.'

'All right. What else happened?' asked Carmichael.

'What do you mean, sir?'

'Well, did they say how they were going to blow us all up? Did they say what they were up to? Identify themselves in any way?'

'No sir. At least, they didn't say what they wanted. They did say that one of the gang was ... n ... no. I mean ... had ... had just completed wiring a bomb in the boot of their car, and she only had to press a button to blow them all to kingdom come.'

'I see. Well, you'd better carry on warning the passengers, steward. There's nothing else you can do for the moment.'

'Yes, sir.' The steward began to withdraw, then paused. 'Oh, there, there's one more, more thing, sir. The girl also said that to, to prove to, to the authorities that they meant what they said, they'd execute three of the passengers in exactly one hour's time.' The words came out in a sudden rush.

He gulped, and hurried away. Already there was a noise of running feet and frightened voices, and Carmichael knew

214

that the opportunity of killing Parker quietly had gone. If he was shot now it could blow everything wide open; on the other hand, another opportunity might well present itself later, especially in view of what was happening up top.

'Right everyone, we'll go to the saloon. See what's happening. Parker, you'll stay close to me. You two, stay out of the way.' He nodded at the Russians, 'And don't try anything clever. Because I'll get Parker and you two before anything else happens. Barber, you go below and try and find that bomb. If this is for real I won't risk the lives of hundreds of passengers. You know all about explosives and booby traps. If you can find the bomb and defuse it try and let me know. We shall then decide what to do about the rest of the situation. Right let's go.'

The two Russians, Parker and Carmichael trooped from the cabin. Carmichael followed them, his hands in his pockets, his right clenching his own gun, his left with Karpov's. Stawizcki's was in his trousers' waist band in the small of his back, hidden under his jacket.

Whatever happened Carmichael was going to shoot Parker. In the confusion, he hoped to get away with it.

Chapter 16

Barber collected the holdall from their cabin and went looking for the stairs leading down to the car deck. By this time
most of the cabins were deserted, the doors left open. As he
reached a flight of stairs at the end of the corridor, one of the
doors opened slowly. His hand was inside his jacket and gripping the gun butt before he knew it.

The frightened faces of the elderly couple facing him
fanned his loathing of terrorists to a white heat. The lectures
he'd attended in the Marines on the atrocities perpetrated by
Black September, El Fatah, the Red Brigade, the IRA and
the Japanese gang whose name he couldn't remember, all
came flooding back. He recalled the senior officer saying:
'Only the fucking Irish call their gang of murdering cut-
throats an army. They give thugs of twenty-one the title of
lieutenant, and if they kill, torture and maim enough people,
particularly women and children, they get made up to major
by the time they're twenty-five.' At that point the bantam-
sized colonel held up the yellow card issued to all soldiers.
'Never go out without this in your pocket, know what's written there and if you want to finish your tour in one piece,
forget the thing ever existed. It was written by shit-house
politicians who care more for themselves and the bastard
Irish than they do for us. If you doubt what I say, then compare compensation payouts to the families of soldiers and
constables killed in Ireland with those paid to the IRA themselves. You men belong to the finest, best trained army in the
world, and you had better believe it. Follow your instinct and
remember one thing; your senior officers are behind you all

the way, standing between you and the so-called do-gooders. Believe that, and you may get home safely.'

This speech had given rise to much discussion among his audience. Many men were surprised that a senior officer should address them in that way; what most didn't know though Barber learnt of it later, was that the Colonel's wife and twin sons had been killed by an IRA bomb planted in one of Belfast's shopping areas.

These thoughts had flashed through Barber's mind before the man said, 'Excuse me, it is true? My name is Smith; my wife and I are going on holiday. Is this some kind of practical joke, do you think?'

His eyes were pleading for Barber to say it was.

'I'm sorry, it's true.' Seeing their despair, he felt constrained to offer some comfort, and went on in a confidential undertone, 'But don't worry – we already have help on board. Say nothing to anyone, and with a little luck we'll all come through all right.' As he turned to go he added, 'Don't tell anyone you saw or spoke to me.'

'Where are you going?' Smith asked unexpectedly.

Barber paused, thought about it and decided, what the hell? If they were going to be blown to smithereens they had a right to know.

'There's a bomb in the car deck and I'm going to dismantle it,' he said, trying to sound completely confident.

'Young man,' Mrs Smith said in a tired voice, 'this is the first time I've been on a ferry, so I read the information sheet they gave us. The doors leading to the car deck are locked. She was right, of course. Barber swore softly. If he went looking for the same door as that used by the terrorists, not only might he not find it, he might also get himself shot in the process.

John Smith suddenly swore. 'Sorry,' he looked at his wife. He glanced at Barber. 'My hobby is locks . . . sort of opening them. If I had my tools with me I could have that door open for you in a jiffy.'

'Yes,' his wife said in an excited voice. 'John was wasted as a Civil Servant. He should have been a locksmith.'

'Or better still a burglar,' he and his wife exchanged a smile, a secret joke shared.

'Stay here,' said Barber. 'I'll be back in a minute with something that might help.' He ran back to their cabin, grabbed Carmichael's overcoat which was slung over the back of a chair, and rifled the pockets. He found the roll of leather with its curious contents and rushed back to the Smiths. 'Will these do it?'

John Smith unrolled the packet and pursed his lips in a silent whistle. 'These are superb. Better than mine. I'll have the door open in no time young man. Ida, wait here. If anyone comes, you start to whistle to warn us.'

'Yes, John,' she said meekly, not wanting to spoil it for him by reminding him that she couldn't whistle. Even if her life was at stake, which under the present circumstances it possibly was.

The heavy door was down two flights of stairs. John Smith took one look at it and gave a nod of satisfaction. 'Simple as falling off a log,' he pronounced, kneeling down in front of the lock. He lay the instruments out before him, picked one up, fiddled with it in the large keyhole and in less than a minute the lock sprang back with a faint click. Smith got to his feet and dusted off his trousers.

'I'd better hurry to the saloon,' he said. 'Good luck, son. By the way, do you know who these terrorists are, or what they want?'

Barber shook his head. 'No idea, thanks for doing the lock, though.'

He waited until John Smith, amateur locksmith, had rounded the bend in the stairs, and then cautiously opened the door. He paused, listening, crouched at the edge of the door. It was so silent he could hear the sea lapping against the hull. Now that the ferry had stopped the stabilisers were ineffective, and the boat, lying beam on to the wind and waves, had begun to wallow gently. A truck was parked next to the door – one of the juggernauts of the road – and Barber, moving as quickly and quietly as he could, crawled

218

under the vehicle's massive chassis. Lying flat on the deck, he carefully searched the area within his view. There was no movement, no indication that anybody else was there. Leaving his holdall, he crawled out to close the door in case the man he was after . . . He paused, his hand on the knob. Why assume it was a man? It could easily be a woman, and he knew from his experiences in Northern Ireland they were far more vicious than their menfolk. It was to the women that the IRA gave their victims to be tortured. Would he, Barber, kill a woman if it came to it? Sod it, yes! he thought savagely, ducking quickly as he realised he had stopped in a half crouch by the door. Just for a second he felt foolish. Perhaps there was nobody there. Perhaps someone had been and gone . . . Perhaps they had never been there in the first place and it was all a bluff.

Keeping well down, he moved along the lanes, past lorries, buses, cars and a few motorbikes. Every few yards he stopped and listened, knowing that in the hollow confines of the car deck his ears would probably warn him of the presence of another person, vital seconds before his eyes could.

From the bows he could see aft down both sides of the ship. There was no movement; the only sound the continual dash of the water against the hull. It was only then that he realised there was a second deck below this one, connected by ladders at varying distances along the centre, and a large stairwell athwartships.

The ladders leading down were mere vertical steel frames, so he decided to use the stairs. They gave more cover, and if he was seen he could always jump over the side and onto the deck below. A broken ankle was better than a bullet through the midriff.

At the top he lay flat on his belly and craned his neck to look down. He heard, coming from the stern, the unmistakable sound of a man working. There was a clink of metal on metal, like laying a tool on the deck, and a slight rustling – perhaps cloth rubbing on cloth. Whatever it was, he knew he'd found who he was looking for.

Barber was half way down the steps when a sixth sense warned Emile Parri of approaching danger. He whirled round, ducking as he did so, and was reaching for his pistol as Barber brought his up to fire. Both men were so busy ducking and firing at each other that they both missed by metres. However, it had given Barber time to dash down the remainder of the stairs and take cover behind the wheel of a car – a Rolls Royce, he noticed – and for Parri to slam shut the boot of the car he was working on, and duck out of sight.

★   ★   ★

The tension on the bridge was almost palpable. Apart from the Master, First Mate and helmsman there were two others, each armed with a Swedish Hsqvarne pistol. The dark skins of both Abdul Muein and Ibrahim Bakr shone with sweat. They hadn't spoken a word since arriving there, leaving Enis Baum to do all the talking, and their silence made them doubly sinister to the three fearful men being held at gun point.

A door behind them opened, and light spilled on to the bridge. Enis and the radio operator stepped out; the former had a 9mm Beretta clutched in her right hand, her knuckles gleaming white from the strength of her grip.

Nobody spoke for a few seconds; then: 'Shut that damn' door,' growled the Master, 'before we all lose our night vision.'

Automatically the radio operator moved to obey.

'No!' Enis snapped. 'Leave it open. How else will we hear when they call back?'

'From the loud speaker in the corner,' retorted the first Mate. 'What else would you expect? We only have one operator, and he can't stay awake all the time.' He spoke harshly, anger taking over from his initial fear. At that precise moment he would have given his soul for a gun and an opportunity to use it.

'Don't worry, Miss.' The scorn in the Master's voice, and his obvious loathing of the terrorists were not lost on Enis,

220

who had always been susceptible to the nuances of atmosphere, and the reaction of others to herself. 'We'll do everything we can to help you. We want you off here as soon as possible, if not sooner. What did they say, Sparks?'

'They said . . .' began Enis.

'Keep silent, Miss. I asked my operator here. He'll give me an accurate account of what was said and not some fantasy of your making.'

Her jaw clenched as she struggled to control her anger. The Master, realising he may have gone too far, was ready to jump at her if she made a move to shoot him. He would have nothing to lose, and everything to gain. With him also, fear had been replaced by a bitter loathing.

'Keep a civil tongue in your head,' Enis said harshly, but she nevertheless let the radioman tell what had happened.

It had taken a few minutes to convince the girl on the other end of the line that this was no hoax, and that the ferry had really stopped half-way across the channel and was in the hands of terrorists. Less than five minutes later there was a telephone link between the terrorists and the Dutch counter-espionage duty officer in the Hague. The latter had been horrified when informed that three passengers would die at three o'clock and had begged for more time, but the terrorists had remained adamant. They would, Enis added, continue killing at the rate of one per hour after the initial three until Jemel Dustein, Hassan Bouza and Wafik Fadami were released and flown by helicopter to the ferry. Further demands would then be made, but a Boeing 707 was to be ready, fuelled, at Schipol to taken them where they wanted to go. The duty officer at the other end said he would do his best to make arrangements but had to contact his superiors. The reply had been that there was only fifty six minutes left.

The tense calm on board the boat was in sharp contrast to the pandemonium that had broken out in Holland. The duty officer had 'phoned his boss, General Max Laurier, who in turn had rung his Prime Minister on a private line. All over Holland men were mobilising for what looked like being the

221

biggest terrorist hijack in European history. Even the top secret Steri team were being called out; a body of men picked for their sharpshooting skills and individual abilities, and formed into one of the most deadly anti-terrorist groups in Europe, personally controlled by General Laurier.

The three man conference was done on the telephone and included Laurier, the Dutch Prime Minister and the Minister for Internal Affairs.

Laurier spoke first. 'Gentlemen, this is a scenario we have played to. You are aware and you know the consequences. I need approval to move.'

'How certain can we be that they are not bluffing?' asked Peter Druckmann, the Prime Minister. He was a sleek looking man, now running to fat. When agitated he ran his fingers through his hair in an uncontrolled motion. His hair was already sticking up on end as a result.

'We can never be sure of that. If they are on a holy Jihad then they are deadly serious and we must assume that they will carry out every thing they say. Because they want the release of the three named then we must assume them to be fanatics.'

'I told you at the time it was a mistake to hold them,' said Jan Schleyer. He was the Minister for Internal Affairs akin to the British Home Secretary.

'There is no time for that now, Minister,' said Laurier hurriedly. He did not want to get into an argument about whether they should have kept the three in prison or not. They had been found in possession of arms and explosives and been convicted of intent to cause an act of terrorism. The law had taken care of the rest. It was the price one paid for living in a democracy. Sometimes the price was exhorbitantly high. Like now. They were in a no win situation. If they capitulated completely then the world press would condemn and ridicule them. If they did something and lives were lost then they would be accused of incompetence at best, at worse, he shuddered at the thought.

'So what do you suggest?' asked the PM.

'We need to play for time. We agree to their demands, set it up and try and find a way out of the problem. That way we will have at least a further six hours, maybe more, before anything happens.'

'Jan, what do you think?'

The Minister took a deep breath, his sweating hands gripping the receiver as tightly as possible. 'I agree. I see no other course for us at this point in time. However, I want it on the record right now that we would do nothing to jeopardise the lives of the passengers. My God, do you realise that there are probably twenty different nationalities on board that ferry? People from all over Europe and visitors from America and . . .'

'We know all that,' cut in Druckmann. 'That is why the ferry is such a good target. It guarantees headlines in every country where one of the passengers originates from. It will be worldwide news within twenty four hours unless we can do something about it pretty quickly. General, you know what has to be done. Get cracking. Put your people in place but do not make a move until I tell you personally. We will keep in contact by phone while I get dressed and get over to your headquarters.' He broke the connection without further ado. The biggest crisis in his political life and he had to leave it to other people. He pitied Jimmy Carter and his problem with the Iranian hostages for the first time. He also envied Reagan and the outcome of the liner hostage when the terrorists had been taken in a daring air manoeuvre by the Americans. For the first time in a long time he prayed with meaning.

It was ten to three when the General spoke to Enis Baum on the ship-to-shore line. He explained the difficulty of getting the prisoners there before midday, and asked for an extension of the deadline for the first three passengers.

To this request Enis replied calmly: 'In less than ten minutes three people will die, and it will be your fault. After that, one every hour as already stated. I suggest you expedite

223

your operation and fulfil our demands quickly, before you have the deaths of too many people on your conscience.'

'Let me speak to the Master, please.' Enis gestured the Captain over and handed him the receiver.

'The Master speaking. Before you ask me, yes, I do believe them.'

'You must be psychic! Christ, we're moving as fast as we can!' For the first time since he'd become head of Counter Espionage five years previously, the General sounded on the verge of panic, which he was. With an effort he pulled himself together. 'Very well. We'll get the bastards there in an hour.' He broke the connection and made two more calls. The first was to his personal helicopter pilot, the second to the maximum security jail where the prisoners were being kept. It was only after assuring the Governor that he himself would be flying in to pick up the terrorists, and would be responsible for what happened to them that arrangements were completed. To hell with the politicians and their indecisiveness, he thought, this decision is going to be mine and hang the consequences. He set up the ambush for the airport.

Enis was smiling.

'Aren't you satisfied now?' demanded the First Mate. 'Do you really have to kill innocent people? You're getting all you want. What's the point?'

'The point? The point is that it will force the issue, keep them off balance; moreover, only by following through on our promises can we ensure success. Too often in the past talking has defeated us. This time there is too much at stake.'

'No one is innocent!' Enis screamed. 'They are all guilty – guilty of indifference. That is their crime, and some shall die for it. And,' she added, 'the first will be British, then Dutch. Then we shall choose a nationality at random. We shall involve the world.'

Mate and Master exchanged glances, then turned away. Each had murder uppermost in his mind.

Barber left the shelter of the Rolls Royce, darted across the
three lanes of vehicles and hid behind the wheel of a lorry.
He listened intently, trying to separate the swish of the sea
from any other noise that might occur inside the hull. Receiving the faintest of impressions that his adversary was moving
closer and outboard, he transferred the gun to his left hand,
dried the sweaty palm of his right hand on the seat of his
pants and transferred the gun back again. He jumped to his
feet and ran forward, leapt onto the bonnet of a Mini,
stepped on to its roof and was falling off in a controlled dive,
screaming like a banshee, before Emile realised what was
happening. From the roof of the Mini Barber had one clear
shot at the terrorist before he was rolling on the deck and
diving into cover. He grinned. Even if he'd missed, he'd sure
as hell scared the pants off the bugger. His instructor in the
Marines had said, 'Always do the unexpected; the expected
can get you killed.' He knew his last move was unexpected, if
nothing else.

Lying flat on the deck, he carefully examined the expanse
beneath the vehicles around him. Nothing; no sign of
anyone. He looked at his watch. 2.45. What had that steward
said? They'd start shooting the first three passengers at . . .
three, was it? No . . . an hour after the hi-jack had begun.
Hell – the time could be up already, and if not quite, then
pretty close. He had to get that sod fast, and there was only
one way; offer a target he couldn't resist.

The hair on his scalp erect, every nerve ending tingling,
Barber stood up and walked towards the last position where
he had seen the man. What a stupid bloody way to die, he
thought – and then concentrated his whole being in surviving.

At the spot where the terrorist had been was a pool of
blood, with a few drops scattered beside it. Barber was turning and beginning to squat when the shot and the hammer
blow on his hand occurred simultaneously, and the gun went

225

flying out of his hand. Instantly he dived, rolled and darted around the back of a truck. His only hope of staying alive was to keep moving.

When he dared to look back he saw his enemy coming steadily after him, limping heavily. Reaching the stairs he had come down earlier, Barber ran up them, nursing his hand against his side. As he reached the top, Emile turned the corner. Another shot rang out, missing Barber by inches, and he swore. After the initial pain his hand had become numb, and was now tingling like a bad attack of pins and needles. He massaged it as he rushed to the door leading to the deck, pulled it open, stepped back, picked up his holdall and darted out of sight to the other side of the juggernaut.

He unzipped the bag awkwardly and scattered the contents on the deck. Next he opened the special compartment in the bottom of the bag and tipped the pieces of gun on to the deck. Quickly he began assembling it; breech into barrel; firing mechanism on to stock. He could hear shuffling footsteps approaching. Fit the lot together and lock in place – leave off rear sight and magazine, no time left. The terrorist was coming into view, his eyes on the door. If he turned his head he'd see him . . .

Perhaps it was the sound of the bullet being inserted or perhaps it was again Emile Parri's sixth sense. Whatever it was caused him to spin around, lifting his gun, as Barber raised the barrel on his right forearm and pulled the trigger with his left hand. The soft-nosed bullet hit the terrorist in the stomach and virtually blew him in half. He was dead before he hit the deck.

Wearily Barber got to his feet and fitting the rest of the gun together, including a short magazine of five rounds, he walked below to find the car and explosives.

★   ★   ★

The saloon was packed with passengers and crew. Babies and young children wept at having been plucked unceremoniously from sleep, while the older ones cowered back, trying

226

to be as inconspicuous as possible. Carmichael, Stawizcki and Karpov were bunched together, Carmichael careful that the other two could not turn on him. Parker was busy sidling away much to Carmichael's impotence and fury. There were six terrorists. Three with automatic weapons, the three girls armed only with pistols. The room was mainly silent except for the occasional child whimpering and parents trying to shush them up. The six Palestinians were on a tightrope of emotions. They were strung so tightly that it would not have taken much to start a massacre. Carmichael stood and watched, gauging angles of shot, fields of fire. Who was the most dangerous? The men with their automatics or was one of the hard looking girls more deadly with her pistol than the weak-looking youth?

After about fifteen minutes people began talking in murmurs, and the noise level slowly increased. Questions were hurled back and forth; all were ignored by the six.

The sudden crack of the pistol shot, fired by Nasima brought instant silence.

'Now you will all keep silent, or the next person will be shot.' She said this in English, then repeated her message in French. All was quiet for a few minutes – and then began something the terrorists had not anticipated and were incapable of dealing with. First a little girl asked to go to the toilet, followed quickly by a young boy. Within seconds nearly all the children were clamouring to go, and then one or two of the older adults. The situation was getting out of hand again, but when Khatun levelled his gun at a child there was instant hush.

'I'm warning you now, no more,' he said harshly. 'If you want to piss, then piss in your pants.'

There were no further interruptions.

The time was 2.50, and Carmichael was getting worried about Barber. No move could be made until the bomb had been dismantled. An explosion in a hold that size would sink the ferry in seconds; there probably wouldn't be time to launch a single lifeboat.

The passengers remained passive, waiting for help from the authorities, sure nothing could happen to them.

Carmichael looked at his watch. Five to two. Where the hell was Barber?

* * *

Down on the car deck, Barber had found a crowbar and, starting in the area where he had first seen Emile, had forced open the first car boot before he realised that a foreigner, if he had wired up his own car, would probably have a foreign registration. The car next to the one he had forced open was also British, but the third one beyond was Dutch. Barber hammered on the boot lid until it was sufficiently dented to allow him space to insert the bar. One heave and it flew open, exposing the explosive mechanism sitting on a bed of plastic explosive with three detonators placed at regular intervals across the white, putty-like substance. Barber grinned. This was the work of an amateur; effective, but simple to defuse.

A signal by radio would complete an electric circuit by causing a lever inside the box to shift, very much like that used to work the tail plane of model aircraft. The IRA were using similar devices in Northern Ireland, but with far greater sophistication, each bomb full of booby traps set for the unwary. Once the circuit was complete the electric detonators would set off the explosive cord, which in turn would sett off a more powerful detonator containing the primary intermediary explosives necessary to set off the main charge.

Carefully Barber withdrew the detonators pressed into the PE. For good measure he pulled out the electric device and crushed it underfoot. He then sprinted off towards the saloon, thankful that he had sufficient feeling back in his hand to enable him to hold the rifle correctly. It was two minutes to two. Gasping as he ran, he prayed he would be in time to save the first of the passengers earmarked to die in the name of the cause.

* * *

The announcement by Nuri Khatun that at two o'clock three people were to be shot was greeted with cries of fear and protest. At first the passengers didn't believe it, but when two men and a young woman were singled out, they were convinced. The three potential victims, who were standing in a group, suddenly found themselves isolated as the others drew instinctively away from them. The girl looked around her in bewilderment, as though she could not understand what was going on. Then, with a little moan, she moved towards the crowd, wanting to lose herself amongst them.

The people crowded further together, to keep her out. They were safe. They weren't the ones chosen by the terrorists. They were going to live a little longer, and the only sacrifice was this young girl they didn't know. Janet was standing further across the room, and the plight of the three brought tears to her eyes. Where was Steve? What was he doing? Why were Carmichael and Parker apart in the room? And those other two – were they the Russians? She had seen them impassively watch the victims be selected. They had to be the Soviets.

The two chosen men were standing quite still, pale as death. One was about thirty, the other in his mid-forties – both men casually dressed, obviously together.

'Move over here,' Khatun ordered harshly. 'Come on – move!' The way he screamed the last word betrayed the stress under which he was labouring.

The girl sank weeping to her knees. She urinated in her terror, and a pool spread slowly around her. Carmichael cursed under his breath. Poor kid. No matter what happened now, her life would be ruined. Her mind would snap, she'd have a breakdown and probably undergo a personality change so radical that her own family wouldn't know her. He had seen it all before.

Janet moved cautiously around until she was close to

Rashid Yagir, ready if the opportunity arose to claw his eyes out.

Suddenly there was an interruption. 'Wait!' said a voice, and all eyes turned to the man who had spoken.

John and Ida Smith had been standing at the back of the crowd, an insignificant couple who had been praying for the young man they had helped to turn up. They had been wondering what had become of him when the shock announcement was made – and then the girl collapsed.

John Smith took his wife's hand and looked at her. She smiled and nodded, unable to speak for a moment. Then, leaning forward and kissing him, she said softly:

'I love you.'

'And I love you too, my darling.' Their eyes met and held; then John called out, 'Wait!' and together they came forward. As they did so another man joined them. He was twenty-five years old, and only seconds before had arrived at a peace of mind he had thought would never be his.

Simon Birdridge had found his God, not through prayer, not through hours of self despair, torturing himself with his own disbelief. He was not forcing himself to go, pushing his courage to its limit; it was none of these things. It had just happened – an awareness of life and death, and of God, his God. For the first time the words 'my Father' meant exactly that, and the prayer had drawn on so often in the past, looking to it for courage, took on a new meaning. 'Our Father, which art in Heaven' . . . Simon was close to tears of joy as he put his hand on Ida's shoulder. The three of them walked together across the crowded saloon, a passage opening before them as the Red Sea parted to let Moses and his people into the Promised Land.

A hush had fallen on the saloon. What was happening? The uncertainty of the passengers was reflected and magnified in the Palestinians. All the guns were pointed at the three advancing people.

'Let them go,' said John Smith quietly. 'We'll take their place.'

230

Khatun looked bewildered, and shook his head. Before he could speak however Simon Birdridge said:

'Do as he says. I am a missionary of the Pentecostal Church, and am ready to die. Can you not see that these two also are ready?'

Without waiting for a reply, he gestured to the two men to help the girl, and together they sidled into the crowd, too numb to appreciate fully what was happening, and incapable of expressing their thanks.

Faced with what amounted to a fait accompli, Khatun, seeing that the time was now one minute past two, cocked his weapon and jerked it to one side. The three understood. He wanted the other passengers out of the line of fire.

Carmichael tensed and suddenly made up his mind. Stawizcki was standing in front, his arms at his sides. Carmichael took Uri's gun from his pocket and thrust it into Uri's right hand. 'Your life and freedom for those two over there.' He nodded at Rashid Yagir, and Mareka Kamal, one armed with an automatic, the other a pistol. Uri half nodded his head. He would do it and then turn the tide on Carmichael. But then Carmichael was aware that was what would happen. He was also ready. Carmichael sidled three feet to his left and carefully drew his right hand with the silenced gun out of his pocket.

Chapter 17

As Khatun raised his gun Barber appeared at the window, and took in the situation at a glance. Carmichael saw him, ground his teeth, urging silently, 'Move, Steve! For Christ's sake move!' Only a few more seconds were left. A few more seconds, that was all, to give Barber time to get round to the other door.

The ferry was rolling more heavily now as the wind picked up. According to the weather forecast, a storm was due. The ferry should have reached Rotterdam before it broke, but now could well be caught in the middle of it.

On the bridge, the Master had persuaded Enis Baum that they would be a lot more comfortable if he was allowed to steam slowly ahead for a mile or two, and then turn back. At first she had refused, but as the rolling increased and seasickness threatened, she was forced to agree.

The few seconds Carmichael had been praying for were provided by the terrorists themselves, as the starting up of the engines, the feeling of getting under way and the immediate lessening of the pitching and tossing of the boat became apparent. For a moment there was uncertainty in the air. What was happening? Barber reached the other door as Khatun recovered his poise and began tightening his finger on the trigger of the 38/49 SMG. As he thumbed over to automatic and safety catch off, Barber smashed through the door with a blood curdling scream that froze everyone in their tracks – but he was too late. So was Carmichael. So was Stawizcki. Nuri Khatun's finger had tightened on the trigger and the gun was firing as Barber shot him through the chest, the bullet entering through the small hole created by the pressure of air that builds up in front of the speeding bullet and exiting through his back, leaving a large ragged hole.

Aman al-Baz's gun was horizontal and about to fire when Carmichael fired. The bullet scattered the terrorist's brains all over the bulkhead behind him. Stawizcki had raised his hand and fired in one smooth movement but had missed his target. Rashid Yagir had been saved by a faint stomach and a trailing shoe lace. He didn't want to see the three people being killed. How could an old couple and a young priest or whatever he was benefit the cause? He had placed his Model 12 SMG across his legs and was bending to tie the lace when the door burst open and Barber hurtled in, screaming.

Stawizcki's bullet passed over Yagir's head by a hair's breadth; the Russian was already swivelling and firing at Mareka Kamal as he registered his miss. This time he hit. The bullet struck the girl in the trachea and almost severed her head from her neck.

Nasima Karami had dropped her gun in panic. As long as everything was going her way she was indeed a hard-nosed bitch, a sadistic bully who enjoyed seeing fear in others. Now, realising that her friends were dying around her, she instinctively threw down her weapon and raised her hands. Unfortunately for her, she was too slow. She knew it was all over, but the knowledge of their defeat was the last thing ever to register. Carmichael had turned, aimed and fired before he realised that it was unnecessary.

Amie Bustani too had seen all their plans dying with her friends. And although bewildered by what was happening, instead of giving in she thumbed her pistol to automatic and fired indiscriminately at the passengers. She was still firing when Barber blew her head off.

At that point Carmichael had sought another target – the one they had come to Holland to kill. He was too late, however. Even as he took aim he saw Parker fall, blood spreading across the side of his pale grey three piece suit. The Superintendent's opinion of Barber, already high, went up a further notch. Barber had also seen Parker drop, and thought Carmichael was one hell of a cool customer to have picked him off in that crowd.

What neither of them realised was that Parker died a hero. He had seen the girl lift her gun and point it to one side of him, where six year old twins were standing, screaming in terror. Acting purely on instinct, he bent to shield the children as she fired, and was dead before he touched the deck.

Rashid Yagir had looked up in bewilderment as the firing started, his laces still in his hands. Horrified, he watched his friends die and Parker fall. The paralysis lasted for five seconds.

Janet, who had also watched, frozen by the violent events, came to life at about the same time as Yagir and screamed Steve's name as the last remaining terrorist raised his gun. Barber spun round, but was too slow to duck or dive out of the line of fire. Janet acted instantly, aiming a kick at Yagir's genitals that brought him to his knees. Through the red mists of agony, he gritted his teeth and raised the gun again. Janet stood there, unable to move, knowing she was about to die.

The rifle was loud in the saloon. For a long time afterwards Janet was to have nightmares of that anguished face flaring up at her before exploding into a sickening mess of blood, brains and bone.

Pandemonium ensued. In the confusion Carmichael acted quickest. He turned on Stawizcki and without warning hit him on the side of his head. Too stunned and half collapsing, Uri was unable to prevent Carmichael removing the gun from his hand. 'Sorry Uri. Just in case,' was all he said. Karpov rushed to his friend's side. 'He'll be all right,' said Carmichael. 'You two keep down and keep quiet. You'll get out of this like I promised.' By this time the saloon had become silent. Barber and Janet hurried to the aid of the terrorists' three victims.

By a strange fluke, John Smith and Simon Birdridge were dead, while Ida, who had been in the middle of the two, was still alive. As he knelt by her side, Barber called to nobody in particular, 'Bring some clean hot water, and something I can use as a bandage.' Then, when no one responded, he looked around. 'You!' he yelled. 'Move your dumb arse!' The man, who had been standing looking down at him, mouth agape, pulled himself together and hurried away. Barber gently moved Ida into a more comfortable position, and as he did so her eyelids fluttered open. She smiled when she saw who it was.

'Is John dead?' she asked softly.

He nodded, too choked to speak. Then, clearing his throat, he said huskily, 'I'm sorry, truly sorry. If I'd been a few seconds earlier . . .'

'You mustn't blame yourself,' she began, then broke off as a paroxysm of coughing shook her.

'Don't talk,' Janet said softly. 'We're getting some water and things. Help will be coming shortly.'

Ida frowned. 'No, no help, please.' Seeing the uncertainty on his face, she went on, 'I'm dying anyway. No no – not through being shot. I have a terminal illness – leukemia – and will be dead soon anyway. My husband, John, he was afraid of . . . of being . . . alone. More . . . more afraid . . .' The effort of talking was becoming too much for her. 'More . . . afraid than of dying, this way, this way . . . is best. Tell me . . . your name . . . young man . . . He . . . we would have been . . . proud to have known you.'

'And I'd have been proud to have known you,' Barber said softly. She smiled, her eyes closed. 'My name . . .'

But Ida was dead.

Carmichael's hand on Barber's shoulder roused him from his sad contemplation of the dead woman's face. He looked up, his expression a mixture of sorrow and rage.

'Come on Steve,' the Superintendent said softly. 'We've still got work to do.'

The bodies were covered, and hot drinks were served to the passengers, who were beginning to get over their shock, and were talking quietly together. A girl, the one who had been the intended victim, sat in a corner in deep shock, unable to speak, and Janet went across to look after her.

'You two men,' ordered Carmichael, indicating two of the crew nearest to him, 'Collect all the weapons you can find and stack them in a corner. You two, keep the other passengers quiet. Open the bar and prepare some food and drink.' He turned to Barber. 'There will be two or possibly three of them on the bridge. They will have heard some of the firing but not our silenced shots. With luck they will think it was the shooting only of the hostages. But we'll have to move fast. They could be up there waiting for confirmation of the deaths or may send somebody down to look. Whichever way it is we don't have much time.'

'What about Parker?' asked Barber.

'He's dead.' Carmichael nodded across the room. The two Russians had already been to look for themselves, and were now retreating to a corner of the saloon.

'And what about them?'

'I promised Uri their freedom. He helped. Without him there would have been a lot more deaths. So leave them, they can look after themselves now.' He suddenly turned to one of the uniformed officers who was sorting out the passengers and organising food and drink. 'You, I want some help.' He took his ID from his pocket as the man warily approached and said, 'Describe the bridge layout to me, as quickly as you can.'

Seeing the Special Branch name on the card reassured him. 'Thank God . . .' he began.

'Never mind that now,' said Carmichael sharply. 'Come on, we haven't got all night.'

*   *   *

Enis Baum tried to appear nonchalant, but the effort was almost too much for her. Had the killings been necessary after all? Whatever one believed, however, one tried to persuade not only oneself but others as well, when it came down to it . . . was it really necessary? Angrily she fought down her self doubts. All was going smoothly, exactly as planned. Within an hour at most, Jemel would join them, and then he

236

could take over. The faith Enis and the others had in Jemel Hassan was touching.

'Get on the radio,' she ordered the Master harshly, 'and inform them that the first three hostages have died. Remind them another will die in one hour's time.' Her two compatriots looked at her with strained faces, and she continued in French: 'Cheer up! It's all going exactly as we planned. We'll soon be on our way.'

'Where to?' asked Ibrahim Bakr sullenly. He was suddenly frightened; they were now well and truly outside the law.

Enis, pretending she hadn't heard, crossed to the door leading to the radio room and listened to the Master establishing radio contact with General Max Laurier. At that moment the General was speeding in his car to the airport. Once there, he would transfer to his helicopter and be flown to the prison.

The news of the death of the passengers was received in silence. When the Master asked for the third time if the General was still there, he affirmed that he was, and said that according to his pilot he could be at the ferry by 4.15 am provided the weather did not worsen. In the meantime, would the terrorists agree to continuing towards the Dutch coast, where it was more sheltered, and a helicopter transfer would be easier?

Enis did agree, but declined to spare the life of the hostage due to be shot at four o'clock. The conversation was abruptly terminated by General Laurier as he arrived at the heliport.

The other two were standing on either side of the bridge facing inwards, covering the four crewmen when they heard the noise and felt the draught as the doors opened. Before they could react, Barber stepped through one door and Carmichael the other. The two Englishmen shot the terrorists at point blank range, and the noise, not of the silenced pistols but of the bodies being flung against the opposite bulkheads, brought Enis Baum out of the radio shack at a rush. The light from the radio room streamed out, illuminating the

237

darkened bridge. The radio room door, which opened outwards, hid Carmichael from Enis's view, but she found herself face to face with Barber. They stared at each other for a full second, then he said softly.

'It's all over. Drop your gun and come quietly.'

Her pretty face distorted into a mask of hatred and she snatched up the firing device suspended at her waist and pressed the button. Nothing happened. She pressed again, in disbelief.

'You're wasting your time, Barber told her, still in the same measured tone. 'I've defused the bomb. There's nothing left.'

'Yes there is,' she snapped, raising her gun. Barber fired instantly but his weapon jammed. Enis laughed, but before she could press the trigger, half her head was blown away, and Barber's head was left ringing from the gun blast that had gone off next to his ear. He turned, not knowing what to expect, surprised to see it was the Mate holding the gun. His face working, the latter fired a second and then a third bullet into the corpse. Barber's hand clamped on the Mate's wrist preventing him firing any more.

'She was an animal,' he said. 'I'm glad I killed her.' He looked defiantly at the others, expecting censure, but none came. He had grabbed Abdul Muein's gun as the latter fell, and turned it to good use.

The Master, quickly recovering himself, said to the helmsman: 'Ring on seventeen knots and turn to an initial heading of one one zero. Sparks,' he ordered the radio operator, 'contact the shore and tell them we're on our way. Oh, and cancel that damned helicopter. Now, perhaps you gentlemen will be good enough to tell me what's going on aboard my own ship?'

They told him ... some of it. At least, they told him a story that sounded plausible. Carmichael was good at that.

* * *

Barber left the bridge and went down to the saloon to find

Janet. He sat beside her for about ten minutes while she coaxed the shocked girl into drinking some hot sweet tea. Then she covered her with a blanket and turned to Barber, who was leaning back, too weary to think straight. The adrenalin that had kept him going all night was just about used up.

'Tell me what it was all about,' she said in a quiet voice. When he did not reply she continued. 'I'm going to get us some strong coffee and a large amount of whisky – the bar seems to be open to anyone who wants to help themselves. When I come back, either you tell me, or there's no hope for us together. I love you, Steve, but I've got to know the truth if we're to stand any chance of making it together.'

She rose and walked away. Barber grinned wearily. Would they make it together?

It took a long time in the telling. Dawn was breaking, and their cups and glasses had been replenished three times by the time he had finished. Janet listened in silence, a silence that was prolonged for several minutes after he had stopped speaking.

'It's not a pretty story when told like that,' he went on at last, 'and if you want out ...' He broke off, and had to cough to cover his emotion. 'If you want out I ... I'll understand. It was fun while it lasted – and the best – and I'll always remember...'

'Shut up, you ass!' Janet interrupted fiercely. 'I don't want out. I'm not going anywhere; at least, if I do then it'll be with you. You are a clot in some ways, Steve, do you know that?' She leaned over and kissed him. 'But I love you all the more for it.'

He smiled contentedly and sat back, closing his eyes for a few minutes...

More than two hours later he felt his shoulder being roughly shaken, and fought his way out of a deep sleep. Carmichael was standing over him, looking as if he hadn't slept at all – which he hadn't.

'Steve, we've things to do,' he said urgently. 'I'll explain

239

later, but listen carefully. Go down into the car deck and get about ten pounds of that plastic explosive from the car. Bring a couple of detonators as well, and the detcord. Have you got that?'

'Sure,' replied Barber, fully awake now. 'What's the time?'

'Nine thirty. There's a fast launch on its way, with Max Laurier on board.' Seeing Steve's blank look he added, 'He's head of Dutch counter-espionage. When he gets here, leave all the talking to me. Look, go and get the stuff and then I'll brief you.' He glanced at Janet, sleeping like a baby with her cheek pillowed on her hands. 'She looks peaceful enough, anyway. I suppose you've told her everything?' Before Barber could reply he continued, 'It doesn't matter, she already knew too much. Now go on – get cracking.'

As Barber threaded his way through the sleeping passengers who had spread themselves out all over the saloon, Carmichael smiled after him. He would make one of Carmichael's best men, though Barber didn't know it at the time.

Strange about the passengers, he thought. Few of them had been able to bring themselves to return to their cabins. There was a feeling of safety in numbers. Even though they had not felt secure with the guns of the Palestinians pointing at them, even though they were willing to ditch others as long as they themselves could stay alive, they still rested more easily, lost in the crowd. Actually some were beginning to wake up, stretching themselves and wandering off to find the toilets or going below to their cabins, to wash or shower.

Barber came back carrying his holdall, the explosives hidden under the clothes he'd scattered when digging out the rifle. He sat beside Carmichael and waited for him to say what was going on.

'Let's go and get some coffee,' Carmichael said. 'My eyes feel full of sand, and it hurts my brain trying to think.'

Strong coffee laced liberally with brandy helped a lot. Replenishing both their cups, the Chief Superintendent said:

'When the General gets here I'll arrange for you and Janet to leave on his launch. It'll get you in a good half hour before the ferry, and away before the regular police and newsmen arrive. One of Max's men will meet you and take you to Schipol; he'll pass you through customs, so you'll have no problem about the gun you're carrying, nor the explosives. Do you have somewhere you and Janet can hole up for a few days?'

Barber nodded, thinking about Dartmouth.

'Good. Stay there until you hear from me. Let my office know where I can contact you. Okay?'

'Clear as mud so far. What about the Russians?'

'They are on their own. They'll be all right. Their passports and documents will hold up.' He changed the subject.

'I have another job for you to do. Let's see . . . it's Thursday today. If I can move things fast enough, I should need you on Saturday.'

'What job?' Barber demanded, frowning. 'I only contracted to do this one, and it's all over now, bar the shouting.'

'You're wrong there, son. It's all part of the same job. The final bit.'

Barber shook his head. 'No way. Any more is a new contract, negotiable.'

'Nope, you're wrong. As of one hour ago you and Janet are agents working on an assignment for me. The records will show that you've been working for me for the last six months, Janet for four. Contracts, pay checks and – most importantly – the official secrets form will all bear your signatures. Oh, by the way,' he added, 'do this one for me, and I guarantee you both a job together.'

'Why the hell did you go to such lengths?' Barber asked incredulously.

'I saw you with your hands together and knew you were telling all. It was the only way I could think of covering her – and then I thought I might as well cover you the same way. And believe me, the covering is cast iron,' he added, his smile taking the sting out of the words.

241

Barber shrugged, 'You're a tricky bastard, I hope I'm making the right decision.'

'I think you are,' Carmichael said.

The throb of the engines was changing, and they became aware that the ferry was slowing down.

'This'll be Max. I'd better go and meet him,' said Carmichael, making to get up.

'Hang on. He'll be a few minutes yet,' said Barber. 'I wanted to say that that was good shooting when you took out Parker. I was most impressed.'

Carmichael chuckled wryly. 'I thought it was you but there are too many bullet holes. I discovered a short while ago that it was neither of us. Parker died a hero, would you believe, shielding a couple of young children from one of the terrorists' bullets.'

'Well, I'm damned!' Barber shook his head, the irony not lost on him. Then he added. 'One more thing. Who were those people? What did they want? Do you know yet?'

Carmichael quickly explained, then hurried away to meet the General.

The Chief Superintendent greeted the tall, gangling man in his early sixties, with white hair, autocratic features and an unmistakable air of command.

'Max! How the devil are you?' Carmichael said, shaking the other man warmly by the hand.

'Hullo James. It's good to see you again. You can't imagine my relief when I heard your voice on the radio. Let's find somewhere quiet, and you can tell me what's going on and how you happened to be here.'

A short while later the General's boat was heading inshore with Barber and Janet on board. Instructions had been passed. No questions would be asked. They would return to the UK without hindrance.

By 16.00 they were on the express train to Exeter. They changed there and were in Dartmouth by 19.00 hours. They had both dozed for the greater part of the journey, speaking little, but even so, arriving at the house, they went straight to bed and slept again until midday.

★   ★   ★

Once free of the ferry and on Dutch soil, Uri Stawizcki thought about what Carmichael had said. To him it made sense, and he only hoped that Andrea Bolkovsky agreed with him. He had been impressed too, by the Englishman's knowledge and even more important, his knowledge of the personalities involved.

Stawizcki fretted all the way to Hanover; the journey seemed endless. They had just made it to the station in time to catch the train. As expected, it was running on time, but even so he kept looking at his watch. He had to talk to Bolkovsky before he heard from any other source what had happened; he had to brief him on what to say, otherwise Bitov could have his balls in a sling. Enschede was past, as was the German customs. Osnabruck was up ahead, and for a fleeting second he thought of trying to telephone his boss from there before dismissing the idea.

Karpov had asked him why he didn't ring from the Embassy in the Hague. He had shrugged, then admitted he didn't trust the staff there. He wouldn't put it past Bitov to have some of the staff reporting directly to him, and anyway, nowadays, even when ordered by the KGB, there was no guarantee their call wouldn't be tapped. No, this way was slower but safer. They would be in Hanover in an hour, and East Berlin by nightfall. There they would have no problem in putting through a private call to Bolkovsky.

East Berlin was bitterly cold after the mildness of the coast. Within an hour of arriving, and after a taxi ride through the drab, depressing streets, Stawizcki got to a safe 'phone and put a call through to his boss. The line was disgustingly bad, and he almost screamed himself hoarse trying to tell Bolkovsky what had happened. However, when he had finished he was relieved to hear the faint voice saying:

'Ring Carmichael from there and tell him I'll be on time.'

* * *

General Max Laurier could not have been more helpful. He agreed not to release Parker's name to the press for eight hours – longer, if Carmichael wanted it, which he didn't – and asked no questions. He was only too pleased to be of help. It put the British in his debt, and one day they would be asked to pay up. He wondered idly what the man and the girl he had helped on their way were carrying in their bag. Oh well, it was no concern of his. Carmichael, as always, had everything under control.

Carmichael himself wasn't feeling so sanguine. He was absolutely exhausted, and determined that when he got home he would take Joan away on holiday for a week or two. He intended looking for his retirement house now, maybe even with a view to taking out another mortgage. It would be expensive, but he could afford it . . . just.

Right now, though, he still had a lot to do. He had to get to Hull as quickly as possible, and then back to London. He needed to talk to his boss, and get him to talk to Fred Pearce, the Permanent Undersecretary at the Ministry; then on to Finland, back again for that meeting – and he needed to mobilise Barber. Christ, he didn't think he could manage it all.

Laurier arranged a helicopter to pick Carmichael up at the Rotterdam terminal and fly him direct to Kermington airport in Humberside. From there he could get a taxi and be in Hull within an hour.

His warrant card whisked him through customs and immigration, and being the only person to be leaving the small airport at the time, he had no trouble in getting a cab. Although the driver assured him it would probably be quicker to take the ferry across the river, rather than be driven all the way round by road – which would also be far more expensive – Carmichael decided on the long way. He slept all the way, and awoke feeling like death when the taxi drew up outside Parker's house. He paid off the driver, then slowly climbed the few steps and rang the door bell.

Chapter 18

As he waited, Carmichael noticed that the smashed glass had been cleared up. He wondered briefly if his instructions had been carried out. Had there been enough time to get a search warrant since he had radioed in?

Presently a young constable opened the door. Carmichael showed his SB card and brushed past, in a hurry to get this over with.

'Inspector Lester is waiting for you in the study, sir. It's . . .'

'I know where it is,' he said, more harshly than he intended. Seeing the young man's crestfallen look, he paused at the door. 'Sorry son, I've had a bad night. What's your name, by the way?'

The constable perked up. 'Hearn, sir.'

'Okay, Hearn. Is Mrs Parker here?'

Upstairs in her room, sir.'

'Good. Will you go up and ask her if she'd be good enough to come down and see me? Tell her it's very important.'

'Yes, sir.'

The constable bounded up the stairs two at a time, eager to do the bidding of a Chief Superintendent of Special Branch. Wait until he told the others at the station; they'd be green with envy.

Carmichael entered the study. A tall morose looking man in an inspector's uniform looked round from the bookcase where he'd been studying the titles displayed there. The Chief Superintendent stepped forward, hand outstretched.

'Carmichael, Special Branch,' he said, noticing the other

246

man's freshly pressed uniform, the kid gloves in his left hand and the disdainful expression on his lean face as he surveyed Carmichael's rumpled suit and dishevelled appearance.

'Do you have the warrant?' Carmichael went on tersely.

'Er ... yes.' The other paused. 'My name's Webster. Inspector Webster,' he went on, emphasising his rank. He obviously expected Carmichael to tell him his own status so that he would know how to address him, but Carmichael chose to let him wonder, replying merely:

'As long as you've got it. I shan't bother showing the lady unless she gets difficult. I've sent Hearn to fetch her. When she arrives I'd like to be left alone with her.'

'H'm. Highly irregular that,' Webster looked affronted. 'I think I should remain. She may also want to contact a solicitor. She has the right, you know.' His tone was that of an instructor lecturing a cadet – which was precisely what his last job in the force had been; teaching young people to become policemen and policewomen. He had been ideally suited to the work, being a devotee of discipline, strict adherence to rules and spit and polish.

Carmichael fixed him with a baleful stare. 'She will not wish to see a solicitor, nor will she wish you to be present. I happen to be a Chief Superintendent, and I don't want you here, understand?'

Webster drew himself up to his not inconsiderable height, positively quivering with hostility.

'Yes ... sir,' he snapped, turned on his heel and marched out, almost colliding with Dorothy Parker as he reached the door. Watching him go, Carmichael cursed himself. If he wasn't so tired he could have handled it better. Still it couldn't be helped. Better concentrate on the matter in hand. Poor woman – he wondered how much she knew about Parker's real background.

'I'm sorry to trouble you, Mrs Parker, but I have some bad news for you,' he began. 'Perhaps you'd like to sit down, before we go any further.' Hell – he always managed things like this so badly. He had hated it when he had first started with the police, and was glad when he transferred to the Service and didn't have to be the bringer of bad news any more. Now here he was, doing it again.

Unexpectedly, she made it easy for him.

'I know what you're about to say.' Her tone did not reveal the hatred she felt for the man standing before her. 'I know about my husband. He told me everything before I left for my sister's, and it has made no difference at all to our relationship. I love him, and always will. I shall also join him in Russia at the earliest opportunity. I care nothing for politics. They are of no consequence to me whatsoever.'

She had been rehearsing her speech for so long that it was impossible for Carmichael to interrupt. Not that he wanted to, there was more than a possibility that she would tell him more than she intended.

'My country as such also means very little to me,' Dorothy Parker went on. 'I don't believe in patriotism, only in love for one's family. My husband is my family. I shall go wherever he is, and live with him for the rest of my life.'

She was clearly wandering from whatever she had meant to say, and confusing herself. Pausing, she shook her head slightly as though to clear it. Her tenseness, the dark shadows under her eyes, were evidence of past sleepless nights. When her husband had been with her it had been easy to be brave; now she was alone, it was the hardest thing in the world. How was she to cope with the press, with television news hounds? What could she say to Simon? She knew she owed it to him to tell him before it became common knowledge, but she didn't know how. How did one tell one's son that his father was a spy? A spy, moreover for the country whose ideology he, Simon, loathed and detested? She shuddered suddenly, and swayed a little.

'Please sit down, Mrs Parker,' said Carmichael, taking her arm and leading her unresisting to the sofa. 'I'm afraid the news is worse than you think.' He paused, then went on gently, 'Your husband is dead.'

She looked at him uncomprehendingly. 'What do you

mean, dead? Don't be ridiculous. He's gone to Russia,' she argued, as though saying it would make it true.

He shook his head. 'No, he was trying to go. He was killed last night while saving two children from being shot by terrorists.'

Dorothy Parker looked at him, her eyes unnaturally bright.

'Tell me what happened,' she said in a controlled voice. 'Exactly as it happened.'

'We were on our way to arrest your husband,' Carmichael lied. 'He'd reached the ferry before we could stop him. A colleague and I went on board, but half-way across the Channel the ferry was hi-jacked by terrorists. There was a gun battle. One of the terrorists was about to fire into the crowd of passengers and your husband, seeing what was about to happen, shielded two children with his own body. Unfortunately he himself was shot dead.' 'Unfortunately my Aunt Fanny,' thought Carmichael. 'Thank God it happened that way.' 'Before he died he told me that he'd left a letter with you, to be opened on his death, if the circumstances warranted it. He said that in this case they didn't, and that I was to come here and get the letter from you before you read it.'

He stopped. Parker's wife sat quite still for several seconds; then she slowly shook her head.

'I don't believe it. I can't believe he's dead. I won't! She screamed the last word, then broke down, sobbing into her hands. The door opened and Inspector Webster put his head in.

'What's wrong? What's going on here? I must protest . . .' he began.

It was all Carmichael needed.

'Get out, and don't come back until I send for you,' he snapped.

'I shall submit a written rep . . .'

'Out, I said – or by Christ you'll end up pounding the beat for the rest of your career!' It was an empty threat, and they both knew it. Nevertheless it made Carmichael feel better to say it, and it was uttered with such venom that the startled Inspector withdrew without another word.

After a few minutes the weeping woman calmed down. 'Do . . . do you have a . . . a hankie, please?'

He handed her a clean white one from his breast pocket, and when she had dried her eyes and smoothed her hair she sat up very straight, resuming her previous air of dignity.

'Thank you. I'm better now,' she said. 'I . . . I think I . . . I'd like to read the letter before I hand it over . . . It . . . it's my last message from him, you see, and somehow, in spite of what he said to you, I'd still like to read it.'

'Mrs Parker, I have a good idea of what's written there, and I earnestly recommend that you hand it over to me without opening it. If there is indeed a personal message in it for you, I shall ensure that you get it. In fact, if you give it to me now, I'll read it and pass on to you anything that is relevant to you.'

'Relevant to me? Chief Superintendent, it's all relevant to me. It's the last letter written by my husband, and I wish to read it. Is that so unreasonable?' Her voice was as cold as her eyes, which regarded Carmichael with unconcealed loathing.

'Please, Mrs Parker . . .'

'No, Superintendent! My mind is made up. You shall have the letter after I've finished with it, and not before.'

'I have a search warrant . . .' began Carmichael.

'Search all you like.' Dorothy Parker's lip curled in defiance. 'You will never find it in a million years.'

Carmichael knew he didn't have the time. There was just too much to do, and he had to have the letter before he left.

'Mrs Parker, does your son know about his father?' he asked. The startled look on her face gave him the answer. 'I think not. I'll make a deal with you. You have one minute to make up your mind before I 'phone him.' He didn't tell her he had no idea where to find her son. 'At the moment your husband has died a hero. He can be buried as such, and no one need ever know the truth. Your son will be proud of him, and cherish his memory. If I tell him what his father was really like I have no doubt he will loathe him for the rest of his days. And that will probably affect his relationship with you.'

Dorothy Parker had become deathly pale.

'You wouldn't do that,' she said softly. 'You couldn't . . .'

Carmichael was at the end of his tether, bone weary with still too much to do. He crossed to the desk, lifted the receiver and dialled the number of his office. The Service could trace Simon Parker more quickly than any other force in the country; could call on more manpower, without having to give an explanation, than even SB, from the constabulary to the customs to the different military intelligence services.

'Wait.' Dorothy Parker looked at him with lacklustre eyes, defeat evident in every line of her slumped body. 'There's no need for that. Take out the third book on the second row of the bookshelf. There's a button behind. Press it, and . . .' She trailed off, watching as Carmichael followed her instructions. The lower wall panelling swung open. She was right – they'd never have found the place, not without taking the house apart.

There were two drawers, both locked. The lower drawer contained a single envelope, addressed to Dorothy.

Carmichael ripped it open, took out the folded sheet and scanned its contents. It was all there, including his, Carmichael's, involvement and the reason for it. Parker had instructed his wife to publish the information, which, had she done so, would have torn Britain apart. The letter was crammed with facts and dates; the original meeting, the Prime Minister's involvement. Carmichael wondered when Parker had found time to write it. After all, he couldn't have learned any of this stuff until he had met with the Russians in the gardens in town. Not that it mattered. The important thing was that he, Carmichael, had his hands on it, and thankfully, it was dated.

The last part was a personal message to Dorothy Parker. Carefully tearing it off, he handed it to her and went away

251

without another word. He paused in the hall to instruct the Inspector to get a doctor for Mrs Parker, and to tell him that he would not be needing the search warrant after all. Then he left the house, flagged down a passing taxi and headed for the railway station.

In the train on the way to Leeds he cat-napped for about ten minutes, too keyed up to relax properly. It was still an effort to waken fully when the train stopped, and disembark to look for a telephone. He rang his office, spoke to his boss briefly and hung up. It was all arranged.

Carmichael slept all the way to Kings' Cross, having taken a first class ticket. He awoke reasonably refreshed, but knew he needed a proper night's sleep in bed before he recovered fully.

The meeting that took place lasted half an hour. Parker's letter, with its obvious implications, clinched the matter. As a result, Carmichael was given a chauffeur-driven car to Biggin Hill, and there transferred to an RAF Harrier.

Under the guise of a night training exercise he was flown to Stockholm, and by midnight was drinking a large whisky in his room in the Hotel Vaux, near the harbour. The place was clean, hospitable and inconspicuous, just the way he liked it. As he was drifting off to sleep he wondered what Andrea Bolkovsky was like in person.

Midday found Carmichael sitting on the terrace of the Hotel Landia, a large hotel near the central square in Helsinki. The European weather was up to its usual tricks, and the day was uncommonly warm. He ordered a cold lager and sat sipping it, enjoying the feel of the sun on his face and preparing himself mentally for the coming encounter.

Although he had never met him, Carmichael had seen photographs of Bolkovsky and recognised him immediately as he crossed the square, pigeons scattering before him. The Russian also picked Carmichael out on the crowded terrace, and pushing through the lunch time groups of businessmen, he held out his hand with a warm, sincere smile.

'I've taken the liberty of ordering vodkas and lager for us

both. Is that all right with you?' Carmichael asked, addressing him in fluent Russian.

'Fine, fine. I see you've done your homework,' Bolkovsky replied, in excellent English. Having established their fluency in each other's language, they both chuckled, and agreed, as they were on neutral territory, to converse in a neutral language.

'How about German?' Carmichael enquired.

'Excellent! For one awful moment I thought you were going to suggest Finnish, which is a language I've never mastered.'

Carmichael smiled. 'Me neither!' Then, becoming grave, he leaned forward and said in a low voice, 'Andrea, you know all about Parker's death and what happened.'

Bolkovsky shrugged, his eyes wary. 'I understand from Uri he was killed by the terrorists. The Palestinians. The news is worldwide. He is a hero. They are ridiculed yet again. I feel sorry for that people.'

Carmichael nodded. 'So do I. However, there is more that I want from you in an exchange. I know you have somebody high in our Ministry, and that he's one of three men. One of those I'm sure is innocent, so that leaves two. I could find him with a little difficulty, but after a good deal of time and effort, and I see no reason to waste either. I'll make a deal with you. Let me present you with my offer, and while we have lunch you think about it.'

He paused. The Russian's face remained impassive, and he said nothing. Presently Carmichael went on: 'It meant a lot to you to get Parker back to Russia safely. Now, not only is he dead but he died a hero. It will be even more difficult now for you to discredit him. In fact we might be able to use any mud slinging you might try as useful propaganda against you.'

Bolkovsky nodded slowly, intrigued now by the astute Englishman sitting opposite him, a man he had learnt not to underestimate. The latter continued:

'I believe Bitov has enough ammunition against you to dis-

253

credit you more than is justifiable after what has happened; however, you're the best judge of that. Now, knowing how you work, I would guess a spy as important as the one in my Ministry would be run by Bitov himself. I have here,' he reached into his jacket pocket and withdrew an envelope, 'written proof that your man is a double agent; that he set the whole thing up. The only thing missing is his name. If you give it to me, I'll not only get you off the hook, but I'll serve you Bitov's head on a plate, complete with an apple in his mouth.' He picked up his glass abruptly, drained it and beckoned for a waiter. 'Same again,' he ordered, 'and bring us a menu, please. We'd like to eat.'

They talked about international politics and the Middle East until they got to the coffee and schnapps. Sipping his Swiss Williams Pear, Andrea Bolkovsky remarked:

'I've always believed it to be a lousy world, Jim, so why are you helping me? You must have an ulterior motive, but I confess I can't see it.'

Carmichael shook his head. 'There isn't one.' He leaned forward. 'Look, just as he was leaving, Uri commented to me that he was surprised by my understanding of the personalities involved in the KGB. I don't want your Number 3 getting to Number 2 and eventually to the top. We in the west would prefer you to stay there just as much as you yourself would. Christ, Andrea – you know what's going on. Unless we can maintain some sort of status quo, keep as many moderate people at the top, on both sides, as possible, we can say goodbye to the world as we know it now. I am a moderate man, and I think you are too. We know the truth about our so-called leaders, what detente really means, the whole works – and we need to work not together, because that's impossible, but in parallel. Do you understand what I'm getting at?'

'Yes Jim, only too well. I think the same as you do – which is why I agree to your proposal.'

When he was given the name he had asked for, Carmichael grunted. 'Thanks. You confirmed what I thought.

Incidentally, he won't be placed on trial.'

Bolkovsky looked at Carmichael dead pan. 'I see,' he said.

Carmichael nodded. 'I think,' he said, as he rose to his feet, 'that we ought to arrange meetings like this on a regular basis, and include the rest of Europe and America; a sort of Top Agents' Congress. Cheerio Andrea. It's been a pleasure meeting you at last.'

'And you Jim. Alles gut.'

They shook hands, then Bolkovsky stood and watched Carmichael go with genuine regret. He was the enemy, and Bitov the friend and ally. What a joke!

★   ★   ★

Carmichael caught a direct flight to London, arriving just before 20.30 hours. His chief was waiting in his office to hear the report on the meeting with Bolkovsky. Afterwards Carmichael rang Barber. When the Chief Superintendent arrived home, well past midnight, it was all set.

★   ★   ★

Pearce, Walters and Chapman were waiting for Carmichael to arrive; Chapman seated in his usual place at the head of the table, the other two placed on either side.

'This is too bad,' Dennis Walters grumbled. 'Another weekend cocked up. Surely all this could have waited until Monday? I know the papers got it all wrong – all that nonsense about Parker dying a hero – but I'm not actually panting to hear the truth at this very moment.' He glanced irritably at his watch. 'Where is that bloody man?'

'He'll be along shortly,' replied Chapman. 'He's had a particularly busy time. I apologise for ruining your weekend again – I agree it is a bit much – but I don't believe this can wait, and I won't be here next Monday and Tuesday. I thought it better to get it over with now, and write finished to the whole sordid business. I . . .' He broke off as the door opened. 'Ah – Jim. Come on in, take a seat.'

'Sorry I'm late gentlemen. I had one or two things to sort

255

out.' Carmichael sat down next to Walters, adding, 'This won't take too long, I hope.'

* * *

Barber left his hired car in the multi-storey car park and walked the mile or so to his destination. He was early and enjoyed the stroll in spite of the blustery wind and threatening sky. The long range weather forecast had promised Britain one of the wettest summers in twenty years, and for once it seemed to have got it right.

He showed his pass to a disinterested guard at the Ministry door and walked in as though he belonged there. He even remembered to address the guard by his christian name, just to prove his familiarity with the set-up. He took the lift to the third floor, got out and walked up another two flights. Then he took a different lift down to the basement garage. As he expected, there were only half a dozen cars parked there, and he had no difficulty in recognising the one he wanted.

As previously arranged, the door was unlocked. Carmichael had seen to that. He reached under the dashboard, located the ignition wires, cut each one, twisted in a few feet of his own wire and reconnected the ignition. Then he threaded the wires under the carpet and as far as the driver's seat; it was a two door saloon, and he pushed the seat forward to make the task easier. Moulding the plastic explosive flat, he inserted two detonators, connected them to the wire he had run, then replaced the seat, smoothed the carpet and left the same way he came.

Waving a cheery farewell to the guard at the door, Barber walked down to the embankment. At a quiet spot, less than half a mile from where he had ditched his weighted suitcase all those eons ago, he took off the wig he was wearing then peeled off the bushy eyebrows. Dropping them into a convenient waste paper bin, he strolled on towards the underground. He had an hour to wait for his train to the west country.

⋆   ⋆   ⋆

The meeting was over.

'Waste of bloody time,' Dennis Walters declared. 'It could easily have waited until next week. Come on, Pearce, I'll give you a lift.'

'Thanks,' replied the latter, rising to his feet. Carmichael stayed where he was. He saw Chapman press a button, and almost at once his secretary came in.

'Mr Pearce,' she said, with a little frown, 'I have a call for you. It's long distance and a very bad line, but the party said it was important. Where would you like to take the call?'

Chapman answered for him. 'Put it through here. Come on Jim, we'll wait outside.' He waved a hand as Pearce started to protest. 'No problem. Come on.'

He led the way out. His secretary was putting on her coat to leave. Chapman drew Carmichael to one side as though to have a confidential word, saying politely to Walters, 'Oh – excuse us, will you Dennis? I'll tell Fred you've already gone on down, and that you'll bring the car round to the front. Okay?'

Walters grunted and stalked out, his face like thunder.

Chapman's secretary was having difficulty with the connection, fiddling with the telephone, impatient to go now she had her coat on. After a few minutes she gave up and apologised to Pearce, saying that his caller seemed to have hung up.

'Never mind Fred,' said Chapman, as Pearce emerged from the boardroom. 'If it's important they'll call back, whoever it is. Oh, Dennis said he'll meet you out front.'

'I'll walk down with you,' added Carmichael. 'It's time I went home.'

He led the way to the lift, followed by Walters and the secretary, Chapman having stayed behind, pleading work to do before he went away. Carmichael thought he felt a slight tremor as the lift dropped to the ground floor, but neither of the other two appeared to notice anything. At the door he

257

said goodbye to them both. You'll have a long wait for your lift home, he thought, hurrying for the underground.

As he sat in the train he remembered Uri Stawizcki's words. 'There's never a winner, we just have to try and keep the status quo.' The status quo; that's what it always came down to in the end. It was all they could ask for. To date, there'd been the longest period of peace in Europe's history. It was a frightening thought.

Recalling the Middle East job he had been working on before all the Parker business cropped up, Carmichael smiled. He had found just the team to send.

Epilogue

On the following Wednesday Carmichael journeyed to Dartmouth to see Barber and Janet. He sat in one of the easy chairs, a beer in his hand and the other two perched side by side on the sofa, waiting to find out what he wanted. He didn't make them wait long.

'I've been in a quandary as to what to do about you two,' he said. 'You know too much to be allowed to run loose, but I can't arrest you or shut you up quietly somewhere. So,' he went on with a grin, 'I have arrived at the only solution.' He paused for effect. 'What I propose is that you both work for me, on a full time, regular basis. Before you answer, let me tell you what I have in mind. There's a little training to undergo, a few weeks, that's all. Radio signals, codes, stuff like that – and then I intend giving you a simple assignment which should start in the Middle East, and will finish God knows where. All you're doing is looking for somebody. If you find him, you simply keep tabs and pass the information on to the Americans. They'll take it from there.' He stopped to finish his beer, then added, 'I suggest you travel as man and wife.'

'Another?' offered Barber. Carmichael nodded, holding out his glass.

'I'll tell you more about the assignment closer to the date,' he went on, watching the cold beer froth into the glass.

'A question,' interrupted Janet. 'How do you know this man, whoever he is, will still be missing in a few weeks time?'

'I don't. But from what I know of the situation, I think he will be.' He shrugged. 'Of course I could be wrong.' The last

259

sentence was clearly not intended to be taken seriously, and his smile further suggested that he was just kidding. You, thought Barber, are a devious, likeable bastard – and I'm not sure which is the correct word order for that description; likeable, devious or bastard.

'Can we think about it?' he said aloud.

'Sure, while we enjoy dinner. Afterwards I'll treat you to a drink at my hotel, and you can tell me your decision.'

Barber laughed. 'Not much time to think is there?'

'By the way,' said Carmichael, ignoring the comment, 'how's your brother doing? Oh, and your sister-in-law. Expecting a baby isn't she?'

'Not any more. I 'phoned yesterday to learn I'm now a proud uncle.'

'What was it, boy or girl?'

'Boy,' said Janet. 'Named Matthew, after Sue's father and, I quote, "Steven, after a bum of a brother," unquote.'

'Congratulations!' Carmichael said sincerely. He felt Phil Barber and his wife deserved one good break – as did Steve, too, if it came to that. 'When's he going to have his operation?'

'More good news,' said Barber. 'He's off to Switzerland very soon. His boss went to see him in hospital and told him not to worry about his job, it'll still be waiting for him when he's fully recovered. In the meantime the company will handle his claim for the serious injury compensation he's entitled to, seeing that he got hurt due to criminal activity. Apparently the State will take care of all bills until he's well, and there'll be some money left over. Sue in the meantime will stay with her parents, who'll be delighted to have her at home for a few months.'

'That is indeed good news,' said Carmichael.

Much later, over the last glass of wine Carmichael looked at them both seriously. 'Now tell me,' he said, 'What have you both decided about the job?'

Barber answered for them both. 'How much is the salary?'

'Mercenary bastard,' was Carmichael's reply.

260

Three months later Barber and Janet were sitting outside a cafe in Beirut. They had just collected two letters from the post office around the corner, and Barber recognised the writing. The top one was from Philip, in Switzerland, the second from Carmichael.

He took a sip of coffee and handed Carmichael's letter to Janet, saying, 'Swap you when you've finished.'

She nodded. 'Okay.'

As she tore open the envelope she wondered what Carmichael had to say. He didn't write often, and she hoped this letter wasn't to recall them or anything; they were pretty close to their target. Carmichael had been right, of course. The man they had come to find was still missing, two months after their night in Dartmouth. He was a leading American nuclear physicist, and when he vanished the CIA thought he'd either defected or been kidnapped. Only later was it realised that the man had had a nervous breakdown. The trail had led to Damascus and then fizzled out, but Carmichael, having accidentally got a lead, was now following it, not intending to tell the Americans until their man had been found, and thus putting them in debt to the British. Remembering their liaison with the Russians, Janet found the attitude to the Americans a sick joke – except that it wasn't funny, no matter how one looked at it.

Meanwhile Barber was reading the letter from Phil.

'Dear Steve and Janet,

How are you both? Well, I trust. I thought I'd drop you a line to let you know how things are going. I am now staying in a pension just along the road from the hospital. It's run by a man called Painblanc, a really nice chap, a superb cook and good company; we manage to communicate via his rather rocky English and my fractured French. We can both say "santé," which is the main thing. His wife is a little odd, very reserved and a dedicated philatelist, but as I get to know

261

her better I realise how genuinely thoughtful she is. There are two children, aged eighteen and twenty-three. The boy's a bit of a tearaway, but good fun, and I'm having a spot of bother with the girl; difficulty in keeping her out of my bed, believe it or not! She thinks all Englishmen are great lovers and doesn't seem to mind about the age gap. Her English is pretty good, as she spent two years in London as an au pair.

Anyway, enough of them. I'm really writing to tell you I'm well on the road to recovery and should be going home in a month or so. Sue sent her love to you the last time she wrote, and says she's looking forward to seeing you soon and to meeting Janet. I think I told you the firm is holding my job for me and taking care of all my expenses through some scheme or other, so there may be some change for you after all, Steve old boy! We'll have to see.

That's all for now. Take care. All the best to you both,
                                   love,
                                   Phil.'

Barber smiled; it was a typical Phil-type letter. Looking up to see if Janet had made out the real meaning in Carmichael's letter, he saw her jaw drop.

'What's the matter?'

'Remember what Carmichael told us about that Russian? Bolkovsky?'

He nodded. 'Sure. Said he was a great bloke.'

'Well...' Janet grimaced. 'He was killed last week in a 'plane crash in Russia.'

'Jesus!' said Barber remembering also what Carmichael had told him about Bitov. 'I wonder if it was an accident?'

THE END